"I'm not sure if I'm lost in the memories of that one night in our past or if I wish tonight were a first."

"I'm not sure, either, Noah," Ava said. "But we can't relive the past, can we? Nor should we automatically believe that the past determines the future."

"Everything about that night is coming back to me, Ava," Noah whispered.

"Perhaps you shouldn't read too much into one simple kiss."

"Maybe," he agreed. "But I would hardly call the one I just experienced 'simple.' I'm not sorry at all that you and I met once before, or that you and I found each other again..."

Dear Reader,

"For the love of a child," one of the most powerful phrases in our language. What any of us wouldn't do for the love of a child. We try to do what's best for the children in our lives. We struggle with each decision and pray we made the right one.

High Country Christmas is Ava's story, the third book in the trilogy, The Cahills of North Carolina. Years ago, Ava made a decision about a child in her life and now she is facing the consequences of that choice. She changes her future and doesn't look back to do what's right for Charlie and ultimately for Sawyer, a young teen being raised by an obstinate and risk-taking single dad.

With the help of her supportive family and the man she comes to love with all her heart, Ava's journey "for the love of a child" will hopefully warm your heart at Christmas and all year through.

If you like Ava's story, please read about her two brothers, who are as different as any brothers could be. *High Country Cop* is Carter's story. *Dad in Training* is Jace's.

Cynthia Thomason

HEARTWARMING

High Country Christmas

—

Cynthia Thomason

Recycling programs
for this product may
not exist in your area.

ISBN-13: 978-1-335-51049-5

High Country Christmas

Copyright © 2018 by Cynthia Thomason

Printed in U.S.A.

Cynthia Thomason inherited her love of writing from her ancestors. Her father and grandmother both loved to write, and she aspired to continue the legacy. Cynthia studied English and journalism in college, and after a career as a high school English teacher, she began writing novels. She discovered ideas for stories while searching through antiques stores and flea markets and as an auctioneer and estate buyer. Cynthia says every cast-off item from someone's life can ignite the idea for a plot. She writes about small towns, big hearts and happy endings that are earned and not taken for granted. And as far as the legacy is concerned, just ask her son, the magazine journalist, if he believes. Please contact Cynthia at cynthoma@aol.com and cynthiathomason.net.

Visit the Author Profile page
at Harlequin.com for more titles.

This book is dedicated to the caring folks at Crossnore Children's Home in Crossnore, North Carolina. Thank you for welcoming me, educating me, and allowing me an intimate look at this warm and wonderful home.

CHAPTER ONE

THE NUMBERS WERE beginning to blur. Ava checked the clock on the wall and was shocked to see the hands indicating one o'clock in the morning. She'd been at this for three hours.

The job would have been much easier if she'd had access to the computers of her deceased father's paper mill company. But the current owner, her uncle Rudy, had denied her request. So Ava spent long hours trying to decipher the financial status of the business by slogging through ledgers the now-retired bookkeeper had painstakingly entered with a number two pencil. And all Ava had determined so far was that something wasn't right. The numbers weren't adding up, literally and figuratively.

Elsie Vandergarten had been a crackerjack bookkeeper in the days when accountants were called by that job-specific name. Ava's father, Raymond Cahill, had trusted her with accounting for every dollar the company took in. A software technician had begun transcribing the figures into the company's computer more than five years ago to satisfy Raymond's techie brother, Rudy. A newly hired comptroller had replaced Elsie when she retired over a year ago when Raymond died.

And now, struggling to find out why her mother's share of the profits had dwindled, Ava had taken it upon herself to examine the company books. Her brothers, Carter and Jace, trusted Ava because she'd always been known as the smartest of the three siblings. The boys figured she would unearth the truth about the creative bookkeeping, and she didn't want to disappoint them, or herself.

Ava leaned back in her desk chair, appreciating the comforting creak the chair's gears made. For three hours her office at the Sawtooth Children's Home had been reassuringly quiet. Nearly everyone else who lived on the sprawling campus was in bed or preparing for Monday's classes. Ava dropped her glasses onto the desk blotter, closed the ledger and stuck it in a large bottom-tier drawer of her classic mahogany desk. She rubbed her eyes with the palms of her hands.

"Whatever you're doing, Uncle Rudy, you are covering your tracks very well," she said aloud. "But nobody's perfect and I'll find it."

Time for bed, she thought to herself.

She stood from her desk and headed for the office exit. In moments she would be in her personal living quarters, a small but cheerful one-bedroom apartment carved out of unused space for the home's chief administrator until she could find a nice house of her own. Having only been in this new job since September, Ava hadn't yet had time for real estate shopping. But after living independently for so long in Charlotte, she was determined not to move back into her old room at the family farm. She stopped in front of a decorative mirror in the office to check the damages of her three-hour vigil.

"Oh no, not another one," she said, lifting her hand to grasp the spiky, coarse white hair that stood out from the others in her dark wispy bangs. "That's the third one this month."

Ava didn't consider herself vain, but really—three gray hairs in a month! She was only thirty-six years old, in good health and completely satisfied with her decision to leave the corporate world of finance in Charlotte. Returning to her mountain home of Holly River to manage the children's facility, which had become a North Carolina treasure, had been the right decision for many reasons. Ava brought her professional business training to keep the school on a steady keel, and she enjoyed her association with the children and staff.

She yanked the offending hair from the others and raked her fingers through the bangs which reached just to her eyebrows. Another quick look convinced her that all the other hairs were a comforting deep chestnut color. She turned off the office light and proceeded into the lobby and the doorway that led to her apartment.

A sudden chilly draft caused Ava to stop. "Where is that coming from," she said softly, knowing all the windows and doors of the administrative office, as well as all residences, were secured at night. The other door leading from the lobby, the one to the kitchen, was open. Unusual, but still that didn't explain a cold late-November wind sweeping through the interior of the building. Nothing should be open, and the security system should have detected anything out of the ordinary.

Ava listened carefully. Hearing no sound, she grabbed an oak walking stick from the umbrella stand by the door and ventured slowly into the hallway. Just a few short steps and she would be at the kitchen, the element of surprise on her side. A soft light guided her way. Nice, but there shouldn't be a light in the kitchen at this hour.

She gripped the walking stick, flexing her hand with each step. All the resident children lived with their "cottage parents" in smaller structures around the campus, so no one would be inclined to visit the main kitchen in the administration building, where Ava lived. All residents could go to their own, smaller kitchen if they needed a late-night snack. The administration kitchen was only used for staff lunches and group meetings.

Ava walked through the kitchen doorway and stopped. The light she'd seen came from the open refrigerator door. A small, slight figure was crouched on the floor in front of the open door. He—or she—Ava couldn't tell since the person was wearing a hoodie, was rifling through food items in the crisper drawer.

Determining that she had probably four inches on the intruder and at least twenty pounds, Ava smacked the walking stick against the door frame and spoke loudly and forcefully. "What do you think you're doing?"

The intruder squawked in a decidedly female way, and fell back on her fanny. Jerking her head around so half her face was visible under the hood, she said, "Good grief, you scared the crap out of me!"

Ava took a moment to process the offending remark before saying, "That's hardly the point. Who are you and what are you doing in here?"

The girl stood, yanked up her jacket zipper. "Nothing. I was just leaving. You can have your precious food all to yourself."

Using the walking stick, Ava blocked the girl's exit from the kitchen to the backyard. She made a quick appraisal. The girl was thin but appeared healthy. Her skin glowed pink from being out in the elements on a chilly night.

"You're not going anywhere," Ava said. "If you're hungry, I'll fix you something to eat, but first I'm getting an explanation."

The girl seemed to weigh her options, and quickly decided that decent food was a fair trade for providing a reason for her breaking and entering, even if that reason were a lie. "Okay, I'll eat."

"Sit down," Ava said, pointing to one of the chairs surrounding the kitchen worktable. Ava took three eggs and some bacon from the fridge, placed a skillet on the stove and began preparing a meal. She kept one eye on the late-night guest while she cooked.

"What's your name?" she asked the girl.

At first the intruder shrugged, but finally she said, "Taylor Grande."

Ava smiled to herself. "Is it a coincidence that your name is made up of two of today's hottest female pop singers?"

"Yeah. My mother had a crystal ball when I was born. She knew I would be famous and wanted to give me a head start."

Remembering the draft when a chill penetrated Ava's bones, she went to the window and yanked down the glass. With a quick twist, she secured the window's lock. "I assume this is how you got in."

"Yep."

"Wasn't the window locked?"

"No. Is it supposed to be?"

"Of course it is. Plus, we have a dependable security system on every opening on every building on the campus. I should have heard an alarm. Our security chief should have registered the entry in his office."

"Looks like somebody screwed up," Taylor Grande said.

Ava transferred the food to a plate, poured a glass of milk and set the meal on the table. "I'll add two slices of toast if you tell me how you dismantled the security system."

"I'll take the toast." Taylor shoveled a forkful of food into her mouth. She followed it with a gulp of milk, and then took an object from her hoodie pocket.

Ava reached for the walking stick when she saw the shiny object, but quickly set her weapon back against the table when she realized she wasn't in danger. "What's that?"

"A Swiss Army Knife. I thought everyone knew that."

"Well, of course I *know*," Ava said. "But

what does it have to do with you breaking and entering?"

Taylor switched a pocket-size knife from the center of the instrument. "Simple. I cut the wire leading to the window alarm." She took another bite of food. "I'm only telling you this because after I finish this meal, I'm heading out and you'll never see me again. And also because you need to update the security around here. Everything should be digital. Wires are an open invitation to people with bad intentions."

"Thanks for the tip." Ava busied herself with making a pot of coffee. She doubted she'd sleep much tonight now that she knew their security system left a lot to be desired.

"That's a great idea," Taylor said, looking longingly at the coffee brewer. "I could use a cup."

Ava scowled at her. "What are you, fourteen?"

"Close enough."

"You should not be drinking coffee."

"Maybe you should have told me that three years ago."

"And another thing…" Ava said. "You are not going out into this weather again tonight.

It's supposed to go into the thirties. Is that hoodie all the protection you have?"

For the first time Taylor pushed the hood from her head, revealing dark blond hair hurriedly tamed into a messy single braid. Her hair was dirty with strands falling over her face. "I'll find a place to sleep," she said.

Ava poured herself a cup of coffee and refused the request to fill a second cup for her intruder. She sat across from Taylor and sipped her coffee. "Do you even know where you are? Do you know what this place is?"

"Some kind of orphanage, right?"

"We don't use that word so much these days," Ava said. "But yes, this is a children's home. Some of our kids don't have parents. Some are estranged from their families. Children come here for all sorts of reasons."

Taylor gave her a curious stare. "Don't get any ideas about me. I didn't come here for anything but food. The truck driver who gave me a ride from Boone pointed this place out when he dropped me off, said I could probably find a free meal. That's all I came for."

"And that's all I've offered you, isn't it?"

Ava said, grateful that the truck driver had pointed this girl to a place of safety.

"Well, yeah." Taylor layered egg and bacon on half a piece of toast and shoved the whole thing in her mouth.

"There is one thing we tend to ask anyone who might be interested in staying here…"

"I'm not interested."

"Right. I know, but indulge me. Where are you supposed to be? Where are your parents?"

"Beats me. As for where I'm supposed to be, that's really just my business." She placed her fork and knife on her plate and wiped her mouth with a napkin. "Thanks for the meal. It was more than I thought I'd get. I figured I'd end up scarfing down some lettuce and carrots from your fridge, but this was way better." She yawned, rubbed her hand across her forehead. "Guess I'll be going now."

"Planning to hitch another ride, are you?"

"A girl's gotta do what a girl's gotta do."

Ava gave her an indulgent smile. "You do know you're not leaving here, don't you?" she said. "My work here is all about taking care of kids, keeping them safe in a smooth-running facility. What would it say about my ability to do my job if I let you go back out into the cold tonight to beg a ride from another stranger?"

Taylor pulled up her hood and stood. "You've got plenty of other kids to take care of, lady. You don't need to make a project of me. I can take care of myself."

Noticing a backpack near the fridge, Ava said, "What's in the pack, your worldly belongings?"

"Stuff. Nothing important." She reached for the backpack. "See ya."

Ava cradled the coffee cup in her two hands. "Suit yourself, Taylor Grande, but here's how I see your situation. You're exhausted. And in seconds you'll be cold through to the bone. You don't really smell like a flower garden. In a few hours you'll be hungry again. I can take care of those conditions for you. I might even be able to get you some clean clothes before you leave."

Taylor swung the pack over her shoulder. "I've got clothes, but thanks."

"Think about this, Taylor," Ava said. "You give me the army knife until the morning in exchange for a bed on my couch tonight and tomorrow we'll reevaluate your situation. If you still want to leave, so be it."

"You won't try to keep me here against my will? I've heard stories…"

Ava sighed. "We're not in the business of hostage taking. Look, you've got to trust somebody, Taylor. You can trust me or the next truck driver who picks you up. For tonight at least, I'm suggesting you trust me."

After what seemed like unending minutes, Taylor said, "Okay. I'll stay. But just till tomorrow."

Ava tried not to look overly grateful at Taylor's decision. "As I said, we'll reevaluate."

Ava picked up the dishes, stacked them in the sink. "One more thing…" she said.

"Yeah?"

"While I'm making up your bed, you take a shower."

Taylor sniffed the sleeve of her jacket. "I don't have a problem with that."

ONCE TAYLOR LAY on the couch, she was asleep in less than a minute. Ava thought about calling her brother Carter. He was chief of police in Holly River, and he would know if any missing kids had come up on his radar. But it was the middle of the night. Carter was at home in bed. And she'd sort of given Taylor her word that nothing would be done about her situation until the morning. Besides, morning would arrive soon enough.

Ava turned on the heat in her apartment and crawled between her covers. She might get two or three hours' sleep if she was lucky. She fell into a restless slumber with her bedroom door open. Taylor's deep breathing comforted her. At least she'd done something for this child for tonight.

The next morning Ava padded around her apartment, making coffee and getting dressed. Taylor was still fast asleep when Ava left to attend to chapel duties. She put a note on the kitchen table where Taylor couldn't miss it. *Taylor, do not leave. I will be back soon.*

During the church service, Ava spoke with Helen Carmichael, one of the "cottage mothers" the school employed to help the children in her charge. Helen and her husband, Mark, were kind people, empty nesters who had sent their own children to college and wanted to lend a hand to others. They lived full-time in the cottage assigned to them for two weeks, and then another couple took over. Each couple only worked two weeks. Managing a home with ten children, even with extra staff to help, was a serious and often painstaking responsibility.

"Helen, you currently have only nine children in your cottage, is that right?" Ava asked.

"That's true. Have you received word that another child is coming?"

"Not exactly, but maybe so." The Sawtooth Children's Home, named for the mountain and the oak trees nearby, had such an excellent reputation that kids from all over North Carolina came to stay there. Often there was a waiting list. "There is one young girl," Ava said. "I think she's around fourteen."

"That would be fine," Helen said. "We've got six under ten and three over ten. Becky Miller is fifteen and she has a vacancy in her room."

With that knowledge, Ava went back to her office, checked to see that Taylor was still sleeping and called Carter.

"What's up, Ava? Everything okay over there?"

"Everything's fine, Carter. But I think I've got a runaway. Claims she doesn't know where her parents are, but I'm not convinced that's true. Can you check your computer and see if a missing girl shows up? This one has dark blond hair, is approximately fourteen, maybe five-four, blue eyes, slim, pretty."

"Where is she from?" Carter asked. "What's her name?"

"Sorry. I didn't get a straight answer from her. Overall she looks well cared for. And I know she came from some distance away."

"I'll see what I can find out."

Within thirty minutes Carter had sent information to Ava's cell phone. Attached was a picture of the young lady who was still currently sleeping on Ava's sofa. She'd been missing for two days from a Chapel Hill address that Ava recognized as upscale.

Ava called her brother back. "That's her," she said. "Does she have any family?"

"Says here she's got a father who's looking for her. I've got to let Chapel Hill PD know. They may want me to pick her up."

"I understand you've got to tell the police. But I'd rather you didn't come here to get her just yet, Carter. I don't want to spook this girl. It's ten-thirty, and I don't expect her to wake up anytime soon. And when she does, I'm sure I can keep her here until we decide what to do. You can come by later, okay?"

"Not much later, but I'll give you a little time," he said.

"Thanks. By the way, what's her name?"

"Sawyer Walsh. And you were right. She's fourteen."

"Thanks, Carter. I'll call if I need you."

Three hours later, Sawyer Walsh was beginning to stir on the sofa. She blinked her eyes open, stretched her arms over her head.

"How'd you sleep?" Ava asked her.

"Okay. Thanks for the bed. I'll be out of your hair in a few minutes. Maybe I can take a sandwich with me."

"I'm sure that can be arranged, but what's your hurry? Why don't you stay here at least for another night? You need more than one or two meals before you continue your journey."

"I should go. I'm supposed to be in California in a week. Got friends there."

Ava had become adept at recognizing lies. The California story was definitely made up. "Oh. California's nice," she said. "But still…"

Ava's argument was cut short by the sound of a motorcycle engine followed by a persistent and loud knock on her apartment door. She turned the lock and opened the door. A man stood in the building's reception lobby on the other side. He had an impressive build, almost an intimidating one, but it was also oddly familiar.

Ava saw the outline of an expansive chest and upper arm muscles under the black leather jacket he wore. He was tall enough to carry off the rough and tumble look, maybe six feet. His dark hair matched the stubble of beard on his face. He appeared tired as if he'd come to the school in a hurry.

Black jeans, a white T-shirt and black ankle boots with an insignia on the sides completed his outfit. A baseball cap covered his thick hair, which was mussed except for an obviously quick attempt to push coarse waves back behind his ears. When he saw her, he removed the cap, releasing strands onto his forehead. Ava swallowed. Something about this man's demeanor and appearance was troubling although she couldn't admit to being afraid of him. She placed her hand over her stomach to ease a tremble that had started deep inside. "Yes? Can I help you?"

"Some guy in a golf cart sent me to this building."

Jack, their Sunday security man, she thought.

"Are you the headmistress of this place?" the man asked.

"Well, we don't use that term so much anymore, but I am the administrator."

His gaze darted all around the doorway. He didn't really look at Ava. "My name is Walsh. I understand my daughter is here."

Of course. This man's sudden appearance was the reason for the anxiety Ava was experiencing. She had been expecting someone to come for Sawyer. Ava ignored the rustling of bed linens behind her. "Walsh? Oh yes. You're Sawyer's father…"

"Bingo." The man pushed past Ava and strode into her living room. When Ava spun around to keep track of him, she saw Sawyer as a flash of sheet and blanket disappearing into the kitchen. Next the back door opened and banged against the outside wall. In four steps Walsh was in the kitchen.

"Sawyer, not another step. Stop right there." His voice was hoarse and seriously angry, his instructions clear and his black leather getup suddenly menacing. Ava shook her head. There was something about that voice. Again, she wasn't afraid, but she was acutely aware of his tone and inflection. Ava knew this man.

Sawyer stopped a few feet outside the door.

CHAPTER TWO

SAWYER SPUN AROUND, a look of anguish etched in her face. She wrapped the bed-clothes more tightly around her, almost as a shield and scowled at Ava. "Thanks a lot, lady. This is what you mean by trusting you?"

"Tay… I mean Sawyer…" Ava fumbled for words. "I'm sorry, but I couldn't let you leave today. You're obviously in trouble, and setting out on the road by yourself, hitching rides, isn't likely to minimize that."

Sawyer flashed a quick hot glare at her father. "And you think turning me over to this man will?"

"I don't know." Ava gave the man a quick appraisal. Though she was beginning to put the clues together, Ava couldn't be completely certain that her instincts about who he was were correct. A lot of time had passed. "I can't draw any conclusions yet."

"Well, I've known him fourteen years, and let me tell you…"

"Cut it out, Sawyer," Walsh said. "Do you have any idea what you've put me through the last two days? I haven't slept. I haven't eaten…"

He took a step toward his daughter. Ava's arm shot out to stop him, a fruitless gesture really because Walsh could obviously snap her bones with a twist of his wrist. "Don't move," she said. "I can have the police here in a matter of minutes." She hoped she could protect Sawyer if need be.

The man still didn't look at Ava. In fact, other than a brief sentence at the door, he hadn't acknowledged her existence. His attention was focused entirely on his daughter.

"Yeah, Pops, one more step and I'm running," Sawyer said. "We'll play a little Catch-Me-If-You-Can."

Walsh put his fists on his hips. "We both know I can catch you, Sawyer. Not much doubt about that."

Ava looked at the stern faces of father and daughter. She'd mediated several ticklish family situations during her two-month tenure as the home's administrator. But none of them had seemed as fraught with as much frustration and peril as this one. "Look, Sawyer, come back inside. I've brought you clean clothes. You can go into the bedroom and change. Then we'll sit down and talk about this."

"Like that's ever done any good," Sawyer said.

Walsh released a long breath. Ava expected him to argue with her, but he didn't. "Do what this lady says or I'll haul you back to Chapel Hill on the back of my bike in nothing but that blanket you're wearing," he said.

Ava shot a glance at Walsh. She didn't especially approve of his threatening technique, but at least he appeared to be supporting her directions to Sawyer.

Sawyer stood on the back lawn for several seconds breathing heavily. Then she yanked the blanket from where it trailed on the ground and stomped up the few steps to the kitchen.

"Do you have any windows in that bedroom?" Walsh asked, keeping his attention on his daughter.

"Yes, but our security system is on. The

windows can't be opened without our hearing a siren." She caught Sawyer's conspiratorial look. "Not from the inside anyway."

Once Sawyer had left the kitchen, Ava realized she was alone with the overpowering presence of the girl's father. A strange tingle worked its way down her spine. She figured she ought to be scared out of her wits, but once more, she wasn't. Maybe because she'd grown up with two brothers, and she'd always thought she understood the male psyche fairly well. But this man, who not only looked like a biker but had driven across the state on a motorcycle, was a truly dominating figure and Ava was intrigued. She couldn't take her eyes off him, just as she hadn't been able to six years ago. Oh yes, she'd known him—too well at one time.

He stood in the middle of her kitchen, his eyes cast down on some spot on her wood floor, his arms crossed over his chest. He almost seemed lost in her small cozy apartment.

"Would you like some coffee?" Ava suggested, hoping he would say yes. She needed something to occupy her hands while she thought about how his sudden appearance might affect her life.

He didn't answer right away. His mind seemed a thousand miles away. After a moment he simply said, "No, thank you."

"I'll have one," she said.

"Suit yourself."

Ava measured ground coffee into the machine. She really didn't want coffee. Her nerves were already on edge, her senses heightened, her mind struggling to maintain a rational demeanor in light of this man's unexpected arrival at her door. What were the odds?

She should be wondering about what she was going to do in her capacity as administrator. The ultimate goal of the Sawtooth Children's Home was the reunification of kids with their families if at all possible. But allowing Sawyer to go with this man? A man who had lied to her when she lived in Charlotte? There was no way she could see herself letting Walsh remove his daughter from her care. She had resources. She could prevent a father from taking his own child if she sensed something about the relationship wasn't right.

When the coffee began brewing, she heard the scrape of a chair on the kitchen floor. She turned to see Walsh sitting, his elbows on her table. "Can I change my mind?" he asked, finally settling his gaze on her face.

Those eyes as brown as an acorn. I could never forget...

"I'd like to have that coffee now," he said.

"Of course." She brought him a cup and set cream and sugar on the table. He used a bit of sugar and took a long sip. Ava studied his full mouth, the movement of his Adam's apple when he swallowed. She clearly remembered when she'd seen him drink something before. In a dark place, in a city miles away. She sucked in an audible gasp and covered her mouth with her hand. There was little doubt left in her mind now.

"How did she get here?" Walsh said after drinking most of his coffee. "Did she tell you?"

Ava sat next to him out of his direct line of sight. She hoped he would keep staring into his coffee. Convinced now that she knew who he was, she didn't want him to recognize her. Thank goodness she'd changed a lot since then. "I don't know about the first two days, but apparently a truck driver brought her from Boone and dropped her off here last night. That's something to be thankful for. It was past midnight when I discovered her foraging in the refrigerator."

He nodded, took another sip of coffee. "Yeah, I'm glad that happened." Just seeing his profile, Ava determined that his face looked drawn, tense. "Do I owe you anything for her care—food, the clothes, whatever?" he asked.

"No. Of course not. This is what I...*we* do here—take care of children in need."

He gave her a quick, piercing stare that made her stomach jump, and then looked back at the liquid in his mug. "That's what you think, that Sawyer is needy?"

"There are many different types of need, Mr. Walsh. No two children are the same, nor do they come from the same circumstances. Besides, your daughter was very hungry when she got here."

"I get that. But believe me, Sawyer is not needy in the usual sense. If she'd put a quarter of her clothes in a suitcase, she wouldn't have been able to drag it across the state."

Ava had to think of Sawyer, not the past,

so she asked the difficult question. "Why is your daughter afraid of you, Mr. Walsh?"

"Afraid of me?" His lips curled up into a cynical grin. "She's not afraid of me. She hates me."

Ava had spoken with kids who claimed to have difficult relationships with their parents, but few had used the word *hate*. It just wasn't in a child's nature to hate the person they depended upon.

Walsh leaned forward and looked at her from the corner of his eye. "Does that surprise you, Mrs…?"

"It's Miss…" She almost said her first name and quickly avoided it. "Miss Cahill, and yes, I'm surprised. Your daughter is obviously independent and clever, and she was visibly upset when she saw you, but I haven't witnessed an emotion anywhere near hate."

His head jerked up. His stare intensified. "What did you say your name is?"

"Cahill."

"No. Your first name."

"I didn't." She paused a moment and then said, "It's Ava."

"Ava, huh?" He rubbed his eyes, stared at

her a moment longer. "The lack of sleep is getting to me," he said.

"Yes, I can appreciate that this has been a difficult time."

"I doubt you can know just how difficult. As far as Sawyer hating me, just wait. I haven't strapped her to the back of my motorcycle yet." He glanced into Ava's short hallway toward the bathroom. "Something I'd better do before it gets much later. Even with the windshield attached and both dash heaters going, it could get chilly out there."

"You'll pardon me for saying so, Mr. Walsh…"

"You might as well call me Noah," he said. "I don't see us becoming pals, but this awkward moment between us entitles us to use first names."

Noah—the name of the man she'd met six years ago. The man who, in one night had changed her life. The man she'd tried so hard to forget because at the time she'd had no other choice.

She struggled to keep her voice steady, to keep her hands wrapped tightly on her mug. To show any signs of the fierce emotions battling inside her would not help any of them.

"All right, Noah," she said, her mind grasping for any topic to lead her mind away from the turmoil it was experiencing. "I can't imagine why you came to get your daughter on a bike. Wouldn't a car have been more comfortable for a drive back to Chapel Hill?"

He shifted on his chair, crossed his leg on the opposite knee. "Comfortable? Yeah, but I got here in just over two hours, and a car would have taken much longer. Plus I can keep a grip on Sawyer the whole way." He stared hard at Ava a moment as if there was something he wanted to say. After a pause, he breathed deeply. "I know what you're thinking. Has this happened before? Well, yeah it has. Gotta say though—" he looked around the comfortable kitchen in Ava's apartment "—this is one of the better places Sawyer has picked."

"Ava! You in here?"

The sound of her brother's voice put an end to further conversation. Ava stood. "I'm in the kitchen, Carter. Come in."

Carter Cahill, wearing jeans and a casual shirt and jacket, strode into the kitchen. Sunday was his day off, so he'd obviously elected not to put on his official uniform. He stopped a few feet into the room and stared menacingly at Walsh. "Everything okay here?" he asked. "There's a strange motorcycle outside. You all right, Ava?"

Noah scowled. "Why wouldn't she be?"

Knowing she had to calm the situation and keep it from escalating into a match of words between the two men, Ava put the past—and her roiling stomach—aside. "This is the girl's father, Carter," she said, standing up. "Noah Walsh. He's come to take her home." Turning to Noah, she said, "This is my brother Carter. He's chief of police in Holly River."

Both men nodded, but made no move to shake hands.

"Where's the girl?" Carter asked.

"I'm here," Sawyer said, coming into the kitchen. She looked rested and well, her hair combed into a ponytail. She wore the clothes Ava had brought her, jeans and a sweatshirt. With her hoodie covering her, she should be warm enough on the ride back to Chapel Hill. The temperature was going into the upper fifties today.

She stared at her father. "Well, aren't you going to put me in handcuffs and cart me out of here? I'd like to get home in time to plan my next escape." Noah started to rise. His jaw muscles tensed.

"Can we all just hold on a minute here?" Carter said. "Ava, I've got some information for you." Speaking to Sawyer, he said, "Can you wait in the lobby awhile, Miss Walsh? And don't try running off. If you do, I'll have the entire police force of this town tracking you down."

"The entire force of this town?" Sawyer said. "Yikes, I'm scared."

Ava gave her a hard stare. "That's enough, Sawyer. Just go into the lobby and wait for us."

Sawyer looked as if another smart remark were on the tip of her tongue, but apparently she thought better of uttering it and ambled from the kitchen with a last sarcastic comment. "I'll be waiting, *Daddy*. Can we stop for ice cream on the way home?"

Once Sawyer had left the room, Ava took a seat at the table. She hadn't realized how weak her knees felt, how clouded her thinking.

Carter began. "I've done some investigating into this situation," he said. "I've discovered that this is the fourth time this year that Sawyer has run away from home." He waited for a reaction from Noah.

"It's true," he said. "She has become impossible."

"Be that as it may," Carter continued, "each time your daughter has run farther than the last. If she tries it again, she could very well slip away from you forever."

"I don't think so," Noah said. "She wants you to believe her life is horrible, but I doubt she'd actually give up the advantages she has for a long absence. She'll always come back."

Ava looked at Carter and, avoiding direct eye contact with Noah, she said. "Sawyer was riding with a truck driver. She hitchhiked from Chapel Hill. Surely as her father, you understand the risks associated with that type of behavior. I mean, she was lucky this time, but…"

A muscle worked in Noah's temple. "You think I don't know that? I see where you people are going with this, but you're way off base. Sawyer won't try this again. She'll be fine when I get her home. She's made her point and knows she scared the…well, scared me pretty good."

Carter's features reflected his skepticism. "For how long?"

Noah sighed heavily as the room remained quiet. "Look," he said. "Sawyer and I have our problems. I travel in my profession. I'm not home a lot, and Sawyer lives with housekeepers—very carefully selected housekeepers that I personally interview. I check their credentials. But Sawyer has a problem with boundaries. The relationships haven't worked out."

He shifted on his chair and leaned forward. "As a matter of fact, we've gone through so many housekeepers that it's no longer a case of me requesting their references as it is the ladies requesting ours. Word has gotten around." He tried to smile, but apparently realized the lack of humor in what he'd just said. "It's not easy to find someone Sawyer will listen to."

"Where is Sawyer's mother?" Ava asked.

Noah frowned. "Currently in a small town outside of Barcelona I believe. Mary Kate and I divorced three years ago. She claimed to need peace and tranquility, and the tension around her relationship with Sawyer could never provide that. They argued all the time."

Ava remembered his confession that he was married when he left her house in the middle of the night six years before.

Noah actually did smile this time. "You may find this hard to accept, but things have gotten easier for Sawyer since her mother left and we filed for divorce. We no longer hear from her, and we're both okay with it."

"You sure about that?" Carter asked.

"I'm sure. Ask Sawyer yourself if you don't believe me. The last few years I was married, Sawyer did not grow up in a happy household. Her mother and I…" He paused. "Let's just say, our family would not have made an ideal sitcom."

"So let me make sure I have this right," Carter said. "Sawyer has no mother in her life, and her father is mostly an absentee parent who leaves her to be raised by a housekeeper."

Noah's lips thinned. "I have to work, man. I make a good living. Sawyer has everything she needs."

Ava and Carter shared a communal look of understanding. Yes, Sawyer had material things.

"Are there any other family members who could help with this situation?" Ava asked.

Noah shook his head. His gaze was fixated on Carter and the hallway where Sawyer had disappeared. He obviously didn't trust either one of them. "My mother is designated legal guardian if something should happen to me. I had to select someone since my profession involves pretty high risk. But right now my mother lives in Oregon. We rarely see her. Mary Kate's mother kept Sawyer for a while. They weren't a good match. She sent her back to me." Noah stood. "If that's all, we'll be on our way now." Turning to Ava, he looked at her for a long, uncomfortable moment and said, "Thanks again for taking Sawyer in last night and for contacting the authorities in Chapel Hill."

One look from Carter told Ava that he was not about to let this matter drop.

"Mr. Walsh," Carter said, "I'm not comfortable with releasing Sawyer to your custody."

Noah sputtered his amused disbelief. "Oh, you're not? Well, sorry, Chief, but that's not your call."

"Actually, I think it is," Carter said. "I see

a threatening situation here, and I'm bound by law to try and prevent it."

"Threatening? I've never touched that child!"

"Maybe you're not the threat, Mr. Walsh, but your daughter's life is in danger from other outside influences. Every time she runs away, she is at risk."

Noah started to speak, but Carter raised his hand. "Not only that, but my wife is a social worker for the state of North Carolina. She works with children and families, and she would never forgive me if I turned Sawyer over to you since she has clearly and repeatedly shown the behavior of a runaway."

"I don't care what your wife is," Noah said. "No one takes my daughter away." He sighed. "Look, Sawyer and I have our differences. I've already admitted to that, but we'll work them out…"

Ava sensed Noah's anger escalating and realized the importance of keeping this situation calm. She spoke in a low, even tone. "Please, Mr. Walsh… Noah, think about Sawyer. Some type of intervention is needed to keep your daughter safe. Maybe you don't realize what happens to kids on the street…"

"Nothing is going to happen to her. I'll keep a closer eye on her."

"Your techniques obviously haven't worked," Carter said.

"I'll set stricter rules. She won't run away again."

"Yes, she will," Ava said. "This is my profession, running a home for at-risk children, and I see the signs in Sawyer that I've seen in other kids. She will keep running away."

Noah stared first at Ava and then at Carter. After several tense moments he spoke to Ava. "Can I see you outside? Just for a few minutes."

Had he recognized her? She didn't think so. There was nothing in his facial features to indicate the past had come back to him. "Yes, of course. We can step out on the back porch for a minute."

"Now, hold on," Carter said. "Anything you need to say to my sister you can say to me."

Noah gave him a sharp look. "Why? Are you suddenly the administrator of this home?"

"Stop it, both of you," Ava said. "Carter,

I'll be fine just outside the kitchen door. You stay here and check on Sawyer."

"Yeah," Noah said. "If she runs away this time, that's on you."

Ava walked out ahead of Noah. When they were alone, she further convinced herself that he didn't recognize her. She had looked much different then. Her hair had been long and highlighted with auburn. She'd worn glasses all the time. She'd been thinner. Besides, a man with his looks and what she remembered as charisma must have had several relationships with women in the last years. Why would he remember that one night with her? "What do you want to talk about?"

He released a long breath. She could see the tension in his eyes, along with something else. Sadness, confusion. He was in over his head with his own daughter, and Ava had never felt a stronger need to help a family than she did at this moment. At the same time, her sense of self-preservation urged her to stay as far away from this situation as possible.

He squeezed his eyes shut. When he opened them again a new emotion made the hint of gold in his eyes seem a deep amber. She sensed his inability to cope with making a decision.

She spoke calmly. "Look, Noah, I know this is difficult for you…"

"Do you? Have you ever given up a child of yours to a complete stranger?"

His question sent a pang of guilt deep into her stomach, the same pain she'd experienced for almost six years now. But she could not tell Noah that. She'd never told anyone, not even her family, about Charlie.

She swallowed, took a calming breath. "I don't want you to think of me as a stranger," she said, avoiding a direct answer to his question. "I care about the children in this home. They are more than a job to me. They are everything. I want each one of them to feel safe and encouraged to succeed."

"I'll bet they do with that brother cop around to back you up. Don't think I didn't see the looks passing between the two of you. I suppose next, a small army of security will enter the discussion."

"First of all, my brother does not come around to 'back me up' as you put it. He has a job, which he's doing this morning, and it keeps him busy. Secondly, we don't have an army of security."

"So you, a single lady, basically run this place by yourself?"

"As the administrator, yes. Why? Do you believe that a woman isn't capable of running a home this size? I'll have you know…"

He put his hands up defensively. "Okay, okay. I apologize. No insult intended."

Mollified, she gave him a brief explanation about how the Sawtooth Children's Home operated. At least she was once again on firm emotional ground. Talking about the school was easy and comfortable. "We have a full-time medical person on campus. We have a cook, three on-site counselors, a gymnasium, school building with fifteen classrooms, each with a qualified teacher." She waited until those facts had settled in before adding, "Each child lives in a cottage with nine other kids, and each cottage has a set of parents in charge. So you see, I don't run this home all by myself."

"I get it," he said. "This is a tight ship. But my daughter is not in need of cottage parents. She already has one parent who just happens to be having a little trouble."

A little trouble? Ava tried logic. "We have room for Sawyer right now," she said. "You will have complete access to her. You can visit her whenever you like. If she agrees, after some time she can even go home with you for a weekend, once we've done a visitation."

Noah responded with a sarcastic chuckle. "Oh? I can see my own daughter on weekends…maybe? How kind of you. This is not happening, Miss Administrator. Not now. Not ever."

A rustling nearby drew their attention to the back door. Sawyer stood in the frame, looking out. Carter was behind her. "Everything okay out here?" he asked.

"Are you almost done talking about me as if I didn't exist?" Sawyer said.

Ava smiled. "What would you like to say, Sawyer?"

She looked down, locking her gaze on the grass. When she lifted her face, she stared at Noah. "I'm old enough to have a say in my own life."

"Okay," he said. "Go ahead. Have your say."

"I don't want to go home with you, Dad.

You're never home, and I hate Mrs. Filmore. She's more like a warden than a housekeeper. And don't think you can just hire another one and I'll be happy." Sawyer looked over the expansive green lawn that led to the cottages. "This place is probably really lame, but it would be better than home. I'm going to stay here, for a while at least."

Ava couldn't bear to see the sense of futility in Noah's eyes. She'd seen it too many times in the looks of parents who'd failed their children in so many ways. She gave him a gentle smile that for some odd reason felt strangely natural and spoke to Sawyer.

"We need to get some things straight," she said. "This place, as you call it, isn't a resort, Sawyer. It's a home for children and teens with special problems. We have rules that must be followed and consequences if they are broken. You will be living with nine other housemates of all ages. Your room will be shared with another resident. You will see a counselor once a week, or more often if we think it's needed. Your cottage parents will know where you go and whom you see. If they deny permission, that's it then."

Ava realized she was painting a rather

rigid picture of life at Sawtooth Children's Home, but she firmly believed that Sawyer should understand that her life would be regimented, and she would have to meet expectations. Maybe the reality of life here was getting through to both father and daughter. At least they were both listening.

Ava could easily believe that Noah Walsh loved his daughter, but their relationship was toxic, and she knew time apart would help them. "Carter," she said to her brother, "you go on. We'll be fine here. I'm just going to take Sawyer and Noah on a tour of the campus. Tell Mama I won't be there for dinner tonight."

Carter tucked his hat back onto his forehead. "If you're sure."

"I am."

He walked through the building, closed the front door. Ava waited until the charged atmosphere cooled down. "Okay, then, shall we take the tour?"

"Why not?" Noah said. "But don't think for a minute that I'm going to simply wave goodbye to my daughter and tell her, 'Take care of yourself, kid.'"

His simple words, "take care of yourself,"

brought back fresh memories of that painful night when he'd said them to her. A glitzy downtown Charlotte bar followed by a night of… She'd never forgotten. That low voice, that sense of desperation in his tone. Those words of regret spoken in the middle of the night. "Take care of yourself." He'd whispered those words in her ear just before the same voice had said, "I'm sorry. You deserve better than a guy like me. I should have told you. I'm married, for now at least. Maybe once I get things straightened out…"

"Just go," she'd said, letting anger and shame rule her reaction. Regret washed over her as she pulled the bedsheets close around her chest. She'd turned her head, let the tears slip onto her pillow. "Just go, Noah. Go."

It hurt to look at him now. The memory had haunted her too long. She couldn't stare into his piercing eyes and see the man who'd caused her to be someone she'd never been before on a night that turned out to be the beginning of the most soul-searching journey of her life.

But time had changed them both, and today the issue was about Sawyer. Noah's attention was fixed firmly on his daughter, as it should be. So much so that other than a few tense silences, he hadn't shown any sign of knowing who Ava was, or who she'd been.

CHAPTER THREE

SOMETHING ABOUT AVA was strangely familiar. Noah felt as if he'd known her before, but that wasn't likely. She wasn't the sort of woman he was drawn to, though lately his "sort of woman" was becoming a mystery.

When dating, he tended toward women who had a laid-back personality, were quick to laugh and appreciated his sense of humor. Since his divorce, Noah had dated several women. Coincidentally, three of them had been named Ava. This attractive, but opinionated woman seemed to judge him with a glance and a word. No way would he have dated a woman who sweated the small stuff.

In one moment Ava had gone from being in control, calm, even kind—a woman who searched for solutions to difficult problems. Now she almost seemed like someone who was hiding something. First, she was looking him directly in the eye and then she was looking anywhere that didn't include him in her line of sight. Had she changed her mind about keeping Sawyer? That would be okay with him. He would take his daughter home, if he could get her to go.

He'd been so relieved when the Chapel Hill cop called with information on Sawyer. So, on practically no sleep, he'd left his house figuring he'd race to this little town of Holly River, pick up his daughter and give this parenting gig another try. He'd told Mrs. Filmore to plan on both of them being home for dinner.

He knew Sawyer didn't care for the housekeeper, but she'd never liked any of the women he'd hired, four in the last year to be exact. They'd all come highly recommended. Strict? Conscientious? Sure. That's what he'd wanted in a competent housekeeper, one who wouldn't let his clever daughter make the rules, and then bend them when they didn't suit her. He'd wanted a kindly grandmother type who could relate to Sawyer on a personal level but be able to wield a strong sword when Sawyer's lack of discipline called for it.

Now he was on the verge of firing this

latest woman who, Sawyer claimed, as always, was more wielder than relater. Maybe he'd keep Mrs. Filmore on until Sawyer decided life at the Sawtooth Children's Home wasn't any more to her liking than life in Chapel Hill. In fact, she might decide it was far worse. This change of heart might happen in less than a week.

True, Sawyer didn't care for the housekeepers, and she'd probably be happier if the only person she had to answer to was her dad, but she'd never complained about the many material things her absentee father's job provided. She couldn't have the lifestyle she'd grown used to if she had a parent who was home all the time sitting behind a desk, but couldn't make enough money to keep paying off a fancy home in an exclusive suburb and credit card debt. Sawyer needed to learn the meaning of trade-offs. He sure as heck had, and it was time his daughter mastered one of life's toughest lessons.

And besides, he'd seen enough of Ava Cahill to know that she wasn't going to be a pushover. Until he'd actually looked at her and found her reluctant to look back, he'd decided Ava was strong, authoritative and the most powerful figure at the home. Her word was apparently law, and Sawyer might decide in a few days that she couldn't cope with the regimented lifestyle of Ava's rules.

As the threesome prepared for the tour, Ava seemed to have returned to her role as by-the-book administrator. She hadn't looked at Noah since they went out the front door of the administration building. The only view he had of Ava was her rigid back as she walked in front of him and her dark hair pulled tightly into a bun. He could almost believe she'd forgotten he was there.

Ava and Sawyer walked together and Noah followed. Ava kept up a steady stream of conversation with his daughter, pointing, waiting for a reaction from Sawyer that was probably never going to satisfy her. Maybe Ava loved this place, but Noah knew his daughter. She was probably already planning her next escape.

"Let's take the golf cart," Ava said, approaching the vehicle left by the front entrance. "It's probably warmed up enough that we'll be comfortable. Besides, the campus is rather large, and we need to cover quite a bit of ground." Logical Ava, back to analyzing, deciding, but without the sensitivity of the person he'd met when he first arrived. The woman who claimed a personal and heart-felt relationship with all the children under her care. Where had this Ava gone? Had she ever really existed?

Sawyer quickly climbed in the front seat next to Ava, probably to avoid sitting with her father. Noah took the rear seat and angled his body so he wouldn't miss any of Ava and Sawyer's conversation. He was still the father, and he wasn't about to give up any of his parental rights without knowing what Sawyer was getting into.

"So what's the story of all you Cahills?" Noah said as a way of breaking the ice and asserting his presence. "How many are you? Do you more or less run this town?"

Ava drove the cart around the side of the building. She still hadn't looked at him. Her attention was on her driving as if the windshield had asked the question. Good grief, it was just a golf cart. What's the worst that could happen if she made a driving error? They'd have to circle a sand trap?

"I don't see what my family has to do with

your leaving Sawyer in my care, but okay," she said. "I can satisfy your curiosity."

"I appreciate that," he said.

"You met my brother Carter, who is chief of police. His wife is Miranda. As Carter told you, she's a social worker. My other brother, Jace, runs the family Christmas tree farm. His soon-to-be wife is Kayla. Then there's Emily, Miranda's daughter, Nathan, Jace's son, and my mother, who lives just outside of town. Of course, we need to add in numerous uncles, aunts and cousins." She headed toward a field where people had gathered. "Satisfied?"

"What do you think of that, Sawyer?" he asked his daughter. "In our family it's just you and me. Do you wish there were more of us?"

Noah waited for the answer. After an uncomfortable few seconds, Sawyer just said, "No. One dictator is enough."

Ava stopped at a grassy area. Tables were set up and folks were helping themselves to food and drinks. Many of the younger ones wore Sawtooth Home sweatshirts on which was proudly displayed a large, sturdy oak tree, obviously the origin of the name.

"What's going on here?" Noah asked.

"This is our typical Sunday gathering," Ava said. "The kids and the cottage parents get out of cooking and doing dishes as long as the weather is nice, and we have a picnic on the grounds." She parked the golf cart out of the way of the festivities. "Have a walk around if you like. Grab a hot dog. I'll just be a minute."

With no further explanation, Ava walked toward a dark-haired young boy. The child, probably no more than five years old, trotted over to her. Noah wasn't an expert on kids, and he couldn't get a good look at the kid's face, but he decided the boy looked well dressed and well cared for if not especially happy to be eating hot dogs on a crisp Sunday afternoon.

Ava knelt down in front of him, held his hand and talked to him awhile. After a short time, she stood and spoke in a loud voice. "Run off and have a good time, Charlie. It's a beautiful day for doing anything you want." The child didn't run. He ambled away, and he didn't look like he was going to have any sort of a good time.

Ava dusted off her black pants and readjusted the red sweater set she was wearing. She watched the boy for some time until Noah came up beside her. "So he's one of the residents I guess," Noah said.

Startled, almost as if she'd forgotten her purpose with these newcomers, Ava whirled to face him. "I thought you were getting a hot dog."

"Actually you *told* us to get hot dogs, but I don't live here and decided I didn't have to follow your order. I don't know what Sawyer is doing."

A wave of her hair escaped her bun and caught on some lipstick. She quickly tucked the errant strand behind her ear. For some reason Noah was fixated on the gesture. Ava Cahill had nice lips, he thought, though he couldn't understand why he would spend so long looking at them or imagining what a lucky man might do with those lips.

She cleared her throat, pulled the lapels of her sweater more closely over her breasts and crossed her arms, which brought her back to administrator mode. "Yes. He's a relatively new arrival. His parents died in a plane accident."

"Wow. Tough," Noah said.

"Yes, it is. I try to give him special attention when I can." She started walking toward the tables where Sawyer had obviously decided that an overcooked hot dog was better than no lunch at all. Noah walked beside her.

"So this kid is actually an orphan?" Noah said.

Ava swallowed, looked straight ahead. "I told you we have children here from all walks of life and many different situations. Little Charlie is just one example of a resident who has no home to go back to."

"I can see why you get wrapped up in their lives," Noah said. "Every story is its own personal tragedy."

She stared up at him with striking blue eyes that he somehow knew would be just as beautiful in the near darkness. In daylight they matched the sky on this beautiful fall afternoon. "You have no idea, but today we need to concentrate on Sawyer's story."

Slightly miffed, Noah said, "My daughter's story is hardly a tragedy. We're just having some temporary problems."

"Perhaps," she said vaguely. "Suit yourself about the hot dog, but I think I'll have one before we continue the tour."

She walked away from him, stopping often to speak to various people. Nearly every day Noah looked down upon the earth from two to five hundred feet in the air, perched on a narrow tower of steel and cables. He knew what it was like to feel dizzy, but never before had he experienced the kind of dizzy that Ava Cahill displayed.

She seemed to be everywhere, talking to kids, adults, staff members. She responded to folks calling her Miss Cahill, Ava, and from the younger ones, Miss Ava. She gave everyone time, a smile, a word. Her energy was impressive. He found himself wishing that some of it were directed at him. She didn't seem nearly as concerned with convincing him of the benefits of living at Sawtooth as she was convincing Sawyer. Despite what Ava might believe, Noah knew his daughter, and they would both be a hard sell. After lunch, Noah, Sawyer and Ava climbed back into the golf cart and continued the tour. They saw a school building, an auditorium, a gymnasium and a science lab. Sawyer seemed observant enough, even interested, though she asked no questions. Noah, on the other hand, asked plenty. No way was he going to leave his daughter in a strange place until he knew everything that made this home tick. And even then, he wasn't sure what decision he would make.

Ava answered each question in a crisp, concise, knowledgeable manner. Her voice was steady. She didn't waste words.

They ended the tour at one of the cottages. This one was painted a soft gray with white trim. Walking inside, they found a lounge area with two television sets, comfortable seating, a game table and toddler toys tucked away in colorful crates. A few of the seats were occupied since hot dog time had ended.

"Let me show you what will be your room if you decide to stay, Sawyer," Ava said, directing them to a stairway off the lounge.

Noah noticed that the doors leading to bedrooms were open. This fact alone should make Sawyer rethink her decision. At the house in Chapel Hill, one would have thought his daughter's room was a field office for the CIA, as she not only kept her door closed, but locked as well. He'd assumed all teenage girls wanted their privacy, and he respected Sawyer's, only gaining entry to her area when invited. Had that been a mistake on his part? Should he have been more of a snoop?

They entered a room with two twin beds, two dressers, two desks, two closets. Standard dorm room equipped. Both beds were made, but one bed had girlie pillows and a few stuffed animals on it. The other bed was obviously waiting for an occupant.

"You met Becky at lunch, didn't you?" Ava asked Sawyer. Sawyer indicated she had. "If we all decide that you are going to stay here, you'll be sharing this room with her."

"How do you feel about that?" Noah asked his daughter. Not only had she never shared a room, he couldn't recall when she'd ever had to share anything.

Sawyer managed to shrug one shoulder with indifference.

"How soon is all this going to take place?" Noah asked Ava, a tingle of panic snaking down his spine. He finally had to accept that this change of address might really be going to happen, and he would be faced with returning to Chapel Hill without her.

"We should get Sawyer settled in right away," she said. "You can send her clothes and personal items from Chapel Hill. In the meantime, we can provide the bare essentials. Our kids wear jeans and Sawtooth School T-shirts to class, and we have plenty of those."

A uniform? Noah watched Sawyer's face for any signs of rebellion. If there was one thing he knew about his daughter, it was that she was not a uniform kind of kid. She hated regimentation of any type. Once again Sawyer's face was unreadable. Did she think she was trading one Mrs. Filmore for another equally restrictive one? Was she planning to escape out the open window over the dressers and shimmy down a gutter? She had to recall that Ava said all the windows were protected by a security system.

"So, what do you think, Sawyer?" Ava asked. "Would you like to give Sawtooth Home a try?"

"Sure. I guess."

Not a ringing endorsement, Noah thought. She had to be planning something.

"Let's all go back to the administration building and start on the paperwork. I've arranged for one of our counselors to meet with you this afternoon, Sawyer. You'll like

Mrs. Marcos. While you're talking with her, your father and I will fill out the necessary forms for a voluntary resident."

Noah couldn't hold his tongue. "That's what you think she is, a *voluntary* resident?"

At last he knew what a sharp look from Ava was like. "Of course. All our residents are here because this home is preferable in one way or another to their previous environments. No one is forcing your daughter to stay here, Noah," Ava said. "I believe she is willing to give this a try."

Noah stared at his daughter's face once again. She gave him an innocent smile—one he'd seen many times in the past. And one he didn't believe for an instant. He figured she'd hop on the back of his motorcycle the minute he turned the key. "Sure," he said, deciding to call her bluff. "Let's go fill out those papers."

When they returned to the administration building, Sawyer went to her appointment, and Ava led Noah into her office. "Have a seat, Noah," she said. "This will take some time. We need to go over Sawyer's medical history, her previous grades, her food preferences and allergies, anything you can think of to help us make the transition easier for her."

He'd thought the Ava he preferred, the kind, all-children-are-important Ava might return when it came time to do paperwork. But no. This woman was disciplined, almost cold. She still didn't seem able to look him in the eye. That bothered him more than a little. Was she hiding something about herself or this "perfect" school she claimed to run?

"Remember, right now this is only temporary, until we can evaluate Sawyer's needs and the problems in the family. When we feel that Sawyer can return to a healthy home environment, we will discuss letting her go with you."

"Gee, that would be terrific," Noah said sarcastically. "How much is this going to cost me?"

"We're funded by the state and private donations," Ava said. "Certainly we appreciate every donation we get, large or small."

"Message received," he said. "Okay, then, ask whatever you need to. I'd like to get this finished and maybe have a nap this afternoon."

Those beautiful and somehow unforgettable blue eyes shot him a perplexed look. "A nap? Aren't you returning to Chapel Hill?"

"I've decided to get a room in town for a few days."

"We really don't advise…"

"I know what you're going to say, but I think it would be wise for me to stick around awhile."

"Why do you think that?"

"No offense, Ava, but my guess is that Sawyer won't be here in the morning, and I'd just as soon be closer to the action when I have to go pick her up again."

CHAPTER FOUR

THERE WERE SO many ways Noah Walsh was pushing Ava's buttons—emotionally and even frantically and with strong memories that had never gone away. Little did she know that when she decided to help Sawyer, she would be standing face-to-face with the man who'd left her shamed, panicked and pregnant six years ago. She'd thought that if she intervened between him and his daughter, he would agree to the home's terms and her advice and leave. But he was proving to be an extremely stubborn man.

Though difficult, Ava had to remember her role in this drama. She was the administrator of a children's home, and the residents were her biggest concern. So she did her best under the ticklish circumstances to talk Noah out of staying in town, saying that once a resident decision had been made, it was best for the child to begin adapting immediately. All this was true, and while Noah nodded the whole time she talked, the unforgettable piercing intensity of his eyes told her he wasn't going to change his mind. He signed the necessary papers with a warning that if Sawyer decided at the last minute that she didn't want to stay, he expected the papers to be torn up. And then he left Sawtooth determined to find a comfortable room for the night. At least she was reassured that he hadn't placed her in his life six years ago. But then again, had he? And if he stayed, would he?

Ava spent the evening with Sawyer, helping her to settle in, finding out what items she would like sent from home, introducing her to other residents, especially to Charlie, though Ava was careful not to send up any hints as to their connection. She wondered if they would naturally get along or if inherent sibling rivalry would become apparent. The irony that the two children were blood relatives didn't escape Ava's thought processes for one minute.

She hoped the two kids would at least have an amiable relationship since they were living in the same cottage. They would be encouraged to get along just like all cottage bunkmates were. As long as Ava was careful, as long as she followed the advice of the counselor, Mrs. Marcos, the two children would never learn of their strong ties until, and only if, the time was right.

And hopefully Noah wouldn't remember the time he spent with Ava in Charlotte either. It was only one night. It had started in a dimly lit cocktail bar and ended in her dimly lit bedroom. She had changed since then, not just physically, but in many ways. She'd been so careful today, once she realized who Noah was, to keep their past a secret, and not offer any clues that might cause him to remember. She told herself again that he must have had numerous relationships since then. Why would he remember a woman dressed in a business suit in a Charlotte bar?

Sawyer was quiet during most of the introductions Ava made at the cottage. Perhaps she would become more talkative as time passed. Later, sitting quietly in Sawyer's room, Ava helped the girl decide on the courses she would take as a freshman in the high school. She would start school bright and early the next day. All residents were urged to establish routines as soon as possible.

When Ava went to bed that night, her thoughts turned to Noah, the man he was now—strong, decisive, determined, but perhaps lost in knowing ways to deal with his daughter, and the man he was then—charming, cocky, ultimately irresistible. He had appealed to all her senses that night in Charlotte. She'd flirted with him, teased him, tempted him—all the things she normally didn't do with any man. He'd stirred her from the inside out, warmed her to her core.

But Ava had to deal with Noah, the man he was now. The frustrated father of a teenager who needed a champion on her side. For Sawyer's sake, Ava had to remember her purpose. She couldn't think of Noah as anyone other than a man who needed to get his daughter back. True, he was no longer married, but that didn't matter now. He'd gone from her bedroom and her life without a forwarding address. They'd had their moment and now it was too late to go back. Ava had made a heartbreaking decision when she discovered she was pregnant, and now she would spend the rest of her life making it right for Charlie.

She wished she understood the complexities of the relationship between Sawyer and Noah. Was he really such a terrible father? Was Sawyer truly such an impossible child? Of one thing, Ava was extremely confident. Sawyer would still be there in the morning, despite her father's dire prediction. She wasn't nearly as confident about Noah, who might change his mind after one night in a Holly River bed-and-breakfast. Somehow she couldn't picture him settling into a place full of country charm and cuteness.

She wondered where he had found a room, what he was doing, what plans he might be making, and most strangely, if she would see him again soon. Her rational side urged her to hope that she would not see him. Maybe he hadn't even taken a room and had returned to Chapel Hill, leaving his troubled daughter behind. The possibility that he had stayed, that she might be seeing him, encountering that oddly mesmerizing blend of power and uncertainty, caused her to spend a restless night.

Ava started Monday with the gratifying

knowledge that Sawyer hadn't decided to leave Sawtooth and, in fact, was in class, wearing the standard uniform of jeans and a Sawtooth T-shirt. Needing a diversion from the odd and unpredictable occurrences of the day before, Ava was glad she had accepted an invitation from her brother Jace, to meet at the Holly River Café. They were going to discuss family matters, specifically the welfare of their newly discovered half-brother, Robert, with whom Jace had established a bond.

Ava arrived at the restaurant thirty minutes early. She sat at a table for two and ordered a coffee. Not five minutes had passed before she heard the familiar low tones of someone behind her.

"So, is my daughter still in Holly River?"

Ava spun around, nearly upsetting her coffee mug. "Oh, Noah, you startled me."

Dressed in the same jeans he'd worn yesterday but with a fresh shirt under his black leather jacket, he looked calm, relaxed, demonstrating the exact opposite of the gymnastics going on inside her at his unexpected presence. Maybe he had put enough trust in Ava to allow himself to get a good night's sleep. His hair was still damp from a shower. He finger-combed a few strands from his forehead.

"Is this seat taken?" He pulled out the other chair.

"I'm waiting for someone, but he's usually late, and I'm early," she said.

Noah took a seat. "Is this a business meeting?"

"More a family one," she said.

He signaled for the waitress, and Allie, girlfriend of Sam McCall and a friend of all the Cahills, who'd recently got her job back at the café, came over. Ava thought Noah would order a coffee, but he scanned a menu quickly and decided on the Big Mountain Breakfast of eggs, pancakes and bacon. For a moment Ava was jealous. She hadn't eaten the café's specialty in years.

When Allie walked away, Noah leaned back in his chair. "Since we exchanged cell numbers and you didn't call, I assume my daughter didn't run away last night."

"You assume correctly. Sawyer is right now—" she glanced at her watch "—in her ninth grade earth science class."

"Great. Understanding the earth will open

up new avenues for her escape act. It's a big planet."

"If you don't mind me saying so, Noah…" Her index finger involuntarily shot out toward his chest, a habit she'd tried to break for years.

He backed away from the offending finger. "I think I might mind a bit," he said.

She placed her hand on the table. "I understand that your joking about your daughter is just a defense mechanism—"

"Actually, you're wrong," he said. "Believe it or not, Sawyer is my number one concern. She has been since her mother left five years ago."

"If that's true," Ava said, "why are you away from her for long periods at a time?"

He frowned. "What did she tell you?"

"Not much. Only that you are basically an absentee parent."

"I suppose my schedule could look that way to her. The truth is, I'm gone at the most for a week at a time. And I try to make up for my absences by staying home a few days in between, only taking jobs close to Chapel Hill. The rash of hurricanes this last summer kept me away from Sawyer more than I would have liked."

He shrugged. "Of course, things don't always work out the way I want them to. I suppose it's just human nature that forces us to adapt to sudden inexplicable happenings in our lives."

His deep stare made her squirm in her chair.

"Don't you agree, Ava?"

"I'm not sure."

"I mean we can be going along just fine. We know what we're about, where we're headed, and then boom, something totally unexpected, something we're not prepared to deal with changes the entire course of our lives."

She looked away from him, cleared her throat. "I don't understand what you're trying to say to me, Noah. How does this philosophical meandering relate to your daughter?"

"It doesn't, not this time. It relates to you."

"Me?" Ava felt the muscles in her chest tightening.

Seemingly relaxed, he leaned slightly forward. "When were you going to tell me?" he asked. "Were you ever going to?"

"I don't know what you're talking about."

"I'm talking about a night in Charlotte six years ago. A chance meeting between myself and a young woman in a cocktail bar. A night of lovemaking that made me feel like a heel for not being completely honest with her."

"You must have me confused with…"

"Not going to work, Ava. You can try lying. You can make up a completely different scenario, but I know." He rubbed his chin while the waitress brought his coffee. "I had a dream last night," he said. "All evening I tried to figure out why you didn't look directly at me, why you seemed sort of familiar. And then, as dreams often play with our lives, the truth came to me."

There was no point denying it. He was as sure of her identity as she was of his. She remained silent, not knowing if he was angry, confused, if he would say something as innocuous as "How the heck have you been?"

What he did say was spoken in a calm, rational way. "So, you got your hair cut."

She touched a few straight strands at her shoulder. "Yes."

"And the glasses? I kind of liked the whole

librarian look you had that night. Hair in a tight topknot thing, dark-framed glasses. But now you can see?"

"I still need glasses for close work," she said. "But I've had laser surgery."

He moved his hands from his shoulders downward to his knees. "And what's all this? More curves, fewer angles. You're softer."

His memories made her uncomfortable. He had recalled so many details, and she had assumed he'd forgotten about her the minute he left her apartment. "I've gained a dress size," she said. "My mother's cooking, I guess."

He stared at her as if he were looking at a painting in the Louvre. "Looks good on you."

She had to move the conversation away from the past before she revealed too much. So she said the one thing she felt he needed to know, the one thing he might have misunderstood about that night. And the one thing that would lead them away from thoughts of continuing where they'd left off. "You should know, I don't make a habit of indulging in one-night stands. That night was out of character for me. And when I recognized you yesterday, I felt a return of the guilt."

"You don't have to excuse yourself to me, Ava," he said. "I never once thought I was one man in a string of many. In fact, I left your house feeling like someone very special."

"Nevertheless, I did feel guilty." She checked her watch. This would not be a good time for Jace to walk into the café. "Well, then, I'm truly glad this is out in the open, that there are no misconceptions. We both need to realize that the current situation we're facing is not about either one of us. It's about Sawyer."

He gave her a small smile she couldn't interpret. After a moment, he said, "Okay. Back to Sawyer."

"She should do well at Sawtooth," Ava said. "And while we're on the subject of your relationship with your daughter…"

"Were we on that subject?" he asked.

"We should be, Noah." She took a sip of coffee and wondered why it suddenly tasted bitter and seemed to stick in her throat. But she knew. This had to be one of the most awkward conversations she'd ever had in her life. "Since your occupation is at the heart of Sawyer's problems, why don't you tell me what you do for a living. What is your job description?"

"Job description?" He cocked his head as if he were thinking of words to describe what he did. "Let's see. Looking at dirt from four hundred feet in the air. Clinging to steel poles in twenty-mile-per-hour winds. Checking power circuits to assure I don't electrocute myself. Coming face-to-face with the beady eyes of hungry baby birds. And that's not even taking into account the bees."

Ava pictured a string of telephone poles as she tried to put the clues together. "I didn't think we had many linemen these days, or telephone pole technicians. Isn't everything underground cables now?"

"Not everything, but mostly, yes. Unfortunately what I do involves keeping cell phone service running smoothly. That's totally different from making your landline work. I'm one of the guys who climbs to the top of cell towers, those scrawny, skeletal structures of crisscrossed poles that reach high into the sky."

She let the mental image sink in while

he obviously waited for a reaction. "You do know what cell towers are?" he asked.

"Of course. I guess I just never imagined climbing them. That must be very difficult."

"It gets easier once you get your first fifty or so structures under your belt."

Amazingly she was beginning to relax. The conversation about his job was a safe topic. "Is there a name for what you do?"

"I'm a tower climber. It's fairly simple and direct. I suppose you can add crew foreman and cell phone technician to my title. Tower climbing takes guts. The second part requires a lot of training and skill."

"Isn't it dangerous?"

"I'd put it up there with lion taming and fire swallowing...without the thrill of being in a circus."

Ava wasn't comfortable criticizing anyone's occupation. After all, she quit her high-paying corporate job in Charlotte to manage eighty youngsters who needed direction and purpose in their lives. Many of her friends had thought she was a fool. Of course, they didn't know that a big part of her decision was Charlie. Once she'd learned of his parents' deaths, she immediately began plans to become part of his life. The Sawtooth Home seemed like the perfect opportunity. Since she had an open adoption agreement with Charlie's parents and knew of their deaths, she urged the state to send Charlie to the school. Getting the administrator's job was just the icing on the cake. Ava would have returned to Holly River no matter what.

She'd gotten the job at Sawtooth Home because of her administrative skills, but she soon discovered she had a strong emotional attachment to the duties, primarily because of Charlie, but not just because of him. Every one of the eighty kids was special to her.

She tapped her finger against the side of her coffee mug. "Would you agree that your choice of employment is one of the reasons for the estrangement between you and Sawyer, and in fact, the main reason she runs away? We've established you're gone for long periods."

His food was delivered to the table. He tucked his napkin into his shirt collar. "Need to go clothes shopping today," he said. "As for my daughter having a problem with my job, yeah, I suppose she does. But her complaints seem to go away when she needs new clothes, the latest smartphone, or an iPad." He snapped off a piece of bacon and rolled his eyes as if he were communicating with heaven. "Bottom line, Ava, I make pretty good money hanging off towers."

"Is this the only job you've had, as an adult, I mean?"

"Nope. I suppose you can count the four years I spent in the belly of fighter planes as a technician in Afghanistan with the Air Force. Followed by a year in technical training school."

"Afghanistan. Another dangerous job," she said.

"No complaints from me. I was with a great crew. Everyone knew their job and did it well." He took a bite of egg.

She gave him a sharp look of disapproval. "I know you're trying for cool, calm and collected, Noah, but I'm seeing a pattern here."

He stopped chewing and stared at her over his suspended fork. "What kind of pattern?"

"One of taking risks and not behaving seriously, or at least considering how your choices affect the people around you."

He frowned. Maybe she'd gone too far.

"You're not suggesting I have some sort of

death wish, are you?" Noah asked. "Because I don't. And, also, I happen to be highly trained and skilled in a service people like you need every day, people who complain if they can't text the pizza place to get their order in. I'm also well paid to do this job."

She scowled at him. "I get it. But I do use my cell phone for much more important matters. Although, the pizza in this town is pretty good."

He smiled.

"Has Sawyer ever asked you to quit this job?"

The smile vanished as his lips hardened. "She's a kid. She can't control what I do with my life or the choices I make. Especially if I make them with her best interests in mind. Believe me, that's more than my parents did."

"I'm sorry to hear that, but it doesn't mean you have to make the same mistakes they did."

He sat ramrod straight in his chair. "Are you listening to me, Ava? I'm not making the same mistakes. Sawyer has everything she needs. She can reach me whenever she wants to. Yeah, I'm gone sometimes, but when I come home, I'm her father in every sense."

"Okay, but I've found that too often children are left out of family decisions. Families work better when everyone has a say in what's going on."

"I'm not sure I buy into that, Ava. There has to be one person who ultimately makes the decision. Is this *equal say* philosophy how you Cahills do it?"

She couldn't answer with complete honesty. Her father not only made decisions for himself and his wife, but for his children as well. And just recently she and her brother Carter, had surreptitiously gone through their mother's papers to discover why Cora was suddenly pinching pennies. But that was for a good reason. "For the most part," she finally said. "At least since my father died. If Sawyer has a problem with your job, she should feel free to express her concerns."

He released a sarcastic chuckle before wiping his mouth. At least he had relaxed a bit. "Believe me, Sawyer doesn't feel inhibited expressing her concerns about anything. And she doesn't have a problem with my job. Her complaints are about the wicked witches I've left in charge of the household when I'm not around."

"And does she have a point about these ladies?"

Noah lifted his fork and aimed it casually at Ava. "I'd be happy to show you the references I've gathered on all these women," he said. "Even the paper they're printed on is squeaky clean."

Ava took another sip of her lukewarm coffee. "Still, something is causing Sawyer to run away from home."

"Yes, and she could run away from your home as well. Sawyer has a way of viewing everyone in a position of authority through the same lens. You could be the next wicked witch."

Is that what he thought of her six years ago? No, she didn't think so. He had treated her as if she were unique, special. But that was then. "I suppose I could. But, Noah, something has to be done. Sawyer's behavior is dangerous."

"You think I don't know that?" He set his napkin on his empty plate. "You think I haven't considered giving up my job to stay home?"

"Have you?"

He pulled some bills from his wallet and

tossed them on the table. "Of course. But here's the bottom line. Sawyer has a problem with authority. She always has. That's why her mother left. Maybe if I were a 24/7 dad, I could control her better, but I don't really believe that. Trust me. To my daughter I'm the lesser of two evils. I'm slightly more compassionate than her self-centered mother, and I'm a bit more tractable than the housekeepers I've hired."

He slid back from the table, the chair making a harsh scraping noise on the wood floor. "I've come to accept my role in Sawyer's life. Money provider, swinging door dad. It is what it is. Do I worry about her? Of course. Do I lose sleep over her? Every night. Do I chase her all over the state of North Carolina when I have to? I do. I keep bringing her home. I pray her street smarts will keep her safe. I hope the next time I hire someone, it will work out. As far as Sawyer and I are concerned, our life together is one big trial and error."

His eyes pierced into Ava's heart with a sadness she'd never have expected from him. She almost always blamed the parents when a child became difficult to control. And her first instinct was to blame Noah Walsh. Maybe she'd been too hasty. He wasn't a perfect parent, but he suddenly seemed a caring one. Just as he'd seemed a caring man that night…

Was he willing to do what had to be done to repair the relationship with his daughter? She hoped so, but it was too soon to tell, and she didn't relish the thought of working so closely with him. She'd only kept their past a secret from him for twenty-four hours and he'd figured it out. Could he also tell that she was keeping an even bigger secret?

He stood and pointed at the money on the table. "That should cover your coffee."

"Noah, wait."

He grabbed his leather jacket from the back of the chair and hung it over his arm. He didn't say anything, just stood there waiting.

Why had she stopped him? What had she intended to say? She didn't know, but she didn't want him to leave after confessing to the problems he dealt with every day with Sawyer. She wanted him to know that there was hope for any relationship if feelings were genuine and both parties were open and honest. But she was just an administrator. Her skills were in the field of organization and decision making. She wasn't trained to help families with deep emotional trauma. But she wanted to help this family.

After an uncomfortable silence, she said, "What are your plans now? Are you going back to Chapel Hill?"

"Nope. I'm sticking around. Took a few days off work and arranged for a stay at… of all places…the Hummingbird Inn across the street. Cute."

"What do you hope to accomplish?"

"Who knows? Maybe something. Maybe nothing." His eyes narrowed. "Nothing against you, Miss Ava, but I'm going to be here for a while just in case."

Was he saying he didn't trust her to take care of his daughter? "Just in case what?"

He shook his head. "Boy, are there a lot of answers to that question. Nice running into you again, Ava. Who would have thought…? Oh, wait, to be honest, I thought about it a lot." He turned away, and with a strong and purposeful stride, headed to the door. He nearly bumped into Jace coming inside.

Jace ambled over to the table, one eye on

Ava, the other on the retreating figure of Noah. "Am I misreading this situation or did that guy with the leather jacket and Harley-Davidson boots just get up from your table?"

"About time, Jace."

"So who's the guy, and is that a twinkle in your eye?"

How wrong he was. If anything, the twinkle was a telltale tear about—well, any number of things. "It is not," she said. "I just squeezed some lemon into my water and a drop squirted onto my face." She blinked to prove her lie.

"So does he have an actual motorcycle to go with his bad boy outfit?"

Ava described the noisy, large, black motorcycle that pulled up in front of her office the day before.

"Lots of chrome?" Jace asked.

"I don't know. Does it matter?"

"Only that at one time in my wasted youth I might have idolized this fella." Jace took a seat. "So what's the connection between you and Bad Bart?"

Ava scowled at him. "His name is Noah Walsh, and our connection is a business one.

We have a mutual concern about a resident at the home."

Jace paused as he considered what she'd told him. "Could that be the breaking and entering criminal who showed up the night before last?"

"Carter told you? I'm not surprised."

"We're your brothers, Ava. You hardly ever need our help but we can't stop watching out for you."

"The cross I have to bear."

He smiled.

"Yes. Noah is her father."

Wanting to get away from the topic as quickly as possible, Ava opted for a new subject. "How are Nathan and Kayla?"

Jace's smile broadened. "My son is fine. Getting good grades, something I never did, and making friends, something I did too much of. As for Kayla, she can't wait for the next three and a half weeks to fly by so she can make an honest man out of me."

"Thank goodness for Kayla," Ava teased. "Glad someone finally came along who had the gumption to make something of you." Ava was only partly kidding. Jace had pretty much avoided family responsibilities for years, but since meeting Kayla and Nathan, he had decided to make their mother's dreams come true and take over management of the family Christmas tree farm. Now he worked two jobs, one at the farm, and one at his original business, High Mountain Rafting.

Ava signaled for a refill of her coffee mug. "How are the wedding plans coming along?" she asked her brother.

Jace ordered a cup. "You're asking me? I'm just the groom. The Crestview Barn is locked down as the venue and I've heard Mama and Kayla talking about flowers and stuff. That's all I know. And Nathan is stoked about being my best man." Jace chuckled. "A ten-year-old in a tux…how cool is that?"

Jace had only recently met his child. He'd never known that the relationship he'd had in college had produced a son. He hadn't seen the boy's mother again, and truly never even thought about her. But as she lay dying, she asked her best friend, Kayla, to find Nathan's father and see if a relationship could result between the two. Turns out Susan, Nathan's mother, had strong intuition. Now the relationship had become a threesome.

"How is Carter taking the demotion from best man to groomsman?" she asked.

"He's okay with it. We'll be a small group of incredibly debonair guys at the altar, Ava. Me, Nathan, Carter and Sam McCall. Can't have a Cahill wedding without McCall."

Ava couldn't argue. She and Kayla's best friend and one cousin would have tough competition measuring up to the groom's side. "It will be a beautiful Christmas wedding," she said.

"Yeah. Don't I hear Mama say that about every other day. I just want it to be over with."

"It will be in just under four weeks. Twenty-seven days and counting, Jace. You'll officially be a husband, new father with a lot to learn, entrepreneur and Christmas tree farm operator." Ava smiled. "Who would have thought it?"

"Not me for a lot of years," Jace said. "But I'm kind of liking being a tree farmer. Though I hope I'll have a few days off after the holiday rush."

Ava smiled. "I think you can count on some time off, Jace. This may be your first year running the farm, but you'll find out that people usually don't buy trees when Christmas is over."

"Very funny."

"Now why are we here this morning?" Ava asked. "What's going on?"

"Okay. Well, I was just thinking. What with the wedding coming up and all, I figure it would be good to spend a little more time with our half-brother, Robert. You know he just had a birthday? He's thirteen now."

"Right, I remember," Ava said. "I have met Robert before."

"Just that one time," Jace said. "He hadn't started school then. No one but his mother could help him cope with his autism."

Ava would likely never forget the day she and Carter had driven to Wilton Hollow to investigate Gladys Kirshner, a woman to whom their mother, Cora, had been sending fifteen hundred dollars a month since the family's patriarch, Raymond Cahill, died. Almost nothing Raymond had done in his life surprised his three children, but this—infidelity, a child born out of wedlock, a secret buried for over a decade. Wow. They were still reeling from the shock.

Cora had made her husband's debts her

debts, and she'd continued his child support payments to Robert without question and without telling her three children why she'd suddenly canceled vacations and maintenance on the family home. But Ava had snooped and discovered her father's secret family, and she and Carter had confronted Gladys about Robert's care and the expenses their mother kept paying. At first, Gladys hadn't been receptive, but now the two families had worked out an agreement and Robert was clearly benefiting.

A lot had happened since then. Jace, the least likely of the three Cahill offspring to feel family empathy because of the second-rate way their dad had treated him, had taken to Robert and had had some success in a relationship with him. Jace had gotten Robert into a great school with special education services, and Gladys had been able to go back to work part-time, giving her a chance to grow and eliminating some of the burden from Cora. But despite these strides, the two families had fundamentally remained separate. Apparently Jace wanted to change that now.

"What are you proposing, Jace?" she

asked. "Are you seriously thinking of inviting Gladys and Robert to your wedding?"

"I am, but I'd like us all to get to know each other better before that."

"Jace, have you thought about how this will make Mama feel? Our family and friends will be there. Gladys and Robert will be the glaring truth that Daddy was unfaithful to Mama."

"I talked to her about it. Mama is okay with Robert being at the wedding." He waited for a reaction from Ava. When she remained silent, he added, "He's our half-brother, Ava. We can't pretend he doesn't exist."

"I would never do that, Jace. It's just… I'm still worried about Mama."

"Ava, I've been seeing Robert every week for almost six months. Kayla and Nathan have met him. He's been doing well at Blackthorn School. He and I relate well. The doctors all say…"

"Okay, okay," Ava said. "He should come to the wedding. I realize you've grown close to Robert, and this will be your big day. You don't need my permission to ask Robert to your wedding if that's why you wanted to meet me here this morning."

"No, that's not why. I want Robert and Gladys to come to Mama's for dinner this Sunday and I need to know it will be okay with you."

The Cahill Sunday dinner, a cherished sacrament of family ritual and warmhearted sentiment. Ava chuckled. "Well, heck, Jace, why not? You've gone this far. Mama said she's tired of having turkey since Thanksgiving, so she's planning on a big Italian meal. There should be plenty."

"Great." He reached across the table and patted her hand. "I knew you'd understand. You should invite your new boyfriend, what was his name again... Harley Davidson?"

"Noah Walsh, and he's not my boyfriend. Can you even begin to picture me with a guy like that?" Suddenly her mind took a leap back six years when the unnatural and improbable had happened. Suddenly it wasn't so hard to imagine Ava Cahill with a guy like that.

Jace put some folded dollars on the table and signaled to Allie that he was done. When he started to rise, Ava said, "Wait. I was just thinking. Maybe I'll bring someone to dinner also. Maybe I'll bring Sawyer. She might benefit from being around a normally abnormal family."

Jace chuckled. "You got that right. But why stop there? Why not bring her hunky daddy along, too? I've noticed lately that you could use someone to talk to."

"You're being ridiculous," she said. Putting Noah and Sawyer together in a social setting could have benefits for both of them. But she simply couldn't consider it. The less time she spent with Noah, the better. And the time she was forced to be in his company should be all about Sawyer—the child he knew about. "And besides, it isn't a good idea," she added.

"Have you asked anyone to go to the wedding with you?"

"No, and you should give up on the idea of Noah coming with me. No way could I wear that dress I've got and straddle the back of a motorcycle."

"You could be the hit of the show," he teased.

Ava watched her brother leave. No, Noah could not be invited to the Cahill family home. Eventually she hoped to bring her precious little Charlie to a Sunday dinner, which would add yet another branch to the Cahill family tree. But she said it often enough to counselors and parents at the school. All families are different. There is no such thing as normal anymore.

CHAPTER FIVE

FOR THE NEXT two nights, Ava tossed around the idea of inviting Sawyer to the Cahill home for Sunday dinner. By the time she went to her office on Wednesday morning, she'd decided that, yes, there could be positive advantages to having the girl as part of a safe and friendly family circle. She wouldn't tell Sawyer about the plan until Saturday. That way Noah would have little opportunity to hear about the invitation that didn't include him. She had enough to deal with just knowing he remembered their one night together.

Did her decision not to invite Noah have anything to do with her recent memories of his piercing eyes, rumpled dark hair, ingenuous clueless nature that suggested he needed guidance in his life and relationships? Or her memories of six years ago—soft, skilled hands, toned body, charm that didn't quit. No, of course not.

Her decision was strictly logical. Professionally Ava was in the business of helping children. Personally, she avoided awkward and embarrassing situations, especially ones that could lead to unhappy endings.

Ava was sitting at her desk thinking over the exact way she would propose the invitation to Sawyer when she decided to head to the children's section of the library and visit with Charlie. She made it a point to speak to him every day, but Wednesday was when his kindergarten class went to the library and the boy seemed comfortable there. With a book in his hand he almost appeared like a child who hadn't had his world turned upside down.

Someday this will all be different, Ava thought as she walked the brick pathway to the library. Charlie will come to her with confidence and trust and, if she were lucky, maybe even love.

She spotted him across the room. He looked, well, precious, the one word that always came easily to Ava's mind. In jeans, perhaps a size too large, and a Sawtooth

Home T-shirt, with his jacket hanging over the back of a chair, and his dark hair sticking out every which way from the wind, he was the boy she longed to hold and to love.

"Hello, Charlie," she said, giving him her best smile. "It's so nice to see you."

He looked up, kept the book open on his lap. "Hello, Miss Ava."

"What are you reading?"

He showed her the cover of the book. Cheerful Randolph the Rabbit, wearing a bib and holding a fork sat amidst a mound of carrots. A good day for Randolph, and Ava hoped also a good day for Charlie.

Charlie's hair, dark but slightly lighter than Ava's, settled stick straight to his eyebrows. Both of them had been blessed with thick hair, though neither had the blessing of soft, silky waves. But Charlie's father... Don't go there, Ava.

"Can I sit with you for a moment, sweetheart?" she said, not the least uncomfortable using a term of endearment. This traumatized child needed attention, love, caring, regardless of the fact that he was Ava's own son.

Her gaze stayed on Charlie's face, especially his sad, round blue eyes. What she would give to see that sadness replaced with the natural exuberance of childhood. Children should be happy, always looking forward, not backward. But Charlie had a long way to go before his innocent vision could see anything but loneliness and fear, the benchmarks of his traumatic past. A tragic plane accident had claimed the lives of the two people Ava had entrusted with the privilege of raising her son, and now he was alone.

Ava settled on a plump pillow next to Charlie. "How is everything in your kindergarten class?" she asked him.

"Okay."

"You still like Mrs. Cramer?"

"Sure."

"Everything okay in your cottage?"

"Yeah."

"I look forward to our visits on Wednesday, Charlie. Is there anything you'd like to talk about?"

"No."

"Can I do anything for you?" For once, she hoped he would think of something. Her conversations with him were so similar. He was okay, he needed nothing, he was doing well… Ava knew it wasn't true.

He sat forward in his chair. "There is one thing, Miss Ava."

A chance to help her son. Ava was beyond encouraged. "I'd be happy to help if I can," she said. "What is it?"

"Do you think I could get my very own soccer ball?"

"You want a soccer ball?" She would have lassoed the moon and painted it with black stripes if she'd thought it would bring a smile to her son's face. "Don't you have sports equipment in your cottage?"

"We do, but the bigger kids play with the ball, and I never get a chance to kick it. If I had my own, I could practice."

"Then I shall see that you have a soccer ball, sweetie, just as soon as I can find a really good one."

"Okay."

She started to ask another question, but was interrupted by another Sawtooth Home resident approaching. "Sawyer," Ava said, surprised to see the teen in the library at the youngest ones' special time. Something must have happened, and it wasn't good.

She spoke softly to Charlie. "You know Sawyer, right? She's in your cottage."

"I know her, but she doesn't use the soccer ball."

Ava smiled. Sawyer came forward, handed a note to Ava and stood with her arms crossed over her chest, a typical teen pose of belligerence. "What's this about?" Ava asked.

"Read it," Sawyer said.

It was more a dare than an invitation, but Ava unfolded the note which had been handwritten by Mrs. Carmichael, the current cottage parent of Sawyer's residence. Ava read slowly, careful to grasp the details. When finished, she turned to Charlie. "Would you excuse us for a moment, Charlie? Sawyer and I need to go outside and talk for a few minutes."

Wide-eyed, Charlie said, "Are you coming back?"

"Absolutely. As soon as I've spoken with Sawyer. You continue to enjoy your book, okay?"

"Okay."

Ava walked outside of the library before she frowned at Sawyer.

"Go ahead," the girl said. "Start yelling."

"Is it true, Sawyer? Were you smoking?" Ava asked her.

Sawyer tapped her foot as if Ava was keeping her from something important. "I'm practically an adult and can make my own decisions, so what's the big deal? I'm not stupid. I know smoking is bad for me."

"Sorry to have to tell you, but all that knowledge is not going to get you out of trouble. Let's go to my office."

Once they were seated in Ava's office, the tension only increased.

Sawyer scowled. "So what's my punishment?"

"Are you aware that tobacco in any of its forms is strictly forbidden on this campus?"

"I read the book of rules you gave me, all six boring pages. But I had a partial pack left, and I figured why should it go to waste?"

"This will result in disciplinary action, Sawyer."

The girl didn't flinch. "What will you do, deny my smoking privileges?"

Ava felt her internal thermometer rise. *Stay calm*, she warned herself as her desktop intercom buzzed. "What is it, SherryLynn?"

"Someone's on the phone for you, Ava. His name is Noah Walsh. He's Sawyer's…"

"I know who he is."

"He says it's important."

Still frustrated with Sawyer, Ava said, "Put the call through."

Panic flooded Sawyer's eyes. She waved her hands frantically and mouthed the words, "Don't tell him." With a quick slash of her index finger across her throat, she added, "He'll kill me."

"Good morning, Noah," Ava said.

"Where is my daughter? I've been trying to reach her for the last twenty-four hours."

"Coincidentally she's standing right here in front of my desk," Ava said, her voice even.

Her statement was met with a sigh of relief. "Please put me on speaker," he said.

Ava did as he asked. Noah's voice was low and hoarse, an indication of his obvious stress. "Are you playing games with your cell phone again, Sawyer? Because if you are I'll take it away from you…that's if the warden at that school hasn't already done so."

"I didn't take her phone," Ava said. "She's not allowed to have it on in class. Perhaps…"

"Was she in class at eleven o'clock last night?"

"Well, no, of course not."

"Sawyer?"

"Sorry, Dad. I might have ignored a couple of your calls. I haven't been in the get-a-lecture mood lately." She looked at Ava. "Though it seems I'm getting one anyway."

"I don't want to hear about your moods, Sawyer. Did it occur to you that I might have something important to tell you?"

"Like you're going away again, or you're shipping me home to another one of your coven of housekeepers?"

Noah didn't respond for a moment. "I'm not shipping you anywhere. But yes, I am going on a work trip. There's a storm brewing in the Atlantic, an early winter wind event. I've got to be there."

"Figures. Bye."

"Thanks for your concern. And while we're on the subject of lectures, what are you being lectured about in Ava's office? What did you do?"

"Nothing. It was all a big misunderstanding."

"I'm sure it was." Another pause. "Ava? The truth, please."

Sawyer gave Ava a pleading look, but Ava couldn't lie to a parent. Besides, she needed to know if Sawyer might have more cigarettes hidden somewhere. "The cottage parent caught Sawyer smoking, Noah."

"Oh."

"Oh? That's all you have to say? Do you know where she might have gotten the cigarettes?"

"Gee, I'm not sure," he said. "Maybe from the faculty lounge?"

Sawyer sputtered with surprised amusement.

"This isn't a laughing matter, Noah," Ava said. "Tobacco is forbidden anywhere on campus, and use of it is a serious infraction."

He breathed deeply. "Right. I know. Sawyer is aware of my opinion on smoking, and she also knows that I will punish her for even thinking of taking up that habit."

"I'll take care of it," Ava said.

"And, Sawyer, remember to leave the dang cell phone on. When I'm away, I like to know I can get a hold of you."

Ava looked at Sawyer who gave her response via a severe pout. "Okay, Dad, geez!"

"I've got things to do," Noah said. "Heading out right away to the Outer Banks. Anything else you need to tell me, Ava?"

"No, I guess not." And then she recalled her plan to invite Sawyer to the Cahill home on Sunday. She should tell him now since he was leaving town anyway. "Oh, there is one other thing."

"Yeah?"

"I was going to suggest to Sawyer that she come out to my family's home in the country for Sunday dinner. My mother always has plenty of food and welcomes the company. My brothers and their families will be there, and maybe another relative or two."

"Okay. If Sawyer wants to go, that's fine with me."

"So if you need to speak to her on Sunday, she'll be with me."

"Seems safe enough," he said. "Chances are I won't be back by Sunday, so again, Sawyer, leave the cell phone on."

Ava took her phone off speaker mode. "So you're going to the Outer Banks?" she asked Noah, though she knew his where-abouts were hardly her business.

"Yep. Big windstorm predicted. I've got to have a crew there in case cell service is lost, which it probably will be. MaxiCom has to be ready."

She recalled the details he'd given her about his job, the risks involved. "Take care of yourself," she said. "We… I mean Sawyer will be anxious to hear from you when your work is done."

"Yeah, right. She'll be on pins and nee-dles. Anyway, take good care of my kid. Somebody has to."

"Of course. It's what I do." Maybe once he left Holly River, he would just keep going and return to Chapel Hill, where he could resume his life.

The realization that she might never see him again brought an unfamiliar ache of emptiness to Ava's stomach, not unlike the pang of guilt she felt six years ago. But why should she feel regret? She hadn't known him before that one night. He'd left without giving her a phone number or address. And, he'd been married. Yes, she had a big se-cret that she would never tell him, but otherwise, he should mean nothing to her. Except, strangely another connection now existed between them. Now they were connected through Sawyer and both father and daughter needed guidance.

The only sentiment she should be feeling for either Walsh family member was sympathy and a desire to help, not this sudden sense of loss that Noah was going away.

"I suppose that's it, then," she said. "You can keep up with Sawyer's activities by contacting her cottage parents."

"Are you saying I can't contact you?"

"I didn't mean that. Naturally you can. I just thought it would be easier…"

"Frankly, Ava, nothing about this whole situation seems easy. But I get that. I'm not so easy myself. And by the way, thanks for having Sawyer out to your family home. I hope she enjoys herself with all you Cahills."

"Goodbye, Noah."

Ava hung up the phone. She'd almost forgotten that Sawyer was in the room.

"You see?" Sawyer said. "So typical. He doesn't care about anyone but himself."

For a moment Ava struggled to connect the dots between what she'd just heard from

Noah and what Sawyer said. "What do you mean? Why do you think that?"

"Did you hear? There's probably a storm brewing in the Atlantic, and he's got to be the one in the thick of it. Does he think about anyone else's welfare? No. He's got to be the first to climb a stupid tower to restore cell service as if the president is going to give him a medal or something."

For the first time Ava heard something in Sawyer's voice that confirmed everything she'd believed about the girl. Sawyer didn't hate her father. She was afraid for him. "He's performing a service," she said. "What he's doing is important."

"Yeah, like he was performing a service when he flew missions over Iraq. Like he's helping the world when he drives eighty miles an hour on that stupid motorcycle or races his speedboat in competitions on Lake Alfred." Sawyer huffed an indignant breath. "You can believe what you want, Ava, but I know my father. He's a dumba— Sorry, stupid thrill seeker who only cares about his own stuff."

"I'm sorry you feel that way, Sawyer."

"Yeah, well, I'll get over it. I always do."

Only she didn't, and Ava now understood. "Do you want to go to my home on Sunday? You'll enjoy it."

"Sure. Why not? Can I go back to class now?"

"Yes. We'll discuss your punishment for the cigarettes later. I have to go back to Charlie."

"Great." Sawyer started to leave, but stopped and turned around. "You need to pay attention to that kid, Ava," she said.

"Oh?"

"Yeah, he's always losing things, and the rest of us have to go around finding them, like his shoes this morning."

"He's only five, Sawyer," Ava explained.

"I get that, but his mind always seems to be wandering. Sometimes I sit with him at supper and all he does is push his food around. And he always leaves things behind." Sawyer sighed. "I'm just sayin'…he seems distracted a lot."

So Sawyer had noticed it, too.

She'd love to give a lot more attention to Charlie. It's why she'd given up a corporate job in Charlotte to run the school. It's why she woke up every morning and went to sleep every night thinking about the baby she'd given up for adoption. It's why she ached to tell Charlie the truth. But not now. Not while he was so vulnerable. And not while the one therapist Ava had confided in advised against it.

Ava followed Sawyer from the office and returned to the library. Charlie had moved on to another book, and she stood quietly for a while just taking in the wonder of this precious boy. If she had to say, Ava would claim that Charlie looked more like Jace than anyone else in her family. But no doubt, he had Ava's eyes, so blue, so wide, so needing to trust a world that had let him down.

Someday, Ava, she told herself. *When the time is right.*

CHAPTER SIX

SUNDAY MORNING DAWNED with a crisp fall breeze and a bright sun. Ava looked forward to dinners with her family though her mother never ceased to remind her that she was living in a cramped apartment on the Sawtooth campus when she could have had her old room back in the sprawling farmhouse. Lately, however, Cora Cahill had stopped pestering her daughter about her life choices, accepting that Ava would do what she wanted. "You always have, sweetheart," Cora would say.

Ava planned to pick Sawyer up at her cottage and bring her to the farm. She hoped Sawyer liked heaps of Italian food, today's fare. Who didn't? Lasagna and spaghetti were always a safe choice to feed a dozen people. Noah Walsh wouldn't be there, and Ava kept telling herself to be grateful that his work had taken him away. After all, she and Noah were as different as two people could be. The risk taker versus the responsible. She'd known that from the first, but that fateful night he'd been exciting, unique, exhibiting a kind of charm that she'd never encountered before.

At one o'clock, driving her mini SUV, Ava swung by the cottage where Sawyer and Charlie lived. She couldn't wait to bring Charlie to the farm. But it was too soon. Cora had instincts that were almost scary. She would be certain to notice those blue eyes, that thick straight hair so like Ava's, the strong jaw like Jace's.

Sawyer came outside almost immediately and climbed into the car.

"Everything okay?" Ava asked. The girl's look of disbelief was her answer. "I guess not." She headed down the sweeping drive to the main street that would take them to Hidden Valley Road in fifteen minutes.

Ava had the car heater on low as they zoomed past the trees now bare of their autumn splendor. Soon the branches would be covered in snow. While beautiful, it was a stark reminder of the long, bitter winters in the mountains. Still, a white Christmas Eve would be the perfect setting for the wedding at Crestview Barn, where her brother Jace would be joined forever to Kayla McAllister.

Jace had found his happiness in Kayla and Nathan, the son he'd only just met a few months ago. Now they would share a future bright with family companionship and, perhaps, more children. They might end up as happy as her brother Carter with the love of his life, Miranda; Miranda's daughter, Emily; and the child they were expecting in the spring. Ava, the oldest of the three, was still alone. She'd never married. She'd never even come close. She wondered now if, like bad luck, happiness might also come in threes. If so, could it soon be her turn?

If only she could reconcile the problems at the paper mill their father had owned and managed for so many years. After Raymond Cahill's death almost two years ago, the family had assumed the profits from the mill would keep Cora comfortable for the rest of her days. But Rudy Cahill, Raymond's brother and current head of the mill, seemed never to be around when Ava wanted to question him about the mill's financial stability. She had invited Rudy and his wife to the family dinner today, but they had declined. They always did.

"Enough is enough, Uncle Rudy," she said under her breath. "I'm showing up this week, and I'm going to get some questions answered."

Before they reached the house, Ava passed a car coming the other direction. She recognized Gladys Kirshner at the wheel. No one else was in the car, so Ava figured she must have dropped Robert off and left, apparently not yet ready to be with Cora in a social setting. Unfortunate, but understandable, Ava thought.

When she pulled in front of the farmhouse, Ava realized her mother had taken the Christmas decorations from the attic. White lights hung from the porch eaves. A Snowy Mountain wreath was on the front door. She wondered who had helped her mother put up these things. Probably Carter who seemed to be full of Christmas spirit this year.

Ava recognized every car in front of the house. Going inside, she found Jace, Kayla, Nathan, Carter, Miranda and Emily, Robert, who stood closely by Jace, and of course Cora. Everyone welcomed Sawyer as Ava knew they would. Sawyer was almost congenial. She even agreed to play a board game with Em, Nathan and Robert. Ava wondered how Noah, with his dry sense of humor and chip on his shoulder would have fit in.

"She seems like a sweet little thing," Cora said when the two of them were alone in the kitchen taking care of final preparations. The others, wearing heavier jackets than usual, braved the outside with bottles of beer or mugs of hot chocolate, and sat by a fire pit in the open air.

"She's doing quite well at the school actually," Ava said, smiling at Cora's reference to "sweet little thing." Cora didn't know she'd uttered a profound exaggeration.

Always the concerned social worker, Miranda entered and asked, "Is this the girl who ran away from home?"

Ava indicated that yes, Sawyer was the runaway. She wasn't surprised that Carter had told his wife about the incident.

"I understand she has at least one parent."

"She has a father, but he's not home all the time. His work takes him away a lot." Just mentioning Noah made the image of his face spring into her mind. No denying he was a handsome man. He had been six years ago, and he still was. And she wondered how he was doing now that the worst of the storm had past. The weather on the Atlantic coast had been dreadful. She hoped he was safe.

"Is he a caring man, at least during the times he's with his daughter?" asked Miranda.

Ava wasn't sure how to answer. "He is, but they have problems, mostly with communicating." Though Ava trusted Miranda, she didn't feel free to discuss the specific issues between father and daughter. Instead she smiled at Cora. "Remember what it was like to have teenagers, Mom?"

Cora chuckled. "A crisis every day, and most times I felt like I didn't have a clue how to deal with them."

"And we turned out okay," Ava said. "Sawyer will, too."

"So what do you think of Sawyer's father?" Miranda asked.

That was the million-dollar question. "He's…different. He's…"

Kayla entered the kitchen. "He's a hunk according to Jace. Kind of a biker type, right?"

"A biker type?" Cora said. "You mean he rides a big ol' motorcycle right through the middle of peaceful towns?"

"No, nothing like that, Mama," Ava said.

"When did Jace meet him?" Cora asked, the question laced with suspicion.

"Now, Mama, don't make anything of this. It was a chance meeting when I was talking with the father. You know I meet lots of parents."

"Of course you do," Kayla said. "But do you always meet them over coffee at the Holly River Café?" She began shredding lettuce into a huge salad bowl. "Believe me, I think it's great. Jace and I both wish you'd find someone special."

"And this fella might be him?" Cora said.

"No, Mama. I just told you not to make anything of this, and here you are, practically accusing me of having a boyfriend."

"Well, Kayla's right," Cora added. "Hate to say it, Ava, but you're thirty-six years old. And if you'd like to have a family of your own, you'd better take finding someone a bit more seriously."

"Mama, stop it. This man isn't anyone I would consider seriously. He just happened to be in the café when I was. That's all there is to it."

Cora smiled. "Okay. I'm not sure I would choose a biker fella for you anyway."

"Lots of good guys ride motorcycles," Miranda said. She winked at Ava. "It's not like he rides with an outlaw group, right?"

"I don't know what he does!" Ava said, her patience wearing thin. Good grief, you'd think at thirty-six, she already had one foot in the grave. "I'm trying to help his daughter, not him. Can we please change the subject?"

"Here's a change," Cora said, handing Ava a stack of twelve plates. "Set these on the table, please, and come back for the silverware."

Dinner was the typical noisy, rowdy affair with dishes being passed, wineglasses being filled, and curious questions being thrown at Cora about dessert. Sawyer seemed to fit in quite well, laughing at things the adults said and paying attention to the children when they wanted her to. Ava was glad she had decided to invite her.

After dinner some of the adults returned to the backyard with the kids, stoked the fire and watched the younger ones roast marshmallows. Since winter would arrive in less than a month, the days were growing shorter, and by four o'clock dusk had already started to settle. It would soon be too cold for the family to stay outside. Ava was ready to call them in when she heard a knock on the front door.

"Who could that be?" Cora asked, attempting to shush the family's fourteen-year-old Labrador. "I've just about got all the leftovers put away."

Ava headed to the door, followed closely by Buster, who growled softly. "I'll find out." She opened the door to see Noah standing on the threshold. She almost wouldn't have recognized him. Gone were the leather biker gear things replaced by a pair of dress jeans, an oxford shirt and a suede jacket. He wore polished loafers on his feet. And in his hands he carried a bottle of wine and bouquet of flowers.

"What are you doing here?" Ava asked, trying to control the constriction she felt in her lungs. Noah looked so good. She recovered quickly, grabbed Buster's collar. "I mean, aren't you supposed to be working?"

He passed a suspicious look at the big dog. "Will he bite me?"

"Not unless he's really hungry," Ava said, releasing Buster with a pat on his head. "Now then, why…"

"Finished the job," he said. "I know I never got an official invitation to this family affair, but I thought these little tokens might earn me passage inside." He held the flowers and wine out to her and she took them.

"The flowers are lovely," she said. "Mama will love them." And the wine was a fine vintage that couldn't have been purchased at the local drugstore.

Having not been officially invited in, he stood just outside and tugged his jacket closer around his chest. "So?"

"Oh, I'm sorry. It's cold. Come in." She backed up a couple of steps and opened the door wide.

"Sawyer still here?"

"Yes. She seems to have enjoyed herself."

"I can imagine. If ever a place looked like a cozy, welcoming home, this house is it. Kind of exudes charm and warmth. I'm sure Sawyer can appreciate that."

Wiping her hands on a dish towel, Cora

came out of the kitchen. "Who's this, Ava? A friend of yours?"

"This is Sawyer's father, Mama." Ava hoped her mother would avoid making a biker comment.

Cora's eyes widened. "The biker guy?"

So much for hoping. "Actually he seems transformed today," Ava said.

Noah stuck out his hand. "Noah Walsh, ma'am."

Ava handed the flowers to her mother. "He brought you these, Mama. I'd say the wine is for all of us."

Cora took the flowers and sniffed some petals. "Can't tell you the last time a young man brought me flowers. Call me Cora, and what'll it be, Noah? Spaghetti, lasagna or both?"

"Whatever you can spare, Cora. I haven't eaten since breakfast."

"Give me ten minutes to heat up a plate, and then have Ava show you to the kitchen. The dining table has already been cleared, but we always have room in the kitchen."

My goodness, Ava thought. *Attitudes change quickly in this place.* She stood next to Noah. The cold air from the open door made her shiver. She couldn't come up with anything to say or do.

"Mind if I close the door?" he asked.

His question shook her mind from an obvious stupor. "Oh, what's wrong with me?" She shut the door. "Come sit by the fire. You must be freezing."

He settled on a sofa in front of the crackling flames. Ava sat next to him. "How did you find this place?"

"Asked the first person I saw in town who looked like a local. Got a quick and overly detailed answer." He smiled. "Though I had a bit of trouble picking out a bank of rhododendrons at the end of November."

"True, but you should see them in April. Shall I get Sawyer?"

"Not right away," he said. "First, why don't I get a progress report? No more smoking incidents I assume."

"No. Sawyer lost her television privileges for a week, but I don't think the punishment was too harsh." Ava smiled. "She said she never watches TV."

"Next time take away her cell phone. It doesn't mean much to her when I'm trying to

call, but otherwise it's her lifeline to well…
everything."

He angled his body so he was facing Ava
squarely. She slid away from him a couple
of inches. "How's she doing in her classes?"
Noah asked.

"Okay, I guess. I usually don't hear unless
a student is failing in a subject."

"No news is good news."

"Absolutely."

Ava tapped her knee with her index finger
while her brain struggled to come up with
an interesting topic. She was spared having
to invent small talk when Carter came in
the room.

"Oh, hey," he said. "How you doing?"

"Okay."

"Sorry about the day we met. Things were
a little tense. You understand I was just doing
my job?"

"As long as you understand I was just
being a dad. I'm not always good at it, but
that day I was trying my hardest."

Carter chuckled. "Now that I'm a dad, I
understand how difficult that can be."

Whispering at the doorway made Ava look
toward the kitchen. Standing in the entry

were Miranda and Kayla, apparently taking in the newcomer and making comments. Finding the interest in Noah just slightly embarrassing, she checked her watch. "It's been ten minutes," she said. "Mama will have your supper ready."

They all moved into the kitchen. Noah sat. Cora put down a plate loaded with pasta and her own delectable sauce. Miranda brought a basket of bread. Kayla scooped leftover salad from a bowl onto a smaller plate. Then they all just stood there as if the arrival of Noah Walsh were the most exciting thing ever to happen in Holly River. Well, maybe it was.

"For heaven's sake, quit staring," Cora said. "Let the man eat. Don't you all have something to do?"

"Sure," Miranda said. "We can join the kids by the fire."

"Don't tell Sawyer I'm here just yet," Noah said. "I don't want to spoil her fun."

Miranda shot him a look of total confusion. She'd probably never thought of her presence as a spoiler to Emily's fun. "Whatever you say."

Ava was left to keep Noah company while

he ate. Cora stood at the sink pretending to tidy up. She didn't like to miss anything.

Fifteen minutes later Noah had nearly cleaned his plate and swore he couldn't eat another bite. He might have devoured everything in sight if he hadn't stopped every few minutes to compliment Cora on her cooking.

"You finished just in time," she said. "The kids are coming in."

Noah set down his utensils and stiffened in the chair when Sawyer stepped inside, followed by the Cahill clan. Sawyer stopped and stared at him a moment, looked at Ava and said, "What's he doing here? You didn't invite him, did you?"

The faces of the adults registered shock. Not surprising, since Ava was quite certain neither Emily nor Nathan spoke about their parents in such a disrespectful way.

She started to answer, to suggest that Sawyer watch her tone, but Noah raised his hand. "No, Sawyer, she didn't invite me, but she did tell me you were coming here. Since I got back to town a day early, and since I know you have school tomorrow, I thought I'd come out here to spend some time with you."

"Whoopee. I'm just tingly all over from your fatherly concern, *Daddy*."

Ava stood. "Sawyer, that's enough."

"It's all right, Ava," Noah said. "My coming here is a surprise."

Sawyer's bottom lip trembled. She frantically searched the room for anywhere to attach her gaze, anywhere other than her father. Ava was truly concerned for the girl.

"Why are you all staring at me?" Sawyer demanded of the adults. "I'm only half of this freak show."

Miranda took both Emily and Nathan by their hands. "Come on, kids. Let's go finish that game of Yahtzee you started earlier." She urged Robert to come with them and quickly ushered them out of the kitchen.

Cora brought a glass of water to Sawyer. "Here, honey, drink this. You'll feel better."

"Sorry, Cora, but water doesn't help. I've actually drunk stuff much stronger and still felt like crap…"

"Sawyer!" Ava had had enough. "You don't have any call to speak to my mom like that."

"Don't you all get it?" she said. "He wants

you to think he did this great thing by coming here today. A day early! Like he really sacrificed to be with me. Well, I know better. In fourteen years I guarantee you he hasn't sacrificed a thing for me."

Her voice kept rising as her anger threatened to explode. "The only thing my father cares about is himself. His stupid job where he can play a hero by climbing towers. His stupid motorcycle that he drives like a maniac and somehow doesn't even get a ticket. His speedboat that he hasn't even taken me on because—" her voice switched to high-pitched sarcasm "—it's not safe, Sawyer. You can't go. You stay home with one of the witches.

"Everything he does is all about him. His stuff. His need for speed. His rep as the bravest climber on the crew." She took a few steps closer to the table and leaned over toward Noah. "What about me, *Dad*? When is it my turn to show up on your radar?"

Ava couldn't bear to keep looking at Noah. Pain was etched in his features as if Sawyer had physically hit him. He let out a breath he'd been holding. "Sawyer, that's enough.

We'll discuss this another time, another place."

"Why? Because you don't want these people to see what you're really like? Too late. They know now. I wouldn't care if the whole world knew what you were like."

A sob tore from her throat. She covered her mouth and ran from the room. Ava heard her stomping up the stairs to the second floor.

Noah pushed his chair back and moved to follow his daughter.

Carter took his arm. "That's probably not such a good idea."

Noah jerked his arm free. "I'm her father. I know how to handle her. She'll calm down in a minute."

Carter scowled at him. "Clearly you don't…"

"Stop this both of you, before you say something you'll regret," Ava said. "Noah, Carter's right. Tensions are high." She applied a lighter touch to Noah's forearm. "Let me talk to her. I'll come down and let you know what's happening."

"I hope you get through to her," Noah said. "Because I came home early for two reasons.

One was to see Sawyer. The other was to sign a six-month lease on that little house next to the children's home. I'm here to stay."

CHAPTER SEVEN

"HERE TO STAY." For a moment Ava could only stare at Noah. Those certainly had not been his words six years ago. No, those words had been "I'm sorry. I'm married." But, then, what more did he owe a woman who clearly was willing to spend one night with him, no strings attached? That was then. Tonight, thank goodness, Noah listened to Ava and Carter. He slumped in his chair and stared at his hands. Maybe he was calmed by the comforting touch of Cora's hand on his shoulder.

Ava decided she could use a comforting hand as well, though no one in this house would know why. Noah living next door? How was she going to cope with Charlie's father living so close? She'd already begun to change her opinion of Noah and think of him as a sympathetic figure. He had handled the realization that they'd known each other before with calm and rationality. That was a point in his favor. But as a father, he was a man who wanted to do the right thing but didn't have a clue how to go about it. A man who perhaps couldn't cope with being a father and never would. How could Noah, with his parental track record ever be a father to a troubled five-year-old?

And now her baby's father was moving in next door to try and make amends with the daughter he'd somehow lost along the way. And Ava would see him often, and each time she would think of her precious Charlie. She would never tell him about Charlie now, not when his parenting skills were so in question. If even *half* of the animosity and hurt Sawyer felt toward her father was real, well, she couldn't risk exposing Charlie to such a toxic relationship.

Just a few days ago, Ava had considered that maybe Noah was selfish because he couldn't see his daughter's viewpoint and didn't want to try. Now she didn't believe that. She believed he was as lost as Sawyer. Maybe he mentally ran from her as much as she physically ran from him. If there was a way to help these two, Ava wanted to bring them together and give them both hope for their future, a future that wouldn't be next door to Sawtooth Home.

After several uncomfortable seconds, Ava said, "How can you do this, Noah? What about your job? Don't you have to live in Chapel Hill?"

"Nope. As you well know, I drive long distances to reach a job site anyway. Why not leave from here instead of Chapel Hill?"

"How do you think Sawyer will react to this news? Doesn't she like living in Chapel Hill? Doesn't she have friends?"

"I suppose the town is all right. It's me she doesn't like living with. But I hope she'll get used to it. If nothing else, Ava, you have convinced me that I need to do something now or I may never mend the rift between my daughter and me. I'm betting establishing myself here in Holly River might show my intentions are positive."

Actually, Ava's first instinct was to believe that Noah's proximity to Sawyer might only increase the stress on Sawyer while she adjusted to Sawtooth Home. But she didn't want to discourage Noah, so she said, "Yes, I suppose it could."

"Are you sure you want to talk to her instead of me going up there?" Noah asked.

"Yes. I won't tell her your plans, but I think she needs a bit of girl talk."

As Ava climbed the stairs to look for Sawyer in one of bedrooms, she didn't know how she would begin to help heal this family.

Ava heard sobbing when she reached the top of the stairs. She followed the sounds to her old bedroom, knocked softly on the door and went inside. Sawyer lay crumpled on the bed, her arms clasped tightly around one of Ava's pillows. She hiccupped loudly and said, "Go away, Dad. I don't want to see you."

"It's me, Sawyer, not your dad." Ava sat on the edge of the bed, threaded her fingers together. "What can I do to help you?"

The girl's answer was simple. "Make him go away. I hate him."

"Do you, Sawyer? Do you really? At first I thought you believed that, but now I'm not so sure."

Sawyer rolled onto her back and lifted teary eyes to Ava. "How can you say that? Do you need another example of how much we hate each other?"

"No. To be quite honest, I haven't especially liked the ones I've already witnessed. But I can tell you what I've discovered so far. Your father doesn't hate you."

"Yeah, right. Like you know."

"What do you want your father to do, Sawyer? What would make you happy?"

"He can quit that stupid job and stay home once in a while."

"So you can be the center of his universe?"

"Maybe. No. I don't want to be the center. I just want a place in it."

"Okay. But there must be something you can admire about how hard he works. He makes a good living, right?"

Sawyer hunched one shoulder. Ava interpreted it as a yes.

"And he's good at what he does. From what you've said, he might be the best at it. You can be proud of that, can't you? It must take a tremendous amount of courage to climb one of those towers."

Sawyer coughed, clearing her throat. "Courage? You think it takes courage? I think it takes blind, freakin' stupidity mixed with selfishness, and anybody who does what he does wants all the glory. Or he wants to die."

Ava put her hand lightly on Sawyer's arm. "Do you believe your father wants to die?"

"No, but I believe he will. Nine climbers have died so far this year, and none of them had worked on the towers as long as my dad has." She sputtered a cold, hoarse sound. "The odds are running out for him. It's just a matter of time. And then it will just be me and the witches. Or me and a woman in Oregon who doesn't even send me a birthday card."

They sat quietly while Ava digested everything Sawyer had said. Then she released a deep breath and spoke softly. "Sawyer, are you afraid your father will die, not because you don't want to be with a housekeeper, but because, deep down inside, you don't want to lose him?"

Sawyer's body trembled. Silent tears fell to her cheeks. "I don't know. Maybe. He's all I have. We never hear from my mom, so no, I don't want to lose him. We argue all the time but in my heart I suppose I… I love him, a little. But he doesn't care that every day he goes up on a tower, he scares me. Doesn't he get that it's just the two of us. If something happened to Dad, I wouldn't stay with one of the witches one day. And I wouldn't go to my grandmother. I'd just leave, be on my own.

"I've tried to tell him that, but he doesn't listen. He thinks he's invincible just because he's had some training. Well I know he's not. Every time he's gone, my mind keeps bringing up images of guys high in the air. I read about it on the internet. I watch videos of tower climbers."

Sawyer stared at Ava as if begging her to understand. "Do you know what the earth looks like from five hundred feet in the air, especially when all you've got to hold onto is a skinny pole?"

Ava squeezed Sawyer's arm. "Have you told him your feelings?"

"Over and over. But he doesn't take me seriously. And he just says, 'Don't worry, Sawyer. I'll be fine.' But he doesn't know that. How many other climbers have said that to people who lo…need them, and then they didn't come home."

Sawyer inhaled, held her breath a moment and said, "If something happened to Daddy, I'd be alone. Completely alone." She stared up at Ava. "That's why I run away, you know. I'm practicing for when I have no one else. I'm trying to show him what it's like to lose the only person that cares about you. And every time I see him, I think, is this the last time? And it makes me so angry."

Ava opened her arms and Sawyer fell into them. She buried her face in Ava's shoulder and cried out all her frustration. Ava held her for minutes, lightly stroking her back. Sawyer's fears were real. She wondered if Noah had ever held his daughter this way.

After a while, she leaned back, ran her hand down Sawyer's braid. "Stay up here as long as you need to," she said. "I'm going downstairs. You come down when you're composed, okay?"

Sawyer nodded. "Okay." Sawyer sniffed. "Is he still here?"

"Yes. He's anxious to hear that you're okay."

When Ava came to the first floor, she encountered quiet. Her brothers had taken their families home. Gladys had picked up Robert. Noah sat on the sofa in front of the fire. His eyes widened when he saw her, waiting for an explanation. Those unforgettable coffee-brown eyes reminded her of the look he gave her from across a crowded room six years ago. A look that said he wanted to get to know her. She looked away.

Cora came in from the kitchen. "How is she?"

"She's still upset, but she'll be okay," Ava said.

"The poor little thing."

"Mama, I need to speak to Noah alone. Do you mind?"

Cora headed for the stairs. "It's been a long day. I think I'll turn in, watch a little TV. You two take all the time you need. Just lock up when you leave, Ava."

Knowing Sawyer was upstairs and could come down any minute, Ava suggested a plan. "You haven't seen anything of the farm," she said. "How about a walk to the barn? It's not too cold in there."

She slipped into her coat and handed Noah his jacket. After asking her mother to tell Sawyer they went for a walk, they left by the back door, with Buster following them across the yard.

"I guess I made a pal of your dog," Noah said.

"You're lucky. He doesn't warm up to people over four feet tall very often."

Once inside the barn, Buster curled up

on some loose hay. Ava and Noah sat on an old tack trunk covered by a blanket. "You're right," Noah said. "It's twenty degrees warmer in here than outside."

Conscious of Noah's proximity on the trunk, Ava took a deep breath, crossed her arms over her chest. She didn't want to touch him, not even by accident. The last few minutes had been an emotional upheaval for her, and she dared not let her feelings for Noah from before interfere with what she had to do now. "As you probably guessed," she said, "we need to talk."

NOAH FELT THE muscles clinch in his stomach. Ava's voice was controlled, even, administrator-like. And she was taut, the kind of tautness that came from somewhere deep in her core and had nothing to do with the fact that she was sitting on a hard trunk. Noah figured it was going to be bad.

"You told your mother that Sawyer was okay. Is that true?" Noah asked.

"She was quite upset, but we talked."

"I was worried about letting her come out here with you to a country Neverland. It was too soon for her to connect with your family. You're all like a painting of family ties."

"Noah, her being here isn't the problem."

"Yes, it is. Sawyer has it in her mind that her life is so terrible, that I'm an uncaring, selfish jerk, that every housekeeper I hire is out to get her. She comes now to the breadbasket of America where everybody is nice and sweet, and the food is good, and even the dog is happy. Of course she's only going to resent me more."

"Noah, she doesn't resent you for not giving her a life like I had growing up. And, by the way, my life wasn't always so rosy. My father was a bully who kept everyone on edge. He tolerated Carter, but he hated Jace."

"Where is he now?"

"He's dead. And that boy you saw…the quiet one? Robert is his illegitimate son, my half-brother, produced as a result of my father's infidelity."

Noah looked at the ceiling of the barn, a building that was clean by barn standards, smelled of aged wood and fresh hay. "You're telling me that your father had all this, a wife like Cora, three nearly perfect kids, and he screwed it up?"

"We weren't perfect. No child is. But yes, my father made some terrible mistakes. Trust me when I say that you and Sawyer have a long way to go to end up like that."

"So what did she tell you? That she hates me?"

"No. As a matter of fact, and as I've told you before, she doesn't hate you."

Noah couldn't help chuckling his disbelief. "What about all those adjectives she has for me, like selfish, stupid and a few other choice ones."

Ava shifted slightly. All at once he could see the soft light in her incredibly blue eyes. Her honest, caring blue eyes.

"Yes, she believes you are all those things," Ava said, "or at least she claims to believe them. But I don't think any of them would matter if she didn't also believe that you don't care anything about her."

"Don't care about her? Good grief, Ava, she's all I think about. Sometimes I wish she weren't, but she won't let me stop. She does everything she can to ruin my schedules, mess up my life and basically, just scare me. I wake up every morning, no matter where I am, and hope she goes to school, doesn't get in a fight with a teacher, doesn't smoke a cigarette."

"I'm going to say it again, Noah. Sawyer doesn't hate you. But she's frightened to death that one day you won't be there at all, that she'll be completely alone. That's a heck of a black cloud for a kid to live under."

"Look, my job takes me away, but I always come home. She has no reason to think that I won't."

Ava closed her eyes. When she opened them again, she stared hard at him. "Don't you get it yet? She's afraid you're going to die, that you're going to climb a tower and never make it down alive."

He shook his head slowly, trying to clear the cobwebs of this confusion. "I've explained all this to her, Ava. She knows I'm careful. She's never even met anyone personally who ended up dying on a tower. It's the internet. She needs to quit googling tower accidents and imagining that I'll be the next victim. She knows this is what I do. I've told her countless times that I'm highly trained and always careful. And let's not forget that I make good money doing it."

He tamped his anger by taking a deep

breath. "Did she also tell you that her room in Chapel Hill is crammed with every techie device a kid could want, that she can't even close her closet doors for all the clothes, that she's already talking about what kind of car she wants in two years? Did she tell you that?"

"She's compensating," Ava said.

"What? What does that even mean?"

"She's using material things to fill a void left by her fear of abandonment." Ava sighed. "I suppose now you're thinking that I'm not a child psychologist, so what do I know."

He didn't answer.

"But I believe I know what you're thinking right now."

"Oh yeah? What's that?"

"That Sawyer readily accepts all the things you give her. She seems materialistic, but Noah, things can't compensate for what she is afraid of."

Noah swallowed and felt a burn all the way down his throat. He met her gaze with an equally hard stare. "You sound pretty confident for a woman who's not a therapist."

"I'm not all that confident, Noah. This is entirely new ground for me. I'm the one who does the paperwork to admit new residents. I keep the financial records. I'm the middle-man between parents and teachers. I decide when children can go home for a visit. But a therapist? No. I'm not even close. What is true is that I'm not as close to this situation as you are. I'm able to sit back and evaluate without being emotionally involved."

She leaned toward him, almost tentatively. "But even that isn't a totally honest state-ment. Sawyer got to me in her lightweight hoodie, warning me about our insufficient security system. She's tough and smart, yes, but she's also vulnerable."

His Sawyer vulnerable? Stubborn, obsti-nate, an expert escape artist? These traits Noah could believe. But he looked at Ava and knew that she believed, and suddenly he wanted to be on the same side. This woman, this determined, compassionate, competent woman knew his daughter better than he did. He had known his daughter for four-teen years. Ava had known her a week.

"So what should I do?" Noah asked. "I've already told her about the skills that certi-fied me as a teacher of other climbers. She knows I don't take risks."

"That's just it," Ava said. "She believes you take risks every day. If not on your job, then on your motorcycle, behind the wheel of your speedboat. And the more you take risks, the more she sees it as a way of avoiding responsibility to her. It's almost as if she believes you don't care if you leave her all alone to fend for herself."

Was this possible? Did Sawyer believe he was so unfeeling? He was beginning to see his daughter as Ava did, an insecure, scared, anxious kid who thought her only sense of belonging, her only family would leave her in a plume of dust at the bottom of a tower. "I don't do any of these things to hurt Sawyer," he said. "I keep at my job because it supports us both. I ride a bike and drive a boat because it's what I enjoy. Am I supposed to give all those things up?"

"I'm not saying that," she said. "But I think you need to talk to your daughter. And you both need to understand the importance of compromise."

He stared at Ava's hand in her lap and impulsively reached out and took it in both of his. He suddenly needed a connection with something solid. Compromise. He could do that, couldn't he? He suddenly could picture doing anything that would make this woman respect him. His thumb began rubbing her knuckles, and a memory of doing exactly this in a bar in Charlotte flooded his mind.

"I understand what you're saying, Ava, but I'm forty years old. I can't suddenly become a different person. I can't start a new career at my age. Or at least I wouldn't want to try. And truthfully, I don't want to. Sawyer and I have become accustomed to a certain life, a life I've provided. I have a responsibility to the people I've trained. They depend on me, and I don't want to let them down. At some point Sawyer has to accept who I am and believe what I tell her."

Ava gave him a warm smile that seemed to melt deep down inside him. "And that might happen. But right now she's just a frightened child, a kid who is taking risks that in some ways are even greater than the ones you take. Every time she walks out your door or climbs out a window, her life is a little less safe. But tonight I believe we have taken a step toward understanding. Admittedly that step is toward you understanding her, but that can change."

She kept her hand in his, leaned forward and stared deeply into his eyes. "We'll start here and go forward. I have every confidence that your relationship with Sawyer can be saved."

He felt more optimistic than he had in several years. Was it because Sawyer had such a determined champion in this woman? Was it because he felt Ava was as much on his side as she was on Sawyer's? Was it because he believed, for the first time, that someone could actually stop him from alienating his daughter forever…for his sake as much as Sawyer's?

Whatever, he hadn't felt this close to another human being in a long time, especially not to a woman. "You're amazing, Ava."

"Maybe I can just see things you can't because I'm only the observer. I simply want to make this situation better…"

Too much talk suddenly. Noah's heart was beating. The blood was racing through his veins. He wanted nothing more than to be closer to Ava, to believe in her. He pressed his hand on hers. "You might think that all I'm feeling now is gratitude, Ava, but it's not. I want to kiss you…"

"I don't know, Noah. This is about Sawyer..."

"Right now," he said, "I believe this moment is about us. Finding you again was like a dream. You came into my life when I was at my lowest, and you've given me hope. That's a big thing in my book, Ava.

"Don't we owe it to ourselves to see if what we shared years ago still exists? Because it was strong then. I hated leaving you that night, especially knowing what you must have been thinking of me. I guess, I'm saying I want another chance to make things right." He cupped her cheek and waited. She didn't pull back. In fact, her whole body seemed to lean into him. He threaded his fingers through her silky hair and moved closer, feeling a slight shudder come from her chest. She blinked hard and breathed in short gasps of air.

"Let's not think for one minute, okay? Just feel." He kissed her eyelids, the tip of her nose, and then settled his mouth on hers. Her lips were lush and fragrant with Italian spices. He tasted her, savored her response. When his tongue slipped inside her lips, she let out a little sound and tilted her head to more fully engulf him in their kiss.

He remembered this woman, this feeling.

He felt her hands flatten on his chest before she pushed him away. "We shouldn't be doing this," she said. "This is about Sawyer..."

"For a minute there, it didn't feel like it had anything to do with Sawyer."

She looked down, focusing on some indefinite spot on the barn floor. "Let's go in. It's getting late."

He exhaled a long breath as they began walking. Suddenly he stopped and asked her, "How did that feel to you?"

"It was a kiss," she said. "A nice one perhaps, but one that shouldn't have happened."

"You don't feel strange? Not even a little déjà vu?"

"No. Of course not." She still hadn't looked at him.

"Well, I'd never forget a kiss like that. And I'm kinda convinced that you haven't either."

A tiny smile creased the corner of her lips.

He reached for her hand. Their fingers entwined for a second, maybe two before she took back her hand. "Come on, Noah. Saw-

yer is probably downstairs by now and wondering where we are."

Yes, probably, he thought, following her.
But Sawyer wasn't exactly what he was
thinking about at this moment.

CHAPTER EIGHT

AVA WAS GRATEFUL she and Sawyer had had a calm, productive discussion when they returned to the Sawtooth campus on Sunday night. Sawyer had forgiven her father for showing up unannounced, but of course she was still angry about how he decided to live his life. Noah's life choices were the big issue between the two, and that problem would not resolve itself without a lot of work and effort on both their parts, not to mention compromise.

Also thankful that her schedule was relatively free this morning, Ava proceeded with her plan to visit the paper mill today even though she'd slept fitfully last night. After what happened in the barn with Noah, she was having a difficult time concentrating on anything but the kiss. Noah had said he remembered their kisses, and she had downplayed his assertion.

Unfortunately, Noah was right. Like him, Ava had never forgotten his kisses. They'd kissed and caressed and enjoyed each other for hours. They'd talked about their childhoods, their wants and goals. They'd laughed at the same things. Noah had been so real to Ava that night. She had believed they shared a special bond, one that might grow despite the distance between them. But now everything was different. Now she had Charlie to consider. She couldn't let herself fall for Noah and face the agonizing choice of whether to tell him about his son.

It was best if she simply didn't allow him to kiss her again. But those moments in the barn had been wonderful. She'd run upstairs to spend a few minutes in the bathroom just to try and get her mind on something else. She couldn't allow herself to be so swept away again. Once Noah had gone back to Chapel Hill, she could concentrate on raising their son by herself, which she had planned to do when she took the job at Sawtooth.

Besides, her history with Noah was flawed, based on a few fleeting hours, a mistaken pregnancy, a man who had been married. Last night she had felt a connection. But that other night, at the end, when he walked out of her bedroom, she had felt shame.

Ava pulled into the parking lot of the Cahill Paper Mill. She'd been here many times before. She'd often helped her father with record keeping, preparing invoices, sending overdue bills to customers. Raymond had been proud of his daughter's intelligence and expertise. She'd been the favorite child. She hadn't asked to be, didn't want to be. But it was a fact.

She took her briefcase from the car, locked the doors and went in the front entrance. The smells were the same, the distinct acrid odor of pulp, the smoky, barely contained scent of the boilers, the more pleasing smell of fresh wood. The mill was a decent, hardworking environment. Most of the employees were happy to have jobs there.

It wasn't always that way. Miranda's own father had died of cancer due to his placement in the asbestos-riddled boiler room, a risk he'd known about but had taken to better his family's situation. The tragic consequences had broken Miranda's heart and caused her to break up with Carter when they were teenagers. Thank goodness they'd found each other again.

Ava proceeded down a short hallway to the executive suites of the company officers. Here the smells were subdued as if the toil and discomfort a few hundred yards away didn't exist. A receptionist sat at a polished desk in front of three office doors. The largest door had once led to Raymond Cahill's office, but now belonged to his brother Rudy.

"Why, hello, Ava," EmmaAnn Brubaker said to her. "Haven't seen you here in a while."

"Hello, EmmaAnn. Maybe you've heard I've come back to Holly River to take over managing the children's home."

EmmaAnn smiled. "I did hear something about that. I'm sure you'll do a good job out there."

"I hope so," Ava said, following her comment with some general questions about EmmaAnn's family. That's just what people did in the High Country. They always asked. "Is my uncle busy? I'd like to see him."

"Let me check for you." EmmaAnn picked up a desk phone and punched a button that would connect her to the inner office. She spoke into the receiver, her voice so low Ava couldn't hear her. After a moment she hung up the phone.

"I'm sorry, Ava. That was your uncle's colleague. He said Rudy's gone out for a while. He's meeting with some...prospective pulp buyers."

Right. I'll just bet he is.

"You can leave a mess..."

"Thank you, EmmaAnn," Ava said, passing by the desk. She put her hand on the doorknob. "I'll just go in and wait for him to return."

"But, Ava, you can't do that. Your uncle wouldn't like..."

"It's okay," Ava said. "I won't touch anything, and besides, this office is like a second home to me."

She opened the door, gratified to see her uncle's shocked expression, his eyes wide, his fleshy jaw practically on his chest. He recovered quickly and stood up. "Why, Ava Cahill, my favorite niece. What brings you out here today? Hope you didn't get your feathers ruffled by that little charade between me and EmmaAnn. I didn't understand that it was you out there."

"Of course you didn't, Uncle Rudy," Ava said. "My feathers are fine." She gave him a once-over. In the nearly two years since Raymond had died, Rudy had not fared well. His waist had expanded, no doubt from too many rich lunches and cocktail hours. His face was drawn and road-mapped with new wrinkles. Only a ring of white hair around his scalp remained of his once-lustrous thick hair. He stood and came around the desk.

"How can I help you, today, Ava? Everything okay at home? Cora doing all right?"

"Yes, everyone's fine." She recognized his questions as platitudes, spoken without feeling or expectation of answers. She placed her briefcase on the floor and took a seat even though he hadn't offered one. "I'll just take a few minutes of your time, Uncle Rudy. The family has entrusted me with Mama's well-being, financial and otherwise, and I'm trying to do my best by her."

Rudy leaned on his desk, peered down at her. "Well, of course you are, Ava. I wouldn't expect any less from Raymond's offspring. But you said Cora is doing fine."

"I know I did. And she manages quite well considering that her income has shrunk since

Daddy died. But we're all concerned that she doesn't seem to have the funds to keep the house up. And she canceled her vacation this year."

Rudy slowly shook his head. "I didn't know that, Ava. I'll be glad to help her if I can with a personal loan. Interest free, of course. But I suspect that much of this problem has to do with that kid Raymond had with one of our former employees."

So Rudy did know about Robert and his mother, Gladys.

"I understand your mama has kept up payments to the boy's mother even though the kid's not her responsibility."

Ava tamped her anger. "Robert is an innocent in all this. How dare you, Rudy. I have to say that I don't appreciate your bringing him into it."

"I humbly apologize, Ava. But what can I do about it? I'm not responsible for the boy, either, and Cora can make her own decisions."

"Yes, but we can all help her out without considering a personal loan from you." She leaned over, snapped open the briefcase and brought out one of the ledgers she'd been working on at Sawtooth. The ledger was distinctive in its army green color with brown leather binding. She was certain Rudy recognized it. "I managed to get a hold of some of the records Elsie Vandergarten left when she retired."

Rudy sputtered a surprised chuckle. "Elsie has those books? She must have absconded with them. They're supposed to be under lock and key, Ava. Despite you being family, you're not really entitled to look at any of the books. Those are official company records."

"Oh." Ava smiled. "I didn't know that. Anyway, this is the most recent ledger, the last one Elsie filled in before the company went all digital. I've noticed some interesting facts about the numbers."

"Well, Ava, honey, you can't put much stock in that. Elsie is going on seventy. Her mind was probably playing tricks on her for years. We just never had the heart to let her go."

"I don't know if I agree, Uncle Rudy. This last ledger shows that Elsie's mind was just as sharp as it ever was. The entries are precise, meticulous really."

"Then what's the problem?"

"Some of the major accounts, ones my father specifically worked on for years are missing."

Rudy crossed his arms over his chest. "What are you saying, Ava?"

"The Mendelson account for instance. That was one of Daddy's largest customers. They ordered thousands of dollars' worth of pulp each year. There are no orders after Daddy died. The same is true of Jackson Paper Company and several others."

Rudy cleared his throat, gave her a hard stare. "I don't know what you're implying, Ava, but things changed after Raymond died. Customers left us because he was no longer around even though I tried my darndest to keep them. Truth is, your daddy played with the numbers a bit, giving out favors like Halloween candy. We couldn't continue with those shenanigans. A company can't exist that way."

Ava stared back. "I haven't found evidence of my father's so-called shenanigans."

"Well, your daddy was pretty clever at covering his tracks. His history with Robert proves that." Rudy smiled as if his point were uncontroversial. "And here's another thing,

Ava. Our corporate hierarchy changed after Raymond. Some of the old account holders didn't like that. I'm thinking they weren't getting the discounts your daddy established. Mendelson and some of the others went elsewhere for their paper manufacturing needs."

"I know Saul Mendelson, Uncle Rudy. I don't think he would abandon his ties with Cahill Paper. You are aware that I can call him and ask if he's buying from another mill."

Rudy placed his fists on his hips. "These all sound like accusations of foul play to me, Ava. You're wading into deep water," he said. "I hope you know how to swim."

"My mother's future is dependent upon the continued success of this company, Uncle Rudy. She is supposed to share in the profits according to my father's estate. If there has been a glitch in the bookkeeping, and some of the accounts receivable have been overlooked, I'm sure we can correct it before this goes any further. Restitution can be made…"

Rudy walked around her chair to the door. He turned the handle. "This conversation is over, Ava. I don't appreciate your tone or your accusations." He opened the door wide. "Give your mother my regards."

She stood, plastered a smile on her face. "I will. Thank you for your time, Uncle Rudy. As a return favor, I will give you some time as well. Take a few days to go over the books as you see them. Get back to me and decide if there isn't a way we can make this right."

"I don't need time, Ava," Rudy said. "I'd suggest that you drop this matter before irreparable damage has been made."

"Suit yourself, Uncle Rudy. Still, my offer of a few days stands. Please give my regards to Aunt Rachel."

She crossed the threshold, but turned around at the last moment. "I have several ledgers in my possession, Uncle Rudy. This is the first one I've examined. I'm wondering if they will all be this revealing."

He closed the door behind her without another word.

AVA WAS SHAKING when she got back in her car. Okay, she'd faced her uncle with her suspicions, and he hadn't denied them. In fact, he'd shifted the guilt to her father. Now Ava was even more determined to prove that her uncle was hiding some of Cahill Paper's most important clients and claiming they no longer ordered from the company. Who knew how much money Cora had missed out on according to the profit sharing deal her dad had established. Probably thousands.

Rudy had his chance today. He could have dealt with Ava, admitted his wrongdoing and avoided a confrontation with the rest of the family. And still he had a few days to reconsider his hard-line approach before it was too late for a peaceful reconciliation. Ava, Carter and Jace were going to demand complete restitution.

As she neared the Sawtooth Home, Ava slowed her car. Just a few yards up a narrow lane stood the small but charming farmhouse that Noah had claimed to be renting. It had been built in the 1930s, and had housed a number of families. She noticed immediately that the For Rent sign was missing from the front yard. Also, a black pickup truck stood in the driveway. Attached was a trailer carrying a motorcycle. Apparently her new neighbor had moved in.

The knowledge that Noah lived so close didn't do much to calm Ava after her meeting with Rudy. She was breathing heavily when she pulled into the parking lot of the administration building at the school. The campus was quiet. All the children were either in class or in the day care center. Ava would have time to return messages.

"What's the matter with you?" the home's receptionist, SherryLynn, asked when Ava came in the door. "No offense, but you look like you could spit nails."

Ava drew a deep breath. "Is it that obvious? I just had a confrontation with a family member, but it's fine."

"Couldn't have been one of your brothers," SherryLynn said. "They are both angels."

"Right. You and most of the people in this town are under that impression." She smiled. "Should I remind you that you never had to live with them?" Ava headed to her office. "But no, my problem wasn't with Jace or Carter."

SherryLynn stopped her from going in. "Oh, just a minute, Ava. There's a man in your office. A really good-looking guy wearing a black leather jacket…" She fanned herself with her hand.

Oh great, Ava thought. Just what she needed so soon after the kiss in the barn.

She entered her office. Noah stood from the sofa against the wall and placed a magazine back on the coffee table. "Hi. Sorry to barge in without an appointment, but…" He stopped, looked her over from head to toe and said, "What's wrong? Did something happen?"

She slammed her briefcase on the top of her desk. "Oh, for heaven's sake. I'm fine."

"You don't look fine. You look mad." A slow smile crept over his face. "You're not upset about what happened last night?"

She tried to stare away the smile. "I've hardly thought about it," she said. "Not everything is about you."

"I believe you've made that clear. Well, if you are regretting the kiss, you might as well know that I enjoyed every second of it and I don't regret a thing, except perhaps that it was too short. In fact, seeing you all flushed and rosy today, it takes about all my will power not to do it again."

"Now would not be a good time to try it, Noah. You are right about one thing. I have had a bad day."

As if he hadn't heard her, he continued. "Last night I kept thinking about this funny little thing you do with your tongue. Sweet, really."

"Would you mind not being quite so descriptive?"

"Devil's in the details, Ava. And that was one detail I don't want to forget."

"We can't relive the past, Noah, whether it was yesterday or many yesterdays ago."

"I'm not attempting to do that," he said. "I'm a man who always plans for the future."

A future with Noah? As tempting as it sounded, Ava knew it would never happen. She needed to keep her encounters with Noah on a business level and stop thinking about what happened in the barn.

She walked around her desk and sat in her chair. "What is it you want, Noah?"

"I wanted you to know I'm all moved in next door."

"Fine. I assumed you were when I passed by there earlier."

"I'd like to see Sawyer when she gets out of her last class today. She doesn't know about my plan to stay here for a while. I want to show her the house. I remember when you said I could take her home for visits once someone from the school has checked out my digs and approved the place." He grinned again.

"Maybe you'd like to come over and check it out."

She picked up a stack of pink messages and waved it at him. "Now's not really good for me, Noah."

"I can see that. Okay. I left your mother's place last night and drove to Chapel Hill to collect some things. Also brought some of Sawyer's belongings from the house. Thought she might like some reminders of home."

That was a truly thoughtful gesture. If Sawyer had some favorite possessions, she probably would enjoy having them in her room at the school. "I'm sure she'll like that," she said.

Noah looked at his watch. "Your assistant outside said the last class was over at two thirty. It's two thirty now. If we can schedule the official visitation by a school staffer later, I'd like to take her over to my house for an hour or so now. Not long I promise. Just long enough to have a soda and unpack her things."

"It's not the customary way of doing things," Ava said.

"Come on, Ava. She's not a child. She can make up her own mind about an hour with me, can't she? And if she's unhappy she can always slip away and come back here. It's a short walk, and she's pretty good at escaping."

Ava smiled. "You do have a point. All right. I'll have her cottage mother send her over." Ava tapped a pencil on the desk blotter. "But it's her decision, Noah. If Sawyer doesn't want to go, that's it. No arguments."

But Sawyer did want to go. Perhaps she was enticed by a box of her cherished belongings. Perhaps she felt bad about the scene from the day before. Maybe she'd decided to give her father a break. At any rate, out her office window, Ava watched them cross the grass and disappear into a line of trees on their way to Noah's new house.

THIRTY MINUTES LATER, Sawyer had picked out a small bedroom that would be hers if she ever decided to stay with her father. She picked through the box of belongings Noah had brought and decorated the built-in bookcases. A favorite rag doll, jewelry box, snow globe from New York City, and a music box brought all the way from Germany when he was in Munich on R & R from battle zones in Afghanistan. A few other mementos succeeded in turning the otherwise-plain room into a girl's-only spot.

"So what do you think of the house?" Noah asked her when they were having sodas in the kitchen.

"There's one thing I especially like about it."

Thinking she might say that its proximity to the school would be the positive attribute, Noah said, "Please, tell me."

"It doesn't have room for a housekeeper suite."

Noah smiled in spite of his disappointment. "I'd like you to feel like you can come over any time."

"I can't do that," she said. "Whenever I leave the campus, I have to inform my cottage parents. So far this, and the dinner at Ava's mom's house are the only times I've left. I don't know if I'll get permission to leave so soon."

Noah took a swig from his ginger ale can. "Like that's ever stopped you."

She grinned. "Point taken."

At this moment, Noah felt closer to his daughter than he had since she was a little girl and demanded he push her on the swing set he built in the backyard. He was pleased with his decision to move in next to the school. If he couldn't see his daughter whenever he wanted to, at least he knew she was close, and that was a start. And these new living arrangements made him feel comfortable for the first time in years.

It didn't appear that Sawyer was going to be so turned off by his presence that she would run away again. Noah enjoyed the long-absent familial warmth spreading through him. He and Sawyer had a long way to go. Ava was right about that, but even the longest journey has to start somewhere. And apparently his and Sawyer's was starting in a little town he'd never have imagined himself visiting.

He twirled the can in his hand. "You know, in ten or fifteen years maybe you won't need a housekeeper and you can stay here by yourself when I'm away for work."

"Ten or fifteen years?" she said. "I'll be old by then. I really will need someone to take care of me."

He laughed. "By then I'll be so old we'll both need a caretaker." He wanted to talk to her about her fears concerning his job and his hobbies. A quick look at his watch convinced him that now probably wasn't such a good time for an in-depth conversation. But next time, when she came over, he would address those anxieties. Maybe then she would listen.

"We'd better start back," he said. "Mama Ava probably set a timer for exactly one hour when we left her office."

"Mama Ava? That's funny," Sawyer said. "Considering she's actually not a real mama to anyone. But in a way she feels more like a parent to me than my own mother ever did." Sawyer suddenly frowned.

"What's wrong, kid?" Noah asked her.

"I don't want to get too comfortable with this situation," she said. "Ava is nice and everything. And I'm getting to know some kids my age at the home. But who knows what's waiting around the corner? I could get kicked

out. Or I could flunk out. I'm better off keeping my guard up."

"You're fourteen, Sawyer. You don't have
to keep your guard up all the time."

"Really? My real mother is gone and we
never hear from her. My father is a…" She
smiled just enough to take the sting out of
what was obviously going to be a snide comment. "My housekeepers are minions of evil.
Should I say more?"

"No, that will do." He stood. "I'm going
to walk you back now before Ava calls her
brother and has the entire eight-man police
force of Holly River out hunting for us."

He smiled as he followed Sawyer out the
door. Thinking about Ava did that to him.

CHAPTER NINE

WHEN SHE SAW Noah and Sawyer approaching from the side lawn, Ava went into her apartment. Every meeting seemed like it could be fraught with tension, either concerning Sawyer or the child Noah didn't know about. If she told him about Charlie, which was, she supposed, the honorable, honest thing to do, would he be angry that she hadn't contacted him? Not that she had any way of doing that. But maybe he would say that she should have scoured heaven and earth to find him.

Would he want to have a place in Charlie's life, which could potentially be even worse? Charlie did not need another parent whose lifestyle was so risky. And another recurring problem—would Ava throw caution to the wind and let him kiss her again? That would be so wrong. A woman can't let a man kiss her, not like Noah did, when she was keeping such a huge secret from him.

She heard Sawyer and Noah talk for a few minutes, but she couldn't hear the words. Then the front door to the administration building closed, and Ava came out of her apartment.

"How did everything go?" she asked Sawyer.

"Actually not bad, until the last sixty seconds."

"What happened in the last sixty seconds?"

"Dad told me he's leaving in the morning for a work trip to some remote area near Aiken, South Carolina. Apparently some stupid birds have built a nest at the top of the one cell tower in the area, and super-duper Dad has to get a crew to climb to the top and relocate the nest. It's interfering with transmission or something."

"Are they allowed to do that? I mean, aren't the birds protected?"

"Not when cell phone service is iffy anyway. I guess they've got to follow some special rules or something. They try to preserve the nest and find a safe place for it and not upset the mother bird."

"That's kind of nice, isn't it?"

"I suppose, but here he goes again. He leaves me, his daughter, to go protect some mama bird's babies. I mean, give me a break!"

Ava put a hand on Sawyer's arm. "You forget, honey. I know what's really bothering you. You're afraid for your father. Do you think he'll be the one to take the climb tomorrow?"

"Knowing him, yeah. He's got to get the credit for restoring cell service as well as saving all the endangered wildlife."

Ava didn't want to argue with Sawyer, but she no longer believed, in fact never had, that Noah was strictly a glory seeker who insisted on taking all the risks himself. Yes, he took some risks in his life and his work, but when his feet were on solid earth, he seemed reliable and dependable. When he located Sawyer in Holly River, he stayed close by, in fact, even rented a house with hopes of restoring a good relationship between them. He returned to Chapel Hill and packed some of Sawyer's prized possessions. Ava believed wholeheartedly that Noah cared about his daughter. If he would just quit taking so many chances with his job, Ava knew he and Sawyer would be on the road to mending their differences.

"I'm going back to my cottage," Sawyer said. "I've got some of my favorite music in my backpack and I want to listen to it."

"Okay. Maybe I'll see you later."

Before Sawyer had reached the outer door, the phone in the reception area rang. SherryLynn answered it. A concerned look immediately crossed her normally placid features. "Oh no," she said. "Hold on. Ava's right here."

Ava grabbed the phone. "What's wrong?"

The words she heard from the woman who monitored the day care center turned Ava's blood to ice. "I'll be right there," she said, dropping the phone on SherryLynn's desk. She passed Sawyer and ran out the door.

"What's the matter?" Sawyer called after her.

"It's Charlie," Ava called over her shoulder. "He's upset and throwing some sort of tantrum."

Sawyer hurried to keep up. "I told you that kid needed watching. It's not just the losing things. Sometimes he acts like he's going to have a meltdown."

By the time she reached the day care center, Ava was out of breath and consumed with panic. Had Charlie hurt someone? Had he hurt himself? Forgetting Sawyer was behind her, she burst through the door and into a room that seemed to be filled with chaos though there was only one child present and one staff member. The rest must have been ushered to a safer environment.

Charlie sat in a corner, wedged between a wall and bookcase. He sat cross-legged in the middle of too many paper scraps to comprehend. He was crying, the most pitiful sound Ava had ever heard.

"Why haven't you helped him?" Ava snapped at a staff member.

"Look at him, Ava. He's hysterical. Every time I tried to approach him, he'd get more upset."

Ava walked closer to Charlie. He cowered farther into the corner and wailed. "Please, listen to me, Charlie. Everything's going to be okay," she told him. *Come on, Charlie, you can trust me.*

"He was okay until Mrs. Hubbard left. I was afraid something like this might happen. Lately we've had to watch Charlie so carefully. He's been sad a lot."

Ava shot a quick glance at the woman before returning her attention to Charlie. "Why didn't someone tell me about this behavior?" she asked.

Behind her, she heard Sawyer's voice, "I sort of did, Ava."

Ava slowly crouched in front of Charlie. He refused to look at her, squinting his eyes tightly shut.

"What's wrong, sweetheart?" she said, picking up some of the scraps of paper beside him. They were pages of a book. No, several books. A quick look at the empty spaces in the bookcase told her where the books had come from. "Why did you do this, Charlie?"

"I hate the books!" he wailed. "I hate all books."

Charlie loved books. At least that's what Ava had thought. "But why?" She attempted to put a hand on his shoulder, but he slid farther away.

"I hate this place," he said. "I want to go home. I want my mommy and my daddy."

"Oh, sweetie, that's just not possible." Ava took a moment to peruse the ruined pages. They were all of families, children with their parents, parents together. Happy, well-adjusted families. Charlie had once had one of those, too.

"Do you remember why you came here, Charlie?" Ava said, keeping her eyes on his, holding his attention.

"Someone said my parents died, but that's not true. They wouldn't do that."

"No one wants to die, Charlie, especially your parents. They loved you very much. But it was an accident. Your parents didn't want to leave you."

His voice was reduced to a frail whimper when he said, "It's a lie. They didn't die. They're coming to get me and take me away from here."

Ava held out her hand. "Give me your hand, sweetie. Please. I bet you didn't even really want to hurt the books."

"Yes, I did." He wiped his eyes with the sleeve of his shirt and frowned. Ava's heart broke.

After another few calm minutes, Ava asked him, "Will you come with me now?"

"Okay," he said.

She took his hand and pulled him up. She resisted the urge to hold him close to her, to comfort him. That would come later, but not just then, when he was hurting so deeply because of his mistrust of adults. Now he needed peace and quiet, so she just squeezed his hand and held on tight.

Sawyer dashed forward and slung an arm around her and Charlie.

"You'll be okay, Charlie. I promise," Sawyer whispered in Charlie's ear, but Ava could still hear every word. Charlie nodded.

Ava put her hand on the top of Charlie's head. His dark hair was damp with sweat. His face was streaked with tears. "Sawyer, will you take Charlie back to the cottage? Tell Mrs. Carmichael that I'll be over later to explain what happened. But in the meantime will you stay with him?"

"Sure." Sawyer reached for his hand. At first he knotted his fingers into a fist, but finally, tentatively he tucked his hand in hers. They started for the door.

"You know what?" she said to him.

He looked up at her with wide, inquisitive eyes. "What?"

"I don't have a mom. She didn't die, she left me. But that's almost the same thing, except your mom didn't mean to leave. Lots of the kids in this place don't have parents."

"But you have a dad, don't you?" Charlie asked her.

"Yeah, and I'm always afraid he's going to die. Not like your dad did. Your dad didn't mean to while my dad knows he could die anytime, and it makes me mad."

Ava started to intervene. She wanted Charlie's attention away from death or abandonment. But she never got the first words out.

Charlie stared up at Sawyer in rapt attention. "Why does he do something that makes you mad?" he asked.

"Let me tell you something, kid. Parents aren't always the shiniest block in the toy box. They make mistakes just like you did today with those books."

"What do you mean about the shiny block?"

"I'll explain it all to you when we find some milk and cookies to drown our sorrows."

Ava just stood and watched them. Charlie may not have understood everything Sawyer was telling him, but he went willingly out the door with her. Perhaps shielding youngsters from the truth wasn't always the smartest way to go. Ava sighed with relief as she went about the task of picking up a small mountain of torn paper.

THREE DAYS LATER, on Thursday, December was a week old and Noah had returned from his trip to Aiken, South Carolina, where he'd successfully relocated a nest of baby ospreys to a turtle preservation area. He and two crew members had restored service to the remote properties of horse farms and vegetable growers. He'd assigned a small job to his crew over the next two days with the hope of spending time with his daughter.

With time to kill before the next day, when he'd go to the school and try to make a date with his daughter, he sauntered into the Holly River Café where the smells were too good to resist. He brushed a light dusting of snow off his jacket and removed his gloves, then took a seat at the counter.

After placing his order, he sat with his hands around a warm mug of coffee. The counter was empty except for him. Most of the tables were full. After a few minutes a man came in, one Noah recognized.

Jace came right over, took a seat next to Noah. "How you doing, buddy?" Jace asked.

Noah smiled. At least someone was happy to see him. "Still a bit mortified over the scene that played out between me and my daughter on Sunday."

"It's forgotten, Noah. Heck, even I have a kid now, something no one ever thought would happen, so I know not to expect quiet and peaceful ever again."

Noah chuckled. He liked Jace Cahill. He'd heard almost everybody in town did. "I can't tell you what I'd give for a few minutes of quiet and peaceful with my daughter," he said.

"It'll get better," Jace said, with all the puffed-up wisdom of a new dad. "Remember, kids grow up to be adults and outgrow all their childhood problems. Then they get to act just plain foolish like we do."

"So what are you doing here?" Noah asked. "You and Kayla not having dinner in tonight?"

"Nope. She's meeting with some of the town council at city hall about her run for councilwoman in the special election. I don't know why she's so worried about her chances. She'll win hands down."

"You sound pretty positive."

"Only one other person is opposing her, and he doesn't seem to be taking the election too seriously. His eighty-fifth birthday is the day of the election. I truly believe that what he wants for his birthday is the announcement that he lost. But it seems more fair to have two candidates, so…"

When Jace let his voice trail off, Noah had glimpsed another fact about small town politics. "Does Kayla have aspirations beyond Holly River?" he asked.

"You bet. She hopes to end up in the North Carolina state senate eventually and spend the workweek in Raleigh. Nathan and I will be living like bachelors until the weekends. Like tonight. I dropped him off at Carter's and came to pick up takeout for all of us."

Remembering that Jace had recently taken over operation of the family's Christmas tree farm, Noah asked, "How is the tree business?"

"Couldn't be better," Jace said. "Maybe you heard that I avoided taking over the farm for years. But now that I'm into it, I've realized it's a good thing for me. Making a bit of money and still have plenty of free time for my other business, or at least I will after

Christmas." He laughed. "If we didn't do gangbusters in December, we'd be in a heap of trouble. Two and a half weeks till Christmas and half our stock is gone. Doesn't help that Mama and Kayla have picked out the prize trees to decorate the barn for our wedding on Christmas Eve."

"You're getting married in a barn?"

"Sounds weird, doesn't it? But yeah. Only these days even the oddest places are called *venues*. Believe it or not, Crestview Barn is a wedding venue." He paused a moment before adding, "Hey, you ought to come."

"Me? Thanks, but I'm sure you've got plenty of guests already."

"Always room for one more. You're renting that house next to the school, aren't you?"

Noah nodded.

"Then you're a member of our community. And you've been to Mama's for dinner, so that practically makes you a member of the family."

"Jace," Noah reminded him, "I haven't been invited."

"You have now," Jace said. "I'm inviting you." A huge grin spread across his face. "Just had a great idea. My sister, Ava, doesn't have a date for the big event yet. I don't think she plans to invite anyone from Holly River. How'd you like to be her escort?"

A lot of time had passed since a simple suggestion like Jace's had lit a fire in Noah's bloodstream, but it sounded like a great idea. "I'd like it fine," he said, "but I'm not exactly Ava's favorite person, not that I wouldn't like to be."

Noah wasn't sure why he'd said that, perhaps to give Ava an out. However he knew Ava had liked the kiss the other night.

"I'm not asking you to marry her, Noah. Besides, Ava likes everybody," Jace said. "When are you going to see her again?"

"Tomorrow."

"Great. I'll stop by her office in the morning and tell her what we talked about. Then you just have to do the asking when you see her."

All at once Noah experienced a bout of nervousness he hadn't known for years, not even when he was four hundred feet up a tower. Climbing a tower, riding a motorcycle, racing a boat—these were all activities he was good at, used to. But asking a smart, pretty woman like Ava Cahill on a date, well, that was a totally different, nail-biting experience. Resigning himself to being turned down tomorrow was the only way he'd get through his dinner tonight at the café.

The waitress brought Jace his takeout meal in two huge sacks. "Tell the family I said hi," she said.

"I'll do that, Allie," he said. "And since I figure you're going to see Sam McCall later, you tell him I said hi, too." He stood up, patted Noah on the back. "And take good care of my pal here, okay?"

Noah wished someone would take good care of him. He was the fearless guy who climbed cell towers and balanced in a harness four hundred feet in the air. But he was much more comfortable meeting a woman in a dark cocktail bar or even taking Ava in his arms in a quiet barn and kissing her than he was asking her for a date.

CHAPTER TEN

"YOU DID WHAT?" Ava had heard Jace correctly, but she needed him to repeat the words again anyway. Her Friday had not been going well, and an unexpected visit from Jace and this announcement didn't make it any better.

"Yeah, I ran into him yesterday and I told him to ask you to the wedding."

"Why would you do that? Don't you think I can get my own date?"

"Well, sure, but every time we've talked about who the lucky dude was going to be, you've avoided the topic. I just figured the pool of eligible bachelors in Holly River wasn't offering up too many choices."

"That's up to me to decide," she said. "When I need you to manage my social calendar, I'll let you know."

Jace backed away, holding up his hands as if surrendering. "That's funny. Mama and I didn't know you had a social calendar these days, Ava."

She was furious that Jace had interfered in her life, but even more than that, she was curious. She studied his face as he stood in her office, but nothing was revealed. What had Noah said when Jace made the suggestion? Had Noah laughed? Had Noah made some excuse about being busy on Christmas Eve? Had he…?

Oh heck. She blurted out the question. "What did Noah say?"

"He liked the idea," Jace answered. "He's going to do it. And I think you should say yes."

"But I only know Noah as a business connection. He's the father of one of my residents." Okay, that was a blatant lie. In one way, she knew him much better than other men she had dated. "Why would he want to take our relationship in a different direction?"

Jace grinned in that boyish way that had always made her do whatever he wanted. "Say yes, and maybe you'll find out."

She tapped her pencil on her desk. "Why

did you come over here this morning anyway? Was it just to aggravate me?"

"That would be enough for me," he said, "but Mama wanted me to come and tell you to do your thing with that holiday store online and order up a bunch of white and gold ornaments. She and Kayla have decided on a color scheme for the trees, and we're running out of time. Plan on eight trees, fifty ornaments per. Can you do that?"

"I can do that. And they will be here in plenty of time. I'll get started as soon as you leave me in peace."

He held up two fingers in a peace sign. "Happy holidays, darlin'." And he was out the door, presumably to go to the tree farm, but no one could ever tell for sure with Jace.

SherryLynn buzzed her from the outer office.

"What is it, SherryLynn?"

"That Jace is just the cutest thing. If I were twenty years younger… Oh well. He's even gotten more adorable since he got engaged."

"Oh yeah, he's adorable all right. Is that why you buzzed?"

"No. Mr. Brannigan is on the phone. He says it's important."

Ava had been waiting for her lawyer's call. She'd given him important information after her visit to Rudy the other day, and Brannigan had promised to follow up.

She picked up her phone. "Hello, Terry. You got something for me?"

"I do, Ava. I contacted those half-dozen accounts that had disappeared from the books when the paper mill went to digital recording. You were right. None of those companies had severed ties with Cahill Paper. They've been ordering pulp all along."

"And they've been paying their bills, too," she added.

"According to their CFOs they have. Add up all six clients that we know about, and it amounts to quite a sum." Brannigan sighed. "What do you want me to do now, Ava? I know this is a family matter, but right is right."

"I agree. What do you suggest, Terry?"

"I can send the results of my findings to Rudy today via courier. Of course, I'll enclose a letter threatening legal action. I don't see any reason to wait. Might ruin Rudy's weekend, and yours too, so it's up to you."

"Send it over to him, Terry. And send me

a copy. And don't worry. I can handle Uncle Rudy if he runs over here after getting the package."

She disconnected the call and took a deep breath. She'd given Rudy enough time to apologize and fix what he'd done, and he'd chosen not to. She fully expected this day to go downhill fast.

AVA HEARD HER uncle's thundering voice in the outer office at three o'clock that afternoon. He demanded to see her immediately. SherryLynn did her best to put him off, but Rudy was adamant.

Ava opened her office door. "You want to see me, Uncle Rudy?"

"You're darn right I do." He held a thick envelope in his hand. Without waiting for an invitation, he barreled past Ava and entered her office.

She went behind her desk but didn't sit. "You seem upset."

Rudy threw the envelope on her blotter, set his hands on the edge of the desk and leaned forward. "What the blazes is the meaning of this, Ava?"

Ava didn't flinch. "I was hoping it would

be self-explanatory," she said. "My lawyer is usually quite precise."

His eyes blazed. "I never thought it would come to this. We're family, Ava. I used to bounce you on my knee."

"Oh, I don't remember that. But anyway, Mama is your family, too, Rudy, by marriage, and over the last year I haven't seen much familial compassion from you. In fact, I've seen every indication that you've been cheating Mama out of her profit-sharing money."

Rudy picked up the envelope. His hand was shaking badly. "You're not going to get away with this, Ava. A few clients claim to have paid us some cockamamie sum of money. There's not a thing in this report from Brannigan that couldn't be explained away as a simple accounting error. This would never stand up in court."

"Thirty-five thousand dollars is not a 'simple accounting error,'" she said. "My mother is due that money, and my brothers and I are determined to see she gets every last penny."

"This is hogwash, Ava, and you know it. Your daddy left Cora very well off. That house and property alone must be worth three or four hundred thousand."

"You're talking about my mother's *home*, Rudy, and as far as her children are concerned, it's worth much more than that for us to see her securely staying there as long as she wants to." She thought about reminding him how Cora had forgone repairs to the old house, leaving it looking worn and tired. Instead, she simply said, "Besides, the value of my mother's personal property is irrelevant to this discussion."

Rudy leaned toward her even more, his upper body extending across the desk. "I'll tell you what is relevant," he snarled. "Blood. Family. My brother must be turning over in his grave at this wanton display of greed on your part, Ava. You're going against your own, and that's never a smart move. I have lawyers too, a whole firm of them. They will make Terrance Brannigan look like a student in his first year of law school."

Ava resisted the urge to lean back. She could feel her uncle's hot breath on her face. She steadied her position behind the desk and said, "Fine. Bring them on."

"You've become one coldhearted woman

since you went off to Charlotte, Ava Cahill. This side of you is pure ugliness." He
pounded the desk, sending pens rolling to
the floor and nearly upsetting her desk lamp.

"We're done here, Rudy. You do what you
have to do."

He shook his head and glared at her. "Oh,
we're not done. Not by a long shot." He stuck
out his index finger at her. "You've made a
big mistake, Ava. You—"

Suddenly her office door burst open and
Noah strode in, his eyes clearly begging for
a fight. "Back away from her now," he said.

"Who are you?" Rudy growled. "This is
family business."

"I can see we're all one big happy family
here," Noah said, grasping Rudy's shoulders
and forcibly turning him toward the door.
"I'm giving you one more chance. Back away
or I'll personally escort you out of this office,
and it will be an exit you won't soon forget."

Rudy tried to glare at her over his shoulder. "You have bodyguards now, Ava? Tell
this goon…"

"I have friends, Rudy," she said, drawing
in a deep breath.

"You're going to need a lot of them before this is over," Rudy said.

Noah gave him a little shove, just a hint of what he was no doubt capable of. "Get out," he said.

Rudy stalled just long enough to yank his jacket lapels together. Then he stormed out of the office. Noah stood in the doorway watching until Rudy had vacated the building.

"You okay?" he said, approaching Ava's desk.

"Yes. And thank you. You came in at just the right time. I was handling him pretty well for a while, but my so-called pluck was fading fast."

"You're welcome. My thorny temper and bad manners do come in handy once in a while." He smiled. "I don't mean to be nosy, but that jerk is really a member of your family?"

Ava sank into her chair. Her hands were trembling and she clenched them in her lap. "He is. My father's brother. The Cahills actually have had several black sheep cluttering up our ranks over the decades. I'm hoping Rudy is the last of them."

"Is this anything I can help you with? I don't have a team of lawyers at my beck and call, but I can chase him around town with my motorcycle. Maybe make him see the error of his ways."

Ava unclenched her hands, placed them on top of the desk. She was beginning to calm down. "I'll let you know if I need such drastic measures." She raked her fingers through her hair. "Why are you here anyway? Not that I'm complaining, but I figured you would have left for another job."

Noah pulled up a chair, rested his ankle on the opposite knee. "Not today. Got back late last night. Thought I'd stop and see Sawyer, maybe ask her to dinner tonight, if that's all right with the school's administrator." His smile mutated to a flirty grin. "Thought I might ask the administrator, too."

"It's fine if you want to ask Sawyer, but I'll probably be going through more ledgers to find evidence against Rudy..." She realized that Noah didn't know what she was talking about. "Never mind. I'll have my nose in a book."

"Oh gee, that sounds much better than a

glass of red wine and a prime rib dinner at Brickstones."

She tapped her finger on the desktop. She was being ridiculous. His plan actually was just what she needed. And she wouldn't be alone with him, so she needn't be conscious of every word she spoke, every gesture she made. Since Sawyer would be there, he probably wouldn't even ask her to Jace's wedding. She gave him a warm stare. "Nothing gets to me as much as a good line of biting sarcasm. You won me over with the words 'prime rib.'"

"I wish I'd thought of some great sarcasm the other night when I kissed you. I might have prolonged the experience." His mouth curled up at the corner. "Instead all I could think was how great the kiss was."

Feeling her face flush as if she were fifteen years old again, Ava stared down at the assortment of items on her desk that had been scattered when Rudy pounded the surface. "Well, I'd better get back to work."

"Call Sawyer for me?" he said, rising from the chair. "Tell her I'll meet her outside her cottage in five. And I'll pick you girls up at seven thirty this evening."

"That should be fine," Ava said. "And, Noah…"

He stopped at the door. "Yeah?"

"Thank you for being here today. And for the dinner invitation." She was well aware that he hadn't asked her to Jace's wedding. Maybe he'd had a change of heart.

"Oh, that's nothing," he said. "Tonight after I drop Sawyer off at her place, I'm going to find a nice, quiet spot for just the two of us so I can ask to escort you to your brother's wedding. I hear it's going to be the best barn event of the season."

He was out the door before she could answer, argue, avoid or whatever she thought she might have done. And it was a full minute before she realized she was grinning like a fat cat.

BEFORE GOING TO her apartment to get ready for the evening, Ava stepped onto the well-lit pathways of Sawtooth School and walked across campus to the cottage where Sawyer and Charlie resided. It had been several days since the incident with the meltdown, and Ava had visited with the child often. Charlie's caregivers had reported no more problems.

Her heart ached for the child—her son. She was glad she'd confided in a school counselor, Marjorie Marcos, about her relationship to Charlie. Besides promising complete secrecy on the topic, Margie had warned Ava of traumatizing Charlie unnecessarily. "He needs to accept that his parents are gone, Ava," she'd said. "We don't want to confuse him. We need to judge when he's ready to hear that a new parent is entering his life."

"But when?" Ava had asked.

"We'll know," Margie said. "I'm making progress with him, but he's so young, and his life has been turned upside down."

"I just want to hug him and love him..."

"You can still do that, Ava, with reservation. Now your biggest concern should be getting Charlie to trust you. When he starts confiding in you, talking about his fears, his hopes, then we are making true progress. Tell him too soon, and we're just confusing him, demanding more of his thought processes than we should."

Ava had agreed to exercise patience with Charlie, but that didn't mean she couldn't give him special attention.

She went to his room and knocked lightly on the door frame. As was customary, the door was open. The cottage parents would close it in a couple of hours and leave three night-lights lit, one for each child in the room.

"Is it okay if I come in?" she asked.

"Hi, Miss Ava," Charlie said. "Be quiet. Chip is already asleep."

"I'll be quiet." She stopped next to the youth bed where four-year-old Chip was comfy under his covers and breathing at a slow, relaxed pace. Then she went to the top bunk where Henry, six years old, was propped on his elbows and playing a video game on an electronic device. The cottage parents kept activities varied for the younger children— some outside play, quieter inside crafts and activities, and limited TV and video watching. Henry would have to put down the device when it was lights out.

"How are you, Henry?" she asked.

"I'm good, Miss Ava. But I don't like meat loaf, and that's what we had for dinner tonight."

Ava smiled. "What would you have rather had?"

"Pizza or tacos," the boy answered. "Would you tell Mrs. Carmichael not to fix meat loaf again?"

"How about if I ask her *very nicely* to fix a grilled cheese sandwich for you on the nights she's planned meat loaf? Would that be okay?"

"That would be okay."

Ava bent down to the bottom bunk. "How are you feeling, Charlie? Did you have a good day?"

"Yes, ma'am. I didn't get in any trouble. And I don't hurt books anymore. Mrs. Marcos told me I was just angry that day, and that's okay."

"It is. It's okay to be angry," Ava said.

"She told me to talk to someone next time I feel that way."

"Good. As for the books, I think reading them is a fine idea for now."

Charlie's eyes widened. "Sawyer told me about how she gets mad sometimes. And Mrs. Marcos said everybody has 'motions, but it's not okay to destroy things."

Ava recalled that Sawyer had taken Charlie back to the cottage on the day in question. She wondered now if the two were forming a bond. The irony of a relationship between the two of them was both troubling and heartwarming. Half brother and sister. "Are you seeing a lot of Sawyer?" she asked.

"Yep. She usually sits with me at supper. We talk about stuff. Did you know that her dad makes her mad?"

"Yes, she's told me a bit about that."

"He's a bad person, isn't he?"

Ava sat on the side of the bed. "Oh no, sweetie. He's actually a very nice man. Sawyer just gets upset because his job is kind of dangerous and she worries about him."

"He should get another job, then." Charlie nodded once decisively as if the solution should be obvious to the most obtuse person.

"Maybe he will," Ava said. "Or maybe Sawyer will learn to accept what he does."

"What's his job?" Charlie asked. "Does he get shot out of a cannon like the man at the circus?"

Ava chuckled. "Nothing so terrifying as that, Charlie. Sawyer's father works on high places, that's all."

"You should go see Sawyer," Charlie said. "Tell her what we've been talking about."

She gently ruffled his hair before standing. It was nice to realize that Charlie was learning the benefits of talking out problems. And that he was understanding everyone had them. "I think I'll do that right now. Are you two boys getting sleepy?"

He pointed to a large clock on the wall. "We have till the little hand reaches the seven," Charlie said. "It's not there yet."

"Okay. Good night, then, fellas. Sleep tight."

Smiling as she always did after visiting with Charlie, Ava walked down the hallway to stairs that led to the second floor of the cottage. She thought loud music would lead her to Sawyer and Becky's room, but the hallway was eerily quiet. When she reached their room, she understood why. Both girls were propped on their beds with earbuds stuck in their ears.

Ava knocked loudly.

"Oh hi," Becky said. "Come on in." She got up off her bed and went to poke Sawyer to attention.

"What's up?" Sawyer asked after popping the buds free.

"I just went to see how Charlie was doing and thought I'd check on you two. I don't get into the cottages nearly enough." She glanced around the room. A bit messy, but not bad. Sawyer had arranged a few stuffed animals on her bed and had tacked some posters on her wall. Ava didn't recognize any of the celebs that obviously caused Sawyer to swoon.

"We finished our homework, so if you came to lecture us, don't bother."

"I didn't come to lecture anyone," Ava said. "But good. I'm glad to hear that."

Ava pulled a desk chair next to Sawyer's bed and sat. "I wanted to thank you for all the attention you're giving Charlie lately. I really appreciate it."

"He needs attention," Sawyer said. "Charlie can be a bit freaky as we learned the other day."

"He's had a tough time. But he seems to respond to you. That's a good thing, as long as you continue to be a positive influence on him."

"No promises," Sawyer said. "But I kind of like the little guy. I get him, you know? I feel sorry for him."

"Anyway, thanks," Ava repeated. "How

did your meeting with your father go this afternoon?"

"I knew you were going to bring that up. You're coming to dinner with Dad and me in a little while, right?"

"Yes, he asked. I think I'm included only because he figured you'd say yes if I went along. Do you want to go?"

"Yeah, I guess. It got me out of meat loaf night, and at least if you're there I won't have to worry about my dad chucking me in the back of the truck and hauling me to Chapel Hill."

Ava smiled. "You know he's not going to do that, Sawyer. He signed papers for you to stay here. He rented the house next door. He's fine with this arrangement."

Sawyer screwed her mouth into a pout. "Then why did he tell me he wanted some time alone with you after dinner? What's he planning?"

He's planning to ask me to my brother's wedding, and I don't know what else. Obviously Ava could not give Sawyer that explanation for fear she'd think they were in a relationship, and right now she was a bit upset that Noah had told her he wanted time alone. "I don't know," she said. "Why do you think he's planning something?"

"Fourteen years of knowing him," she said. "Don't let him talk you into anything, Ava, okay? You and I are friends first, not you and my dad. If he wants me back at Chapel Hill, you tell him no."

Ava smiled. "Does that mean you actually like living at Sawtooth?"

Sawyer sniffed loudly. "I mean this place has its problems. It's certainly not perfect, and the rules are ridiculous. But it's better than being under the thumb of the demon housekeepers."

"I doubt you have anything to worry about," Ava said. "I believe your father will let you stay here as long as you want to."

Sawyer rubbed a finger under her nose. "At least my coming here accomplished something," she said.

"What's that?"

"It forced my dad to come to me for once. Instead of forcing me to go back to him."

"You're right," Ava said, marveling at the simple wisdom of Sawyer's statement. "That's a very interesting point." She patted Sawyer's hand, stood and went to Becky's side of the room for a brief conversation. "Have a good night, girls. See you later."

As she walked back to her apartment in the administration building, Ava thought about Sawyer's words again. Yes, Noah renting a home and coming to his daughter was a bigger accomplishment than he probably even realized. Ava considered it a major step forward in improving their relationship. And just maybe, it predicted more changes to come.

CHAPTER ELEVEN

NOAH HAD ARRANGED a perfect evening. Dinner at Brickstones, a bottle of wine for the adults, prime rib for everyone. The fire burning in the stone fireplace next to their table was warm and cozy, the ceiling lights soothingly low. The music from a solo guitarist mellow and sweet. The Christmas tree was twinkling over a smattering of wrapped gifts. And Noah looked so handsome in dress jeans, a button-down shirt and suede jacket.

Even the conversation seemed made to order. Noah asked Sawyer about her classes, and she answered without inserting her usual sarcasm. Ava discussed some activities that were coming up at the school for the holidays, and she asked about Noah's plans for Christmas. At that point the conversation began to deteriorate.

"I might be busy Christmas Eve," he said. "Other than those plans, I'll be staying right here, in my little place next door. What could be more Christmassy than the town of Holly River?" He looked at his daughter. "Sawyer, I'm hoping you'll stay with me, at least on Christmas Day. You'll need to tell me pretty soon what you'd like for Christmas if I'm to get any shopping done."

"Why bother?" she said. "Your work will probably call you away and you won't be here for the holiday anyway, despite what you just said."

Ava held her breath. *Oh, no, Sawyer, we're having such a lovely evening.*

His voice low, he said, "Sawyer, I've never missed Christmas with you, and you know it."

"First time for everything. I've learned not to get my hopes up."

Frowning, Noah called for the check. He walked the ladies to his truck and drove back to the school in silence. When they arrived at Sawyer's cottage he said, "I'm going to show Ava the house, Sawyer. One of the rules of the school is that a visitation must be performed at the home of the parent before any resident is allowed to stay any length of time.

Ava has to see my place before you and I can have a holly, jolly Christmas."

"Whatever." Sawyer climbed down from the truck and headed to the front door of her cottage.

"See you soon, kiddo," Noah called after her.

She flung a dismissive wave over her shoulder without turning around to look at him. Noah put the truck into reverse.

Ava couldn't hide her disappointment in Sawyer. "Thank you for a lovely meal," she said. "It was delicious, and at least one of us should tell you so."

"My pleasure," Noah said. "And you're welcome. I'll just pretend I'm saying that to Sawyer as well."

"You told her we were spending some time alone tonight."

"I did. The visitation isn't just an excuse. You actually do have to check the place out."

"True. I hope Sawyer believes it. She was certain that we were planning some sinister plot that concerns her."

Noah smiled. "In case you haven't noticed, Ava, my daughter can be something of a drama queen, a fact I've pointed out to her a number of times."

"Well, maybe a little."

Noah drove off campus and down the quarter-mile road that led to his rental house. Every one of Ava's senses was alive with expectation. For what? She didn't know. She'd passed this house hundreds of times, but she'd never really looked at it. And now that she was going into the driveway, the only thing she knew for certain was that she wasn't thinking about seeing the house. She was thinking about that other night with Noah and she wondered if the same was true of him.

In a moment she and Noah would be alone in the tidy stone structure. She took a deep breath and wondered what the next minutes, hours of her life would be like. And then, suddenly, the air in front of the truck was sparkling in the headlights.

"It's snowing," she said, her voice soft and reverent.

He looked at her, smiled. "It was predicted. Just an inch or two."

"It's beautiful, the kind of thick, heavy

snow that coats and sticks to the trees and makes the world pure again."

"And sticks to the sidewalks and driveways, too," he teased. "Which reminds me, if Mr. Crocker, who rented me this place, doesn't have a snow shovel in the garage, I'll be heading to the hardware store tomorrow."

She flashed him a pretend scowl. "All that talk of work is ruining my snow high, you know."

"Sorry." He reached over and covered her hand with his. "I'll bet it's still a balmy fifty degrees in Chapel Hill right now."

"Which is why I love the mountains." As they approached the house, Ava noticed multicolored lights in the bushes. "Oh, Noah, you put up decorations."

"Just a few. There's a tree inside as well." He sent her a smile. "I have a friend in the tree business."

He parked the truck in front of the house and turned so he was facing her. His eyes were dark in the low light from the dashboard, but they still reflected that deep intensity that seemed to reach all the way to her heart. He raised his hand and cupped her cheek.

Was he going to kiss her? And was he assuming too much to think that she wanted him to? No. Ava had found herself looking at his full lips throughout the evening, remembering the kiss in the barn, anticipating the next one, knowing she was taking a chance and still wanting to experience Noah again.

He curled his hand around her nape and pulled her close. When his lips touched hers it was déjà vu, complete with the tangle of emotions every time this happened. But all at once Ava didn't care that she'd let him kiss her in the barn or that they were kissing now. She didn't care about anything but the feeling of his lips on hers, his mouth, hungry and possessive, his fingers slipping into her hair and up the back of her scalp.

He moved his head, gently yet persuasively, deepening the kiss. Her senses reeled with the magic of the moment, the snow, the darkness, her feelings. Mostly her feelings. A groan escaped from deep in her throat. He was everything she'd remembered and much that she was only now experiencing. If emotions could soar, hers did. She was lost in the feel of his mouth, the scent of his breath on her skin, the solid pressure of his hand on her back.

When he stopped, his gaze leveled on hers. Ava touched her lips, feeling the dampness that lingered on them. And then he said the strangest, most baffling thing.

His voice hoarse, his lips curled in a smile of pure satisfaction, he said, "I'm not sure if I'm lost in the memories of that one night in our past, or if I wish tonight were a first."

"I'm not sure either," Ava said. "But we can't relive the past, can we? Nor should we automatically believe that the past determines the future."

"That's true," he agreed. "But I'm a man who loves kissing, and I sure did love that kiss of yours." He remembered his first kiss. It was in the fifth grade. How it confused and excited him. He remembered the kisses he shared after the prom with the girl he was sure he'd end up marrying but didn't. He remembered the first kisses he'd experienced with Mary Kate, his wife, kisses that held promise and yet grew tired and compulsory after a short time.

"I'm not sorry at all that you and I met

once before, and I'm absurdly happy that we found each other again…"

"Noah, you shouldn't think in terms of 'you and I,'" she said. "I'm sure you didn't think much about me, or I you before you roared into my life on your motorcycle. During those years apart we both changed and we lived full lives. We're together tonight only because of your daughter."

Noah was suddenly aware that his life hadn't been full at all, and despite Ava's attempts at logical analysis, he didn't believe hers had been either.

"So this kiss was nothing special?" he asked.

She grinned. "I didn't say that. It was nice."

"That was not a nice kiss, Ava. In my mind it was powerful. I remember the effect you had on me six years ago. I left your apartment that night thinking that I was walking away from something pretty spectacular. I wanted to go back, talk to you, explain about my situation."

She blinked, took a deep breath. "What happened that night shouldn't have happened at all. You were married. I was…well, I wasn't myself."

"And yet, here we are together. I'm not going to say I believe in fate, but I can't help thinking this all means something, Ava."

"Noah, don't. Let's go into your house, where I'm supposed to record this as an official visitation."

"Okay. But if we're going to be strictly business when we go inside, then I need to get my proposal over with."

"Oh, I…"

He took her hand. "Ava Cahill, will you allow me to be your 'plus one' at your brother's wedding?"

She pressed her lips together before a smile seemed to appear spontaneously on her face. "I have just one question," she said.

"Sure. Anything."

"Was this your idea, or Jace's?" Her grin widened. "Either way I'm going to say yes, but I'm curious."

"Honestly? Jace brought it up. At first I couldn't see myself crashing a Cahill wedding, but then I thought of spending a whole evening with you, and I was immediately on board. I was worried that you would have already accepted a date or would say no."

"Well, for the record, my answer's an official yes."

"Great." He got out of the truck and came around to open her door. He took her hand so she wouldn't slip on the newly fallen snow and he held it tightly as they walked to his front door where a pine wreath scented the air.

All at once, it was super important to Noah to have Ava like his house. Yes, he was only renting it, but from the day he moved in, he'd felt a sense of belonging. The solid, hardwood floors, the brick fireplace, the comfortable earth-tone furniture, the sofa built for two. Yes, he'd rented the house to be close to his daughter, but since then the simple structure had come to mean so much more.

Before going in, she stopped him on the threshold. "I'm a liar, Noah," she said.

"Oh?"

"The kiss was considerably better than nice."

He cupped her cheeks with both hands and kissed her again, slowly, leaving them both breathless.

CHAPTER TWELVE

AVA STAYED AT Noah's house for almost an hour. She seemed charmed by the place, saying she'd seen the house many times but never imagined that the furnishings would be so nice, the workmanship have such quality. He offered her a glass of wine. She refused. He offered to turn over the television remote control to her. She declined. But when he suggested they go outside and watch the slowly drifting snowflakes, she readily agreed.

Born and raised in Florida, Noah had never pictured himself dusting snow off patio lounge chairs, but that's just what he did. Then he spread two blankets on the chairs and they each reclined, their hands joined between as naturally as the snow fell in December. Ava pulled her faux white fur collar up around her neck and made him think of a delicate snow fairy. While they talked, the trees at the end of his property slowly became blanketed in the mesmerizing stars of newly fallen snow.

"I really should get back," she said after checking her watch. "It's after ten."

He smiled. "Tomorrow's not a school day."

"No, but I'm thinking I might go another round with my uncle Rudy, and I need to be on my game."

The last time Rudy had been in Ava's office was still fresh in Noah's mind. Along with the burst of anger toward the bully, Noah had felt an overwhelming sense of protectiveness toward Ava. He didn't want to think of her alone with the man again, especially on a Saturday when the full office staff wasn't working.

"Maybe I should come over in the morning. I was going to check with you to see if I could take Sawyer shopping, but I don't mind hanging out with you for a while."

"Don't be silly," she said. "Rudy is family. He wouldn't have hurt me when he showed up before. He just wants to intimidate me, make me change my mind about pursuing legal action against him."

"I don't know what's going on," Noah

said, "but I wouldn't want to be on opposite sides of an issue with you stubbornly sticking to your guns. I know you can handle yourself. Still, I'd feel better…"

"No, Noah. I'll be fine. Besides he might not even come tomorrow. Take Sawyer shopping. You two need some time alone, and I know she'll enjoy the attention."

So with plans made, Noah took Ava back to her apartment in the administration building. When he parked in front, he leaned in close to her. "I had a great time tonight," he said.

"I did, too."

He closed the few inches between them and pressed his mouth to hers.

"No, Noah," she said, backing away. "Not here. Not on the campus."

"Why not? Do you think kissing never happens on these hallowed grounds? Over half your residents are teenagers."

"That's different. You and I aren't governed by raging hormones."

He sat straight. "Speak for yourself."

She smiled. "And I have to act like an administrator. What if the security guard drove by? Or one of the cottage parents was out for a late-night walk and spotted us?"

He opened his truck door. "Okay, you win. Maybe I'll just peek my head in your office tomorrow when I come for Sawyer. But I promise I won't come around the desk."

He walked her to the door, waited for her to turn the lock and offered his hand for a firm shake. Gallant and much too friendly. Then he reluctantly said good-night.

Driving back to his house, he thought of Ava, the qualities that made her different from anyone he'd ever met before, the niggling memories that made him remember the last brief time they'd been together. Ava Cahill—an enticing blend of impropriety and decorum. Two Avas. He admired one and he'd become almost spellbound by the other.

"You're in trouble, Walsh," he said aloud. "You, Ava, and a beautiful wintry wedding. And you thought climbing towers was the most dangerous thing you did."

He was still smiling when he went into his house.

THE PHONE CALL Noah got from his boss at Maxicom the next morning brought him back to reality with a crash. Just what he needed, a chance to spend a quality day with Sawyer, and he'd have to end it by telling her he'd be gone for five days straight. Seems the snowfall in Tennessee was not as fluffy and serene as what fell in Holly River. Cables had come loose from their poles in the blustery winds, cell service was sketchy. Five towers in all in the central part of the state needed immediate attention.

He wasn't going to disappoint Sawyer. Not this time. He called a crew foreman and assigned him the easiest fix. Climbers, because of the emergency nature of their jobs, were usually ready to grab their packed bags and travel to wherever they were needed. Noah's pal and climbing buddy, Karl, was no exception. "I'll take care of it, chief," Karl said. "We should get there by early afternoon, and have it fixed by dark. We'll see you on Sunday for the toughest climbs."

True to his word, Noah stopped at the administration building. Ava wasn't in her office, but he left a note.

Good morning, Miss Cahill. Sorry to have missed you. Leaving tonight for

Tennessee and a five-day gig. Still taking Sawyer shopping, but she's not going to like the rest of the story. Good thing I only have one kid, eh? I guess you're right. Parenting is not my strong suit.

He grinned when he thought of her reading the note. They had come to agreeable terms about one thing at least. As a parent, he had his faults. But after this five-day trip, he was determined to pick up where he'd left off with his daughter. He hadn't felt this confident about relating to Sawyer in a long time. He hoped she wouldn't flip out over this latest trip.

AVA RETURNED TO her office after a quick tour of the campus. She often walked the grounds looking for anything that might be out of the ordinary. On this Saturday morning at barely ten o'clock, she didn't find anything unusual. The younger children were playing on gym equipment and marveling at the snow that was beginning to melt. The teens were nowhere to be seen. *Probably still in bed*, she thought.

She walked to her desk and saw a folded

paper leaning against her pencil sharpener. *Miss Cahill* it said. *Personal.*

She picked it up and studied the script. She'd never seen Noah's handwriting before, except for his signature when he filled out paperwork for Sawyer's admittance, but somehow she knew that the note was from him. Bold, clear strokes of the pen reflecting the boldness of the man himself.

She unfolded the paper and read. Disappointed that he was going to be gone for five days, she read on, hoping that perhaps he would be on campus long enough for her to see him once more before he left. And then she read the last part of the note. "Good thing I only have one kid…parenting is not my strong suit."

Something inside of her snapped, a sharp, painful ache that began in her chest and radiated outward. He had no idea how his casual observation would affect her. He had no idea he had another child. But he was thankful that he didn't have any child other than Sawyer. How would he feel if he knew about Charlie? Would he be certain that Sawyer was enough of a problem and a responsibility?

She banished any notion of guilt that she hadn't told him about her pregnancy. He'd walked out of her bedroom and her life after a few hours of intense emotions that she'd never forgotten, not for one instant. Through the blur of her shame she heard him admit he was married, and she let him go. She didn't know how to contact him. What happened that night was completely unplanned and unexpected. She wasn't emotionally ready for what occurred, and he wasn't free to pursue it anyway.

No, Charlie was her responsibility. From the moment she discovered she was pregnant, she loved the life growing inside her. But never once did she think she was the appropriate person to raise him. She was busy twelve hours a day climbing ladders to success. Besides, what did she know about raising a child? She was scared. Petrified of making a mistake. Sure, she had a family, but not one close by. For all intents and purposes, she was on her own. Other moms, other families, could do better for her baby. Her baby deserved better. And now, she and Noah were in two different places about parenting. He knew that he had faults. She'd never given herself the opportunity to find out.

But since meeting him, learning his ways, his confidence, his insecurities, the thought had entered her head that maybe, one day, he could know about Charlie. Once his problems with Sawyer were solved, he would want to know that he had a son. But no, this note, written so innocently, might have been an offhand comment. Or this note might very well reveal the truth of Noah's feelings about fatherhood, and Ava couldn't take that chance. He'd had one child. That was enough, and perhaps because of his flaws, maybe it was too much.

Ava read the note a second time, or perhaps it was a third. She folded the paper and put it in the back of a desk drawer. It was for the best. Noah, with his long absences, his risk-taking lifestyle, wouldn't be a good father for her Charlie anyway. *Her Charlie…* Hopefully one day those words would truly mean something. If she ever told him she was his mother, she would be in his life forever. That's what her Charlie needed after suffering a tragic loss in his young life. Not a parent who risked his life almost on a daily basis, a father who had one child already who feared that each time she said goodbye to him might truly be the last time.

Ava sat at her desk, folded her hands and waited. For what, she wondered. For Noah to "peek his head" in her door for a minute as he promised? For Sawyer to end her day in her usual funk of worrying and feeling abandoned? For Rudy to come by with an ultimatum? This was not going to be a good day. And now Noah would be gone for five days. And in spite of everything, she couldn't deny that she would miss him—too much.

NOAH COULDN'T REFUSE his daughter anything. It was his way of making up for time lost, time that Sawyer couldn't forgive. By the end of the shopping trip, he'd run up his credit card by nearly five hundred dollars. The biggest expense had been a new notebook computer, which he didn't mind buying her. New earrings and shoes and purse— those things had just been fluff, and because of the job she hated, he could afford them.

"You're going to Tennessee in the snow?" she said when he dropped her back at Sawtooth and tried to discuss his plans with her "You're really something, Dad, you know that? So now you're not just climbing those stupid towers. You'll probably freeze to death."

"I am climbing. But I won't freeze to death. Remember, Sawyer, I have all the gear I need to stay warm and safe. I'll be back in five days."

She got out of the truck. "Sure. Whatever. Just go."

He tried. "Sawyer, we've had such a nice day. Let's not spoil it with…"

She held up her packages in both hands. "Yeah," she interrupted. "A great day. And now I know why."

"That's not fair, Sawyer," he said.

"What is fair with us, Dad? You tell me. Is it fair for you to leave? Am I not being fair by criticizing your choices? I guess I'm just supposed to sit quietly and never say anything."

"That's not true, Sawyer. We'll talk more about this when I get back."

Her chin jutted out at a stubborn angle. "Never mind. Just go. I'll see you whenever."

She slammed the truck door. "Five days!" he called through the glass. "Not whenever." If she heard him, he couldn't tell. She didn't turn around and soon entered the cottage door. He backed up and headed down the drive muttering to himself. "Impossible. That's what she is. No amount of reasoning gets through to her."

He was angry, both at his daughter for dismissing him emotionally and at himself for being impatient with her. He drove a bit too fast back to his house. When he walked inside, his phone was ringing. He hadn't even taken his cell so nothing would interrupt his time with Sawyer.

"Walsh," he said. "What is it, Chad?"

He listened to his crew chief complain about the workload, the difficulty of the projects, the narrow time structure they had to work under.

"Let me grab a few hours' sleep, I'll leave at 5:00 a.m."

He could have left then. Maybe should have, but too many climbers had learned the hard way that driving through the night left them tired and careless. Noah liked to ensure that his crew had proper rest and recuperation. Not just for their bodies, which took a serious toll climbing those heights with a thirty-pound bag of supplies attached to them, but emotionally as well. Tower climbers were a particular breed of technical people and at forty years of age, he was still one of them. How much longer could he continue to do this job? His body would tell him.

He had a beer, ate a frozen dinner and tried not to think about last night's meal at Brickstones. When he crawled into bed at nine, he put Sawyer out of his mind and let the void fill with Ava. Not a bad way to drift off to sleep. And not a bad way to fill his mind on the drive to Tennessee tomorrow.

CHAPTER THIRTEEN

NOAH REACHED THE job site at ten o'clock. The sun was shining, but in the foothills of the Smoky Mountains, snow was still thick on the trees and landscape. Not the pretty, thick snow—the cold, about-ready-to-turn-to-ice freezing stuff.

He spotted his crew about fifty yards off the highway in an open field. Their pickup truck was parked close to the tower, which was a tall one, more than four hundred feet. He shivered, imagining the top and hanging on in what looked to be about a twenty-mile-per-hour wind. He was equipped with warm work gloves, a fleece jacket, knit cap and helmet, and fur-lined boots. He'd be fine. He'd worked in worse situations.

Chad, his crew chief, was visible right away. At six foot five, he was easy to pick out in a crowd. Nearing fifty years old, he didn't climb much anymore and never the tallest towers. He managed the guy wires down below and kept his attention on the progress up the tower. If anyone dropped a wrench two hundred feet in the air, threatening to hit a climber below him, Chad knew about it and hollered a warning before it caused damage.

As Noah drove his truck to the site, he noticed something very unusual about the climb. Only one man was on the tower. Bad mistake. Everyone should have a climbing buddy, just like Noah had Karl. Whoever this was, he was going solo. Great. A problem he'd have to deal with right away.

But then, as he got closer, he realized the guy was not only alone. He was minus the most important equipment. Noah jumped out of the truck and ran to confirm his fears. The man had no harness, no helmet, no satchel of work supplies. He was close to thirty feet off the ground, and he wasn't moving. His feet were on two support poles; his arms circled a central pole and he was holding on as if his life depended on it.

And Noah had the sickening thought that it probably did.

He spoke to his crew chief first. "What

the heck's going on here, Chad? Who is that guy?"

Chad's normally placid face was etched with frustration. His eyes remained fixed on the climber. "He's a new hire, Noah. Just came on this morning. Had all the right credentials and convinced me he knew what he was doing. You weren't here, and we needed the help, so…"

"Does that look like he knows what he's doing?" Noah blurted out.

"He's a hotshot, Noah. A free climber. Told the crew this morning that he could shimmy one hundred feet up any tower with no safety equipment. A few of the guys tried to tell him it was senseless to try, but the dang fool set out to prove it."

Noah had met a few guys like this. Free climbers who tested their skill and stupidity by forgoing safety equipment for a temporary thrill. Noah didn't allow such disregard for the rules on one of his teams so he'd never before worked with one. And never before had he been responsible for one. All that suddenly changed.

"I suppose you told him to come down before he kills himself," Noah said.

"I've been yelling at him for the past fifteen minutes," Chad said.

"Great. And when he does come down, you're going to tell him he's fired."

"I should hope the dunce has figured that out by now."

Noah glanced around at the three other crew members who seemed spellbound by the careless act. "Why didn't someone go up after him?" he asked Chad.

"They didn't believe he was in any real trouble." Chad jabbed a thumb in the direction of the tower. "The guy, Rick's his name, convinced everyone he could climb freestyle. Nobody knew he'd get thirty feet up and freeze. And once he got so high, well, nobody wanted to go up and save him."

In this weather, the word *freeze* had two entirely different meanings. The weather was one. Blind, numbing fright was the other, the kind that left a person immobile and unable to act.

Noah uttered a few colorful phrases under his breath as he dashed for his truck and the equipment he could get to easily. He pulled on his helmet, snapped the strap in place, grabbed his harness, stepped into it and buckled it across his chest. Last he put on his gloves and grabbed a couple of cables and lanyards to secure his climb. He chose the strongest cables because he had a hunch he'd be coming back down with about one hundred and sixty pounds of dead weight hanging on to his shoulders.

"You're going up after him?" Chad asked.

Noah stared at the man three stories above his head as he attached cables and lanyards to his harness. "Sometimes it doesn't pay to be the boss. But I figure that idiot has a mother somewhere who expects him for Christmas dinner."

Noah took his first step up the tower. He called out, "Hey, Rick, you okay up there?"

"I can't move," the man said. "It's so cold. My hands are going to slip. I'm going to fall."

And then Noah began talking, saying whatever came into his mind. As he made his way up the climbing poles, hooking his lanyards above him with each step to secure his position for the next ascent up the tower, he continuously talked to Rick. "Got any kids, Rick? No? Where you from? Got a girlfriend?"

Sometimes Rick answered. Most times he

just cried out, "Hurry up and get me. I can't hang on any longer."

Darn fool, Noah thought. If he at least had his harness on, even if his hands slipped, he'd stay attached to the tower. He might swing in this wind, get a few bruises from banging against the tower. But he'd live. As it was now, both of their futures depended on one harness.

Noah had considered taking another harness up with him, but even if he'd been able to manage the extra weight, he would never have been able to attach it to Rick. The funny thing about freezing with fear is that the human body was truly frozen. The victim couldn't move any part of his body. Attaching a harness would have been more dangerous than the attempt to get the guy down piggyback style.

After ten minutes, Noah was breathless. The wind blew ice particles into his face that felt like needles. But he'd reached his target. He hooked the lanyards from both harness cables to a position above him and reached out to put a hand on Rick's back. The wind beat relentlessly. Rick's jacket flapped in the wind, making a racket.

"We're going to get you down, Rick," Noah said. "But you have to listen to me."

Rick's voice was hoarse and trembling. "I'll try. I will. What should I do?"

"I'm going to bring my head up under your arm. Then all you have to do is wrap your arm around my shoulders, as tightly as possible. Can you do that?"

"I don't know. I can't move. I've done this dozens of times, but today, I don't know. The weather. I hadn't planned on… I'm so sorry. I…"

You may have done this dozens of times, Noah thought, *but this is one time too many.* He saw Rick's fingers begin to slip on the pole. "Here I come. Under your arm just like I told you."

Noah had practiced the maneuver, but he'd never had to use it. None of his climbers had ever tried to free climb a tower, especially not in weather conditions like these. He was glad he'd never encountered this dangerous situation before. He would have fired the guy on the spot.

This rescue maneuver was not intended for careless free climbers. This approach was strictly for safety climbers who had all their necessary equipment but had encountered an unexpected problem, a cramp, a broken bone from falling objects, a heart attack. Heck, Noah would have risked his own life without a thought for a guy like that. But this hotshot...

He reminded himself of Rick's mother, ducked his head and met the rock-hard wall of Rick's upper arm. "Loosen up," Noah hollered. "Give me a little space to get under you."

Rick's muscles relaxed just enough for Noah to slip under his arm. He grabbed Rick's hand from the pole and brought his arm around his own neck. He could already feel the weight of the climber on his back.

"That's good," Noah said. "We're attached. Just a few more moves and we're going down together." He could hear Rick grinding his teeth, sucking in quick breaths.

"Now the other hand, Rick," Noah said. "Let go of the pole and bring your hand around to clasp on to the first hand."

Rick didn't move. Noah thought he heard something very like a giant sob. "You've got to do this, Rick. You've got to help me. Hell, man, I don't want to freeze up on this pole with you!"

Rick's index finger slipped on the pole, loosening his grip. It was enough for Noah to grab his hand and pull it around to grasp the other. Now the climbers were head to head with Rick making a sort of choker around Noah's throat.

"Loosen up a bit," Noah said. "Keep holding your wrists just like you are but I've got to breathe, son."

Rick exhaled, and Noah grabbed one of his legs. The foot slipped right off the pole, and Noah hooked his hand under Rick's knee and brought the entire leg around his waist. "Okay, that's good. Now the other leg."

"No. I can't," Rick cried.

"We're almost there, Rick. Lock your other leg around my waist and we'll start down. We'll be on the ground in ten minutes. I've got you. I've got a harness. We'll get down."

Rick whimpered, didn't move. His knees dug into Noah's ribs. His weight grew more cumbersome by the second. Noah had no choice. He forced Rick's other foot from the pole, Rick's last attachment to the tower, grabbed his knee and brought the leg around.

A sharp pain sliced into Noah's chest. He figured he'd cracked a rib. The phrase "I'm getting too old for this..." raced through his brain.

"Okay. Now all you do is hold on. You can do that. Hold on." Every word hurt, pushed by air from a damaged rib. "I'm taking the first step down the tower." Sucking in a shallow painful breath, Noah released one lanyard, placed his boot on the next pole down.

And Rick panicked. He screamed, reached above his head and clutched the second lanyard, the one Noah hadn't loosened yet. The first rule of climbing. Always leave one lanyard attached. Even one cable will hold the weight of one man. And if a guy is lucky, maybe two.

Noah reached up, tried to punch Rick's hand away from the lanyard. He hollered above the wind for him to let go. But the damage had been done. Rick's fingers depressed the clip, the lanyard slipped from the pole. There was nothing attaching both men to the tower. They were both suddenly free climbing. Only Noah had a cumbersome harness and the weight of another human on his back.

His hands slipped. Noah heard the men

on the ground holler up to him. He thought he heard Chad yell, "Call 911. They're coming down."

Noah reacted instinctively. He'd been taught how to fall, how best to hit the ground. He had only seconds. He clutched Rick's arms as they tumbled. Noah remembered two things. Duck your head. Land on your side. Five seconds later his body struck the hard, icy ground and everything went black.

THE CALL CAME into the administrative offices at the Sawtooth Children's Home a little before noon. Ava and SherryLynn were going over some important paperwork that was due on Monday. SherryLynn paused to answer and spoke in a soft, serious tone. "Ava, you better take this. The man says it's an emergency."

Ava picked up her desk phone and connected. "This is Ava Cahill. Who is this?"

"My name is Chad Walker, ma'am. I work with Noah Walsh. Noah told me his daughter is in the home there, and if I should ever need to reach her…"

Ava's blood chilled in her veins. The hand

holding the phone shook. "Yes, that's true. Has something happened to Noah?"

"Sorry to tell you, but yes. There's been an accident."

Ava tried to swallow, but her throat felt as if it had closed. "What sort of accident?" she managed to say.

"Noah fell from a tower. He was rescuing another man, and…"

She didn't need the details. The first five words were enough. "Is he…?" She couldn't say the words. She couldn't contemplate such wretched news for Sawyer, for herself, for Charlie's father.

"He's alive. Taken to the hospital in Daniel's Creek. I don't know any more details right now."

Ava needed to say something. She needed more information for Sawyer. She needed to give Sawyer hope. "How bad was the fall?" she asked.

"About thirty feet, but he was carrying another climber. And the ground was hard."

"Daniel's Creek… Daniel's Creek…" She repeated the name several times as she searched for her cell phone in her purse. How long would it take to google that location? Finally she said, "Where is that?"

Chad Walker told her and estimated it was about a five-hour drive. She looked at her office clock. They should be there by five thirty.

"Hospital's called Daniel's Creek Medical Center," Chad said. "You'll tell his daughter?"

She'd give anything not to have to do that. "Yes, of course. I will bring her to the hospital myself. Thank you."

Thank you for what? she wondered as she hung up the phone. For delivering gut-wrenching news that might put Sawyer over the precarious edge she was perched on already? For breaking Ava's heart, a heart she didn't even know could be broken by Noah's leaving them. For destroying any chance Charlie might have had to know his father?

Her chest hurt. She squeezed her hands together until they ached. But there was no time to cry. She spoke to SherryLynn. "Can you find out where Sawyer Walsh is right now?"

After a few seconds, SherryLynn gave her Sawyer's location. "Have her come to my apartment right away," Ava said. "And, SherryLynn, I'll be gone for a few days. Sawyer is going with me. Refer any emergencies to my cell phone, unless the call is from my uncle. Tell him you don't know when I'll be back."

"When *are* you coming back, Ava?"

"I'm not sure. That call was about Sawyer's father…"

"What happened?"

"I don't have all the information, but he's in the hospital. I'll call you when I know something." And then she went into her rooms to pack a suitcase.

Sawyer was oddly stoic when Ava told her about the accident. Ava worried she was close to becoming hysterical, so she kept talking to her. They drove to Sawyer's cottage, where the girl packed a few essentials, and they were on their way to a place called Daniel's Creek, through a cold, snowy landscape.

CHAPTER FOURTEEN

THE DANIEL'S CREEK MEDICAL CENTER was easy to find. Even without GPS, Ava would have been able to locate the largest, most modern building in the area. Situated between a country cafeteria and a two-story Best Western, the center was a beacon on an otherwise lonely stretch of road.

The trip to the small town had seemed to take forever. Weather conditions forced Ava to slow down for warning signs about ice on the roadway. Sawyer hadn't said more than a few words the entire trip. She stared out the passenger window and appeared to be watching the bleak, passing landscape. Ava knew she was lost in her own thoughts, and Ava's heart broke for her. At some point her emotions would get the best of her, and Ava hoped she was prepared to deal with Sawyer's panic…and her own.

Darkness had already settled when Ava

pulled into the center's parking lot. "There's a motel next door," she said to Sawyer. "As soon as I get a chance, I'll call for a room reservation."

They parked and entered the building. A security guard at the entrance demanded to see their IDs. He took pictures and provided each of them with a stick-on tag identifying them as visitors. Then he told them where to find Noah Walsh's room.

Ava was suddenly frightened of what she and Sawyer might find when they entered Noah's room. How badly was he hurt? Were his injuries evident on his face? Would he be covered in bandages? Thinking she would prepare Sawyer, she asked the guard for an update on Noah's condition.

"I don't have that information here, ma'am," he said. "You can stop at the patient advocacy office and ask if you want to."

"Let's just go to his room," Sawyer said. "I don't want to waste any more time."

"Okay." Ava patted Sawyer's shoulder and they followed the directions to the intensive care unit.

"If he's in intensive care, he's really bad, isn't he?" Sawyer said as they walked.

"Not necessarily. Sometimes patients just need extra monitoring."

"Or sometimes there's no chance they're going to survive a three-story fall and nurses are just waiting for them to die."

"No one is waiting for your father to die, Sawyer. I know this is a small town, but the hospital looks modern and well-staffed. I'm sure the doctors and nurses are watching him around the clock."

From the nurses' station, they were directed down a short hallway to a series of rooms with automatic glass doors that opened with soft hisses that almost sounded comforting. They found Noah's room. A nurse was inside. She was apparently checking his vital signs and recording data on his chart. She came to the door when she saw Ava and Sawyer.

"How is he?" Sawyer asked.

"He's holding his own," the nurse said. "Are you immediate family?"

"I'm his daughter."

The nurse turned to Ava. "And you?"

Ava didn't know how to answer. The man in the bed is my son's father. The man is someone with whom I had a wild, unforgettable night six years ago, and I've never stopped thinking about him. The man is flawed and reckless, but he has found a way into my heart. Finally she said, "I'm a family friend. I brought Mr. Walsh's daughter from North Carolina."

The nurse paused, and Sawyer quickly said, "She needs to come in the room with me."

"Okay. Usually we just allow immediate family, but we can make an exception since you're a minor." The nurse stepped aside, and Ava had her first look at the man who lay motionless on the bed, steel bars on each side of him preventing him from getting up. As if the stationary creature under the covers had any such intention.

Sawyer gave a gasp of shock, wrapped her hands around the bedside bars. "His head. What happened to his head?"

Ava understood her concern. The left side of Noah's head had been heavily bandaged around his temple. His arm was also bandaged, and his left leg was in a cast. She took Sawyer's hand and held it tightly.

The nurse checked a couple of gauges. "We're hoping it's not as bad as it looks," she said. "I don't know if you're aware how this happened, but he fell thirty feet and landed on frozen ground. That would have been bad enough, but he had another man on his back. Naturally the added weight made the injuries worse than they might have been."

"How could it be worse than this?" Sawyer asked. "I mean, he could be..." She gulped. "He's not going to die, is he?"

"I don't think so," the nurse said. "We're doing everything to keep him alive. He's actually doing pretty well...considering."

"But why is his head bandaged?"

The nurse replied, "He landed on his left side, which is actually good news. If he'd landed on his back, well...broken backs take a long time to heal. The bandages you see are covering surface wounds from the impact. Some of them are deep, but most are minor cuts and bruises. Amazing really."

"Why won't he wake up?" Sawyer asked. "Can't he hear you?"

"He's heavily sedated," the nurse said. "Again, not unusual for a fall victim."

"Did you induce the coma?" Ava asked, remembering years before when Jace had fallen from a tree, and the doctors had put him in a temporary coma while his injuries healed.

"No." The nurse walked to the door, and the glass portal slid open again on a near-silent hiss. "I thought I heard the neurologist's voice. He's at the nurses' station now," she said. "But he'll be with you in a moment. He'll be able to answer your questions."

Sawyer stood at the bedside, looking down at her father. She moved her hands as if she would touch him, but each time she returned them to the steel bar. "Does he know we're here?" she asked.

"I kind of doubt it," the nurse said. "Sometimes patients are aware of their surroundings, but Noah's in a deep sleep. That's good, really. He needs time to heal." She smiled at Sawyer. "You can touch him if you like. You won't hurt him. Just avoid the bandaged areas and his chest. He has a broken rib."

Sawyer sniffed and laid her hand on top of Noah's where it rested on the blanket. Ava gave a silent prayer that Noah would respond. A wiggle of his finger, a flexing of his palm. Nothing.

A doctor entered the room and came to the bedside. "Hello. I'm Dr. Kirkland, the staff neurologist. I'm monitoring Mr. Walsh, checking for brain damage, interior bruising or swelling..."

Ava told the doctor who she was and that Sawyer was Noah's daughter.

A great sob came from Sawyer's lips. "Brain damage?"

Dr. Kirkland patted her hand. "Don't worry. I haven't found any. Noah has had two scans and both resulted in encouraging news. We'll give him another tomorrow just to make sure. Plus, he has responded adequately to stimuli."

"So...if all of this is good news," Sawyer said, "why is he still sleeping? Why doesn't he wake up?"

The doctor smiled. "We call that nature's protective way of healing. Your father will wake up when he's ready. He'll probably have a heck of a headache, and he won't be too thrilled with a fractured leg, but my guess is, he'll be happy to be alive."

Sawyer began muttering to herself. "I knew this would happen... I just knew it!"

Ava put her arm around Sawyer's shoulders. There wasn't much she could say right now. Sawyer's dire prediction had come true.

"What about the other man?" Ava asked. "The nurse said Noah was carrying someone down the tower on his back."

"Oh, he's okay. He's down the hall where we watch patients with minimal injuries. He's been complaining about the food and asking for a beer since he got here." Dr. Kirkland took another long look at Noah. "I'd say he ought to be more concerned with buying your dad a beer when they get out of here. Noah saved his life most likely. He definitely cushioned the other guy's landing."

"How long can we stay?" Ava asked.

"As long as you want," Dr. Kirkland added. "But things may not change for a few hours, or maybe even a day or so. There's a motel next door. I'd suggest you go over and get some rest."

"No," Sawyer said. "I want to stay here."

"Okay, then. I'll see you ladies tomorrow. Don't worry. Your dad is going to pull through and hopefully be as good as new. He'll be back to his old self sooner than you think."

"No!" Sawyer cried. "I don't want him to be like he always has been."

Dr. Kirkland gave Ava a confused stare.

"It's okay," she said softly, looking from Sawyer to Noah. "These two have a rather complicated relationship. Thank you, Doctor."

Darkness settled in, calming the hospital around its soothing, soft lights. From Noah's window, Ava could see the motel across the parking lot. Later she would try to convince Sawyer that they should check in. Sawyer needed rest, time to compose herself for when her father woke up.

After a couple of hours Ava suggested Sawyer go to the vending machines down the hall and get something to eat. Noah's nurse had gone on break, and no change had been noted in the patient. All of his vital signs were monitored at the nurses' station a few doors down.

"Sure," Sawyer said. "I could use a cola. What do you want, Ava?"

"I'll take a Sprite and some crackers. We passed a fast-food place down the road. We can probably get burgers there even if it's late when we leave here." She gave Sawyer some dollar bills and watched her leave, grateful that the girl had something purposeful to do. Waiting was so hard.

Ava walked closer to the bed and leaned over the rail. This was her first opportunity to be with Noah alone, and she experienced a profound emotional reaction. As she looked at him, her heartbeat increased, her breathing shallowed, her eyes stung from tears that needed to be shed. She reached through the rails and took Noah's hand in a firm grasp.

What a mess this all was. The irony of Charlie's parent suffering a tragedy like this so soon after his adoptive parents died was devastating. If Noah didn't change his inclinations to accept risks in his job and personal life, how could she ever tell him the truth about Charlie? Another heartbreak might be more than the child could handle.

And Sawyer. The girl hadn't said much in the past two hours, but Ava knew she was suffering with every passing minute. What if Noah refused to change? Would this incident push Sawyer to the brink, cause her to run away again? Or would this event make Noah evaluate his life from Sawyer's point of view?

And what about herself? Her relationship with Noah had taken several unexpected turns. She'd been stunned when she'd recognized him as the man from her past. After the shock wore off, she'd questioned his ability to be a parent, and even his right to raise a child.

Then she'd gotten to know him and understand that he loved Sawyer, but he was stubborn and refused to change according to what he believed were his daughter's unfounded worries. And as she became more comfortable with Noah, Ava recognized what had first drawn her to the man, and those qualities that continued to engage her heart almost like a magnet. Only now she knew him as a kind, sensitive and complicated man who truly loved his daughter. Noah had become much more to Ava than a memory and a troubled dad.

She soothed the skin over his hand with her thumb and entwined her fingers with his. "Come on, Noah," she whispered. "Don't do this to Charlie. Don't do this to Sawyer. You have to wake up. You have to be all right. Noah, please. I think I…" She could have said more, begged him to wake up for her sake, but remembered the nurse indicating that some patients hear what's being said to them. So Ava could not risk admitting that she was very close to falling in love with Noah. Even though it was true, their relationship had problems, ones that wouldn't go away just because she cared for him.

She had remained strong through this day for Sawyer's sake. And she would continue to stay strong until this ordeal was over. She would not give in to the overwhelming need to let her heart rule her head. She would not cry. She would not—

A twitch in Noah's left hand caused Ava to jerk away from the bed. Her gaze went instantly to his face. His eyes were moving under the lids. His lashes fluttered against his bruised skin.

"Noah, are you waking up? Please, Noah..."

His eyes opened and Ava's heart hammered. He stared blankly, only for a moment, before he closed them. And then it happened again, several times—reflex action or a serious attempt at regaining consciousness? Ava could only wait and see. She considered ringing for the nurse, but selfishly decided against it. If Noah were truly waking up, she wanted the first precious remembrance alone with him.

After a few moments, when Ava thought

her heart would leap from her chest, Noah's eyes stayed open for several seconds. His gaze darted around the room, and then settled on her face. His lips moved. A smile?

"Wh…where am I?" he said, his voice husky.

"You're in the hospital. You took a fall."

"Oh." He blinked again several times. Now when he looked at her, he seemed aware, focused. He licked his dry lips and said, "Ava, beautiful, sweet Ava. I was dreaming about you. Don't make me go like this. I want to stay."

CHAPTER FIFTEEN

ALL AT ONCE Ava didn't think her legs would support her. She backed a step away from the bed and sank into a chair. Through the bed rail she could see Noah's face. His features were relaxed, smooth. His eyes closed again. He appeared to be sleeping comfortably.

Don't make me go. I want to stay. Noah's simple statement kept repeating in her mind. When he had opened his eyes, she knew he'd recognized her, but he believed they were together as they had been six years before and he was leaving her alone in her bed. Back then she wouldn't have considered letting him stay, not after he admitted he was married. But almost from the minute she met him in that glitzy Charlotte bar, she knew how the evening would end, with her wrapped in Noah's arms.

She'd been feeling sorry for herself after being passed over for a promotion. And she was lonely. She hadn't had a date in months, and hadn't met anyone who interested her. For a thirty-year-old woman, the prospect of spending every night alone was daunting.

And then Noah Walsh walked into the bar in jeans, boots, a leather jacket that fit him just right. And Ava, her senses buzzing and her confidence suddenly strong, zeroed right in on him. What if? she asked herself, and not finding a reason to answer the question negatively, she made eye contact with him and the rest was the foundation for memories, both good and bad.

Having never seen this man before, Ava understood the risk she was taking that night. But she felt reassured he would never be able to trace her identity in a city the size of Charlotte. They introduced themselves with first names only. They sat at a table for two, had another drink, or maybe two, and talked openly about many topics. Ava discovered that Noah was bright, funny and easy to talk to beyond his obvious qualities in the looks department. And she was flattered into believing he found her charming.

She invited him back to her apartment, where they ordered takeout from a local Chinese restaurant, opened a bottle of wine and kept her selection of dreamy music at a low level. Wasn't it then only natural that after a nearly perfect evening, the next stop was her bedroom, where Ava discovered Noah had other qualities that she quite admired?

By the time both Noah and Ava fell asleep, she had made the extraordinary decision that she had found a man she could see in her life long term. But when he roused her from sleep at three in the morning, planted a gentle kiss on her temple and told her he had to go, she was to learn that the man she had taken a chance with was far from her ideal.

"I'm so sorry," he'd said. "We shouldn't have… I shouldn't have."

What? Through the haze of sleep she wondered why he would have said such a thing.

His voice lowered as he bent toward her ear. "I'm married. It's not a happy marriage, but you're probably going to think all men say things like that to… Well, I should have been honest with you. But you're so great. I couldn't believe my luck in meeting someone like you…"

A sharp pain had sliced into her heart. "Just go," she'd muttered under her breath.

"I want to keep in touch…"

She'd turned over in bed to get a last long look at him, those wide, deep brown eyes, the slight crinkles in the corners, his full mouth. "Get out," she'd said. "I never want to see you again."

He scooped up his clothes from the floor, pulled on his T-shirt and jeans and walked out of her bedroom. And Ava vowed never to be taken in again. And she was glad that she hadn't given him so much as her last name. And when she discovered she was pregnant, she even rented a different apartment, making her nearly impossible to track down if he should try.

And she didn't even try to find him. The thought of having him in her life again, the fear of her giving in another time, the risk of him knowing about a baby… No, these options were not viable. She accepted the pregnancy and took on the responsibility. She didn't even tell her family and requested leave from her job for the last four months of her term.

How many times had she seen him in the past two weeks? Ten, twelve? She'd lost count. But in her quiet hours she had dwelled on every meeting and discovered she wanted to see more of him. They had mostly cleared the air about their past, though there was still a huge secret, but even so, she began to envision a future. And she let herself believe that this time would be different.

Yes, there was Charlie to consider, but sometimes she could actually envision a life with Noah, Sawyer and Charlie, with the secret still intact. It was a fantasy, but she allowed herself to believe in it, just a little, from time to time. But now he'd said her name from his hospital bed and told her he hadn't wanted to leave. He'd been dreaming about her and that night.

What if he wanted something permanent with her? The possibility thrilled her as much as it frightened her. Would she tell him about Charlie? She clenched her hands tightly together knowing the decision she had to make would be the second most difficult one of her life. The first had been giving up Charlie hours after he'd been born.

Sawyer's voice brought Ava out of the stupor that had overwhelmed her. "I brought drinks and some chips," she said. "There wasn't much of a variety."

Ava slowly turned toward her. "What?" She saw the items in Sawyer's hand. "Oh, yes, that's fine."

Sawyer set the items on a table and went to the bedside. "How is he? Any change?"

"Yes, your father opened his eyes."

"Really?" The nurse was just coming back into the room and went to her patient, raised his eyelids. "He's back asleep now."

"Did he say anything?" Sawyer asked. "Did he remember what happened to him?"

"Ah, yes, he spoke. He mentioned that he'd been dreaming. That was about it."

"This is good news, isn't it?" Sawyer asked the nurse.

"Of course. He's starting to come around. With a little encouragement from all of us, I'll bet he'll be holding a conversation in the morning."

"What should we do now?" Sawyer asked. "Should we try to wake him up?"

"I wouldn't. He'll probably sleep through the night. I think you ladies should go next door and get a room. Relax a few hours. You'll need your energy if Noah is alert tomorrow. If he should wake up, I'll call you."

Cell phone numbers were exchanged, and

an hour later Ava and Sawyer left Noah. They took a room at the Best Western, ordered pizza delivery and turned on the TV. Sawyer had accepted that her father was going to live, so she dialed up a comedy movie, and she was soon wrapped up in the action on the screen. Ava pretended to watch, but her mind kept going back to those words. *Don't make me go. I want to stay.*

EARLY MONDAY MORNING Sawyer was dressed and ready to go back to the hospital. As much as Ava wanted to see Noah, she procrastinated as long as she could. "I'll be ready in a few minutes," she said, and took her time getting dressed. "Let's get the complimentary breakfast," she suggested and urged Sawyer to have more than a Danish pastry.

They finally arrived at the hospital about nine o'clock. A different nurse was in Noah's room. "I have good news," she said. "We've already gotten the results of Noah's CT scan, and everything looks good. In fact, we are moving him to a private room down the hall this morning."

"That's great," Sawyer said, going to the bed. "Has he said anything this morning?"

"No. He hasn't awakened, but the doctor and I both believe he will very soon. Especially after he spoke yesterday evening. That was such a good sign."

Sawyer sniffed loudly. "And I wasn't even in the room to hear him."

"You'll be here the next time," Ava said. She wondered if Noah would awaken and begin talking about what he'd been dreaming of. No, surely he won't, she told herself. He probably wouldn't even remember seeing her last night.

"How long do you think he'll have to remain in the hospital?" Ava asked the nurse.

"Well, if he wakes up today, we're going to give him an MRI tomorrow to make certain that the spleen or other internal organs weren't affected by the fall. The first MRI showed no damage. Another one would be conclusive. Then, if everything checks out and if he's feeling better, he'll probably be discharged on Tuesday."

Tuesday? There were complications associated with discharging Noah the next day. Did the hospital staff realize that Noah's home was five hours away, and he lived alone?

Would Noah accept that he couldn't drive his truck until his leg had healed?

"Will there be someone in his home to help him?" the nurse asked, as if reading Ava's mind. "You should contact his primary care physician and ask about a visiting nurse a few days a week."

"I'll take care of him," Sawyer said.

"But, Sawyer," Ava said. "You can't be with him twenty-four hours a day. You have school, and you need to return to some sense of normality. Besides..." She stared down at Noah for a moment and noticed the scruffy beard he'd grown in a few days. He looked more like the man who'd ridden up to her building on his Harley-Davidson that first day. The man who hadn't slept while awaiting word about his daughter. "Besides, I don't think you're strong enough to help him get around."

"He won't need much help, believe me," Sawyer insisted. "He'll try to do everything for himself the minute he gets back home." She frowned down at Noah. "You forget... I know my father. And I want to be with him as much as I can. We have a lot to talk about."

Ava nodded. Indeed they did. But what would those conversations be like? Would Noah realize that he was lucky this time and might not be the next? "You're right, Sawyer. You should be with him as much as you can. We'll work it out."

The nurse left the room and Sawyer and Ava sat in the chairs they'd occupied yesterday. The chairs touching, they would wait for Noah to come back. After a few minutes Ava realized that Sawyer was crying.

"Oh, honey, he's going to be okay."

"I know. That's why I'm crying." She grabbed a tissue and wiped her eyes. "The worst thing happened, the thing I always thought would happen, and he's going to be fine."

"But, Sawyer, aren't you happy about the outcome?"

Her body trembled with a large intake of air. "Yeah. Seeing him like this is awful. I'm glad he's going to be fine, but now he'll go back to work. He'll go back to doing all the dumb things he's always done. He'll think he's invincible. He'll believe that his crew can't go on without him. Nothing will change. I'll eventually have to get used to another housekeeper…he'll be away for days at a time, and I'll always wonder if he'll come home or if I will end up sitting by his bed in another hospital…or worse. Sitting by his grave."

She leaned over and put her head on Ava's shoulder. For the second time since they'd known each other, Sawyer cried out all her frustration. "You must think I'm the most horrible person," she said. "I should be grateful…and I am! But it could happen again, and the next time…"

Ava rubbed Sawyer's shoulder. "Maybe this accident will make him rethink his responsibility to that job," she said. "Maybe he'll rethink his relationship with you. You might be surprised, Sawyer. Your father may wake up in more ways than one."

Sawyer's sobs quieted. "I want you to be right, Ava. I don't care about all the stuff in my room in Chapel Hill. I don't care if he never buys me another thing. I just want him to come home every night."

"I know, sweetie, I know."

The sound of heavy breathing made both of them turn toward the bed. Strange sounds came from Noah's throat as if he were trying to cough. He cleared his throat. His eyes blinked several times.

"Stay with him, Sawyer," Ava said, rising from the chair. "I'll get the nurse."

She was back with the nurse in under a minute. When they entered the room, Sawyer was holding her father's hand and he was looking up into her eyes.

"Shouldn't you be in school, young lady?" he said, and managed to gift her with a beautiful smile that melted Ava's heart.

"Shouldn't you be anywhere but here?" Sawyer snapped back in a voice choked with emotion. "How many times have I told you…"

"I know, I know." He looked down his body. "What's wrong with my leg? I didn't break the darn thing, did I?"

"You sorta did," Sawyer said.

"Oh, terrific." His voice hoarse, he spoke again. "What about the dang fool I tried to get down off the tower? Where's he?"

"He's fine," the nurse said. "He's being discharged today. And if you behave yourself, you could be leaving on Tuesday."

He looked confused. "What day is it now? Isn't it Sunday?"

"Monday. You only lost one day," the nurse explained. "Not bad for a guy who landed on frozen Tennessee ground."

"Sawyer, how did you get here?"

Sawyer stepped away from the bed, turned toward the door where Ava had been hovering. "Ava brought me, Daddy."

He smiled. "Ava…"

She came forward, her eyes blurry at the sight of his beautiful face. Noah reached his hand up to her. She took it in hers. "Welcome back, Noah," she said, amazed that she could get the words out over the constriction in her lungs.

"Ava, you came, too?"

She blinked, stared at him, and released a long breath. He didn't remember what he'd said last night. "Of course. We've all been so worried."

His gaze traveled the length of her, taking in her jeans, her light blue blouse. He was studying her as if he were about to take an exam on all of her features.

"You got your hair cut," he said.

"Ah, no. Not recently." She touched her shoulder-length hair and remembered that it had been long when they'd met before six years ago.

"Looks nice anyway," he said. "Thanks for coming, Ava. And thanks for bringing Sawyer."

Still holding his hand, Ava sank into the nearest chair. He didn't remember what he'd said the night before. Maybe he never would. What if he didn't remember what they had meant to each other these past two weeks? He'd had a head injury after all. And on Tuesday they would all go back to Holly River and take up their lives as they'd been living them before the fall. Well, maybe not exactly the same. At least not for her.

NOAH WAS RELEASED Tuesday morning with strict instructions to take it easy and make appointments with doctors in his hometown. The orthopedist told him he might be able to use a walking boot instead of crutches in a few weeks—an encouraging piece of news since he didn't relish the idea of wearing a tux to a wedding while using crutches.

He didn't like leaving his truck in Tennessee, but since he wasn't permitted to drive yet, he had no choice. One of his crew promised to bring the vehicle to him when they'd finished repairing the towers affected by the snowstorm.

And so, after thanking the staff at Daniel's Creek Medical Center, and after having a few choice words with Rick about his stupidity in free climbing, Noah, Ava and Sawyer got in Ava's car for the return trip. Noah sat in the back seat with his leg elevated. They hadn't gone a mile before Sawyer said, "Dad, you should have fired that guy, Rick."

"Chad has the honors," he responded.

"And next I need to find someone who will fire you."

"What?" Noah leaned forward to better hear his daughter. "No one can fire me. I'm the boss."

"In my opinion Rick wasn't the only one who did something stupid on Sunday."

"Sawyer, I did it to save a man's life."

"I know, and I'm proud of you and all for saving that guy, but why didn't someone else do it? Why does it always have to be you?"

Noah frowned, but he doubted Sawyer saw it. "I thought I just explained that," he said. "I'm the boss. You've heard the expression 'the buck stops here'? If I'd let someone else climb that tower I might have lost two lives, both people I'm responsible for."

"But, Dad, still…"

"Look, Sawyer, we've been getting along so great. Let's save the arguments for when we get back to the house. I'm sure you've been thinking about what to say to me for days."

"You bet I have, and I don't care if I speak my mind in front of Ava. You have to admit she knows both of us pretty well."

He grinned at the rearview mirror. "Yes, I'll admit that."

"And Ava knows how I feel. I'm hoping that maybe now you'll listen to me."

Obviously Sawyer wasn't going to let the subject drop. Ava was quiet. Her attention seemed to be focused on her driving. Noah wondered what she was thinking about his conversation with Sawyer.

"Sawyer, I have to go back to work," Noah said. "You know that. You also know that I have a broken leg, so I'm not going to be climbing any towers for a while."

"So this is the perfect time for you to find a different job."

"Like it's that easy," he said. "Repairing

cell towers is what I'm trained to do. That and maintaining aircraft in a war zone. You want me to go back to Afghanistan?"

She turned her head to give him a typical teen sneer. "Other fathers do safe things. They sell insurance or used cars."

"First of all, I'm not going to do either of those things or anything even remotely similar. Second, you and I have become accustomed to a lifestyle that neither one of us wants to give up, especially you. If I quit my job you can forget about using my credit cards and hanging out at the mall all the time."

He could see that she'd crossed her arms over her chest. "Oh sure. Make this all about me. Make me the unreasonable one."

Noah stared at Ava's profile. She had to be thinking something about this quibbling. Surely she didn't agree that one accident in over ten years was cause for him to quit his job, a job he was good at and one that paid considerably better than a living wage.

Her face was nearly unreadable. Other than a slight twitch at her temple, she could have been going over song lyrics in her head. Her face was also one of the first things he'd thought about when he awoke in the hospital, and now he knew why. For some reason Ava's face had etched itself into his subconscious while he'd been sleeping. He'd needed to see her. He'd needed to know that she was concerned about him, that she cared. The scariest part now was the realization that he needed *her*. And he could no longer deny it.

"Don't you have anything else to say?" Sawyer asked him.

"Sure. Let me just add that in most cases, you actually *are* the unreasonable one."

"Me?" Sawyer's voice had risen to an uncomfortable level. And finally Ava got involved.

"Okay, that's it!" she said. "I've just gotten on the highway, and we still have over four hours left until we get back to Holly River. I won't make it another ten miles if I have to listen to the two of you." She paused. Her beautiful lush lip curled up at one corner. "Don't make me turn this car around."

Sawyer gawked at her with wide, surprised eyes. Noah smiled and hoped she could see him in the rearview mirror. "Yes, ma'am," he said. "We'll be good as gold for the next four hours, won't we, Sawyer?"

Sawyer slumped in her seat. "I guess." After a few minutes she turned to Ava and said, "I'm hungry. I'll watch the signs for the next drive-through place."

"Noah," Ava said, "are you hungry? You can't take any more pain pills unless you've had food."

"I could eat I guess."

"Fine. At least we all agree on something."

THEY MADE IT back to Holly River before the sun set. And considering that mountain daylight lasted no later than early evening, Ava was glad. Noah exited her car by stretching the muscles he hadn't used in five hours and swinging his broken leg onto the driveway. "Can't believe I'm this stiff," he said.

"You fell thirty feet," Ava said. "I can't believe you're still walking."

They went into the house. Ava and Sawyer let Noah use the bathroom while they plumped the cushions on the couch and brought out extra pillows from the bedroom. When he came back, Noah didn't argue when the ladies insisted he lie down. Ava put an extra cushion at the end of the couch to support his leg. "Try to keep your foot higher than your heart," she said. "Improves circulation for better healing."

"Thank you, Nurse."

Ava turned her attention to Sawyer. "Are you staying to fix your father some dinner? I can come back later and pick you up so you don't have to walk back to the cottage in the dark."

"Of course I'm staying," Sawyer said. "And I'll be here all day tomorrow, too."

"You don't have to do that," Noah said. "I'll be fine."

Ava didn't want to have an argument, but the obvious needed to be said. "I understand you want to stay, and I told you we'd try to work it out, but if your dad says he'll be fine, you've missed two full days of classes, Sawyer…"

"I know. I'll make it up. I'm going over to the cottage now to pick up some clothes. I'll arrange to meet with kids in my classes on Saturday morning. They can fill me in on what I missed. By then we should have a nurse scheduled to come by the house to see Dad."

Ava searched Noah's face for a sign that he agreed with her. He responded with a shrug.

Ava supposed he'd had enough drama for one day. Or maybe he was genuinely pleased that his daughter was showing interest in his recovery.

"Okay," Ava relented. "Go on and get your things. I'll wait here until you get back."

Sawyer left and Ava asked Noah if he needed anything. He requested a glass of water. She brought it to him and set it on an end table. "Can you reach it?" she asked.

He gave her a mischievous smile. "I can reach more than that," he said, grabbing her wrist and tugging gently.

She landed on his lap. "What are you doing?" she said to him. "You could be hurting yourself."

"Nope. Pain pills, remember? And all the lab stuff checked out fine. The last thing I'm thinking about at this moment is hurting myself."

She gave him a look she hoped conveyed all her frustration, pretended and fake, at his boldness. The truth was, she felt relieved. He hadn't forgotten that they'd gotten close. "I guess I don't have to ask what it is you're thinking about."

"Nope." He wrapped his hand around her

nape and pulled her close. When his lips touched hers she felt warm and dizzy at the same time.

After what seemed an eternity and no time at all, he leaned back and looked into her eyes. "That's the medicine I've been waiting for all day. Why haven't we had a chance to do that before now?"

"Well, you were unconscious, and after that Sawyer was watching every move you made."

He smiled. "Yeah, she's acting like a mother bird afraid one of her young will fall out of the nest."

"One did," Ava said.

He slowly rubbed her arm, stopping at her wrist where his thumb circled the pulse point. "Let's get some more kissing in before she flies back in here."

Ava didn't even think of arguing. She took his face between her hands, careful not to disturb the remaining bandages, and gave in to the very strong desire to kiss Noah—his lips, his cheeks, the stubble of beard that would probably be gone tomorrow, his eyes.

"I do think you might be feeling better," she said when she wasn't exactly finished kissing him, but knew his daughter would return soon.

He grinned. "Makes me feel a lot better when the moaning is coming from you and not me."

Ava stood, looked out the window. "Sawyer's back."

"Just my luck," he teased.

Sawyer bounded inside. "I have the class work all figured out," she said. "I can stay all day tomorrow with Dad."

Noah smiled, nodded. "Great."

"Oh, by the way, Ava," Sawyer said. "I ran into SherryLynn. She said your uncle was by today. Who is that guy anyway? SherryLynn said he's kinda creepy."

"Don't worry about him, Sawyer. He just wants to pick an argument with me."

Noah sat up straight on the sofa. "I don't like that, Ava. Pick me up tomorrow and I'll stay in your office with you."

"No, you won't," she said. "The nurse comes tomorrow to check you out, and you're not missing that appointment. I'll be fine. We have great security at the home if I need it." She headed for the door, stopping to give Noah one last longing look. His smile told her he'd gotten the message. She'd enjoyed their time together. She was looking forward to more.

"Get some rest, both of you," she said. "I'll check on things in the morning."

When she left, Sawyer was fluttering around Noah as if she truly were that mother bird and asking if he wanted a sandwich. And Ava was thankful that they were all back in Holly River again and Sawyer and Noah seemed to be mending their differences. Ava was pleased with the way this day had turned out, except she figured she'd have to face her uncle Rudy in the morning.

CHAPTER SIXTEEN

ON WEDNESDAY MORNING, Rudy Cahill showed up at Ava's office. She was adding some final touches to the office Christmas tree, a way of avoiding anxiety about his potential visit. Without waiting to be announced, he stormed into her office.

"Good morning, Uncle Rudy," she said, wrapping the last bit of garland around the lower branches of the tree. "What do you think of my tree? Are you ready for Christmas?"

"Cut the nonsense, Ava. How can you talk about holidays when you've sent lawyers chasing my tail, making all sorts of demands?"

"Only demands that you rightfully owe, Rudy."

He strode over to her desk, crossed his arms over his chest. "What's gotten into you,

Ava? Doesn't family mean anything to you anymore?"

"Actually, family means more to me than it does to you."

"Family means everything to me!" he insisted. "I kept quiet and sacrificed for years so my brother could make all the decisions about the company. It wasn't easy keeping my mouth shut. And now my nephew's getting married in a little over a week, and you're driving an even-bigger wedge between all of us." He jabbed his index finger on her desktop. "I've half a mind to skip the whole thing and keep my family away from yours."

Ava maintained a placid expression. "Oh, that would be a shame."

"But I'm a bigger man than that," he said, choosing to ignore her sarcastic tone. "I've always been fond of Jace, and now he's finally made something of himself."

Not finished with the sarcasm, Ava said, "I'm sure your approval will mean so much to him."

"You've caused me enough headaches, young lady," he continued, "but I think I've put an end to this malarkey about me owing money to your mama. I've been head to head with the paper company accountant for days, and this—" he tossed a large manila envelope on her desk "—is the result of hours of work."

Ava picked up the envelope, pretended to study the dates scrawled on the outside. "What should I be looking for in these records?"

"The truth, dang it! The real and factual money trail, not that hogwash you and that senile bookkeeper dreamed up."

"Don't blame Elsie for any of this, Rudy. She simply recorded company transactions until you fired her and put your own super tech genius on the job. I must tell you, he's quite good at following directions and covering his trail."

"Don't think you're going to scare me with your inferences of crooked behavior, Ava."

"I don't think that. I only want to educate you with the veracity of the discoveries my lawyer and I have uncovered."

"Your lawyer!" Rudy scoffed. "Terry Brannigan is a two-bit ambulance chaser."

"At any rate, we'll look these over and get back to you. Perhaps by the wedding date. I'll let you know our conclusions, and

I hope you'll consider bringing a check to the ceremony—not for Jace, but for Mama. It's fine if you simply get a toaster for Jace, so long as you don't come empty-handed."

"I don't understand you, Ava. You used to be my favorite of all Raymond's kids."

She smiled again as SherryLynn came into the office. "I hope to someday regain that honorable status, Uncle Rudy, when all this mess is behind us."

SherryLynn came to stand beside Ava. "You've had a number of calls, Ava. Some of them sound urgent, or I wouldn't have interrupted you."

Ava hadn't heard the outer office phone ring, so she knew SherryLynn was standing beside her to offer support. "Thank you, SherryLynn." Turning her attention to Rudy, she said, "I assume we're done here?"

"Blast you, Ava! You'd better think twice about the trouble you're bringing down on yourself by threatening me."

"I usually think twice about everything I do, Rudy. It's just generally good practice."

He stomped out of her office and slammed the door. Ava put the envelope away with the intention of getting together with the lawyer to go over the fantasy numbers Rudy and his accountant had no doubt come up with. She realized the different effect this visit had had on her when she noticed her hands—they weren't trembling as they had before. She'd stood up for her mother, and it felt good.

AVA AND HER lawyer went over Rudy's papers that same afternoon. They found nothing to alter their findings of the last week. The lawyer immediately drafted a letter to Rudy giving him no option but to pay Cora all the money he owed her. Apparently Rudy thought by coming to Ava's office and intimidating her one more time, she would cave under the pressure. He didn't know her well.

Ava called Noah's house several times during the day on Wednesday. Because of her workload, which had gotten much worse due to her trip to Tennessee, she didn't have a chance to pay a visit during the day. But she talked to Noah. He said the nurse had come, and he was feeling well. Sawyer was doing a good job of taking care of him.

That evening wedding preparations took up all of Ava's time. With the ceremony so close, she joined the women of her family at Cora's house and they worked on decorations for the barn and table centerpieces. Jace and Carter were there as well, and they did an admirable job of ignoring the work going on in the kitchen while they watched a Tar Heels basketball game.

The next morning, Ava was anxious to get to Noah's house and see him in person. When she'd left him with Sawyer on Tuesday evening, her lips had still been warm from his kisses, and her mind didn't let her forget how wonderful Noah's kisses had become to her.

THE NURSE HAD just left. She'd given Noah glowing reports about his progress. That was great, he supposed, but no one, not even Sawyer, who was around so much these days, could help him with the restlessness. He'd never been so inactive in his whole life. As Sawyer so often pointed out, he had the fast toys to feed his adrenaline. And sitting on a sofa all day was just not his thing.

He had too much time on his hands. Ava was busy with wedding stuff. Sawyer was catching up on school work. He tried reading but soon lost interest. And then he'd go back to thinking again. About Ava.

He couldn't shake the feeling that something just wasn't right. He was about ready to admit that he was head over heels about her, but his mind kept going back over the last weeks. Why hadn't she told him she recognized him when he came to her door that day? Was she ashamed of what they'd done? That he'd been a married man at the time? But that had been on him, not her. And he thought he'd explained that.

She'd finally stopped insisting that their relationship was all about Sawyer, and that was progress, but in his gut he had the feeling that something was holding Ava back. What was it? Was there something she wasn't telling him about her family? Some deep dark secret. Or was she still hung up on the feelings of shame?

If Ava couldn't get over her shame, how could they go forward? Noah simply had to know.

AWARE THAT SAWYER was meeting with classmates to catch up on her assignments, Ava called Noah on Thursday and told him she was coming over. He seemed almost relieved. Perhaps he had missed her with the same ache that she'd experienced the last couple of days. She headed over to the stone cottage next door with an overwhelming sense of anticipation. She couldn't wait to see Noah again and prove to herself that he truly was recovering nicely.

She came in via the unlocked front door. Noah came out of the kitchen on his crutches. He gingerly carried a cup of coffee and set the mug on an end table. He looked at her a moment and said, "Hi."

"Hello, yourself. How are you feeling this morning?"

"I'm okay. Going a bit stir-crazy."

She nodded and dropped her jacket on a chair. Noah looked wonderful to her, almost like his former vibrant self. She hoped she looked half as good to him in one of her favorite yellow sweaters.

She noticed he wore cargo shorts that looked as though they'd been through a war, and a T-shirt with a college logo.

"Aren't you freezing?" she asked him.

"Could use a blanket," he said, settling on the sofa. He lifted his broken leg and rested it in the spot where she would have sat. She backed away, grabbed a throw from a chair and draped it over him.

"Thanks."

Ava took the chair nearest him. "So, the visit from the nurse went well?"

"Told you it did. She changed the bandages and a few other things."

"Okay. Good. The bruises on your face are clearing up. Did she say anything about how you're doing?"

"All good. She said I can't hope for a quicker recovery than I'm having. So I guess I have to put up with cabin fever for now. Everything go okay with Rudy?" he asked after a minute.

Thinking she would tease him by throwing his own curt answer back at him, she said, "Told you it did."

"Right. You did."

He searched around the sofa, running his hands behind his body and between the cushions.

"What are you looking for?"

"Had a book here last night. Must be in the bedroom."

She stood. "Would you like me to get it for you?"

"Sure."

She found the book on his nightstand. Before bringing it back, she wondered what was going on. Why was Noah acting so indifferent to her? He hadn't asked her to sit beside him. He hadn't kissed her. Was he hurting? Was he angry about something? Was he going to read the book while she sat only a few feet away from him?

She came back to the living room, handed him the book and stepped back. "Noah, is something wrong?"

He didn't answer. Just stared up into her eyes until her nerves made her restless. She looked away from him but when she returned her gaze, she was met with the same intense glare. "Noah, what's going on?"

"I've been thinking about us, Ava. The two people we are now and the two people we were. When all you have to do is move from a bed to a couch and back again, you have too much time to think." He cleared his throat, paused. "I'm completely confused about who we are now, Ava. I'm into this pretty deep. Sometimes I think you feel the same. But sometimes you seem almost indifferent."

She shifted on the chair. "Noah, if there is one thing I am not, it's indifferent to you."

"Okay. I'd like to believe that. But I can't shake the feeling that you're holding out on me."

"What? Why would you think that?"

"That first day when I came for Sawyer we played this little cat and mouse game. You knew who I was. I didn't connect the dots until the next morning. You refused to look at me directly. And then once the truth was out, it was like this powerful force hit me between the eyes. I'd found you again."

"Yes, and I'm so glad you did. You must know how I feel about you, Noah."

"That's just it, Ava. When I'm holding you, when we're kissing, I feel this strong bond. And then, at other times I sense a disconnect. Lately I've been wondering if you are reliving our past." He cleared his throat. "I just have to ask the tough question. Are you ashamed of what happened between us, because I'm not, but if you are, and if you can't get over it and move on then I think we have to put the brakes on this relationship."

"I'm not ashamed," she blurted and then swallowed hard, trying to break the grip of panic in her throat. *No, Noah, you can't mean this.* Now was the time for honesty, almost the whole truth. "Well, I was at first, mostly because you were married, and I had acted so out of character. But being with you now, even for such a short time, means a lot to me. I care deeply for you, Noah."

There, she'd said it, and the sky hadn't fallen and lightning hadn't struck the house. And Charlie was still playing in his cottage. "I'm no longer looking backward. I'm looking forward with you, Noah."

Please believe me, she thought. *Don't let this be the end.*

His eyes softened. "Ava, if I hadn't told you I remembered you that morning in the coffee shop, would you ever have told me?"

She rubbed her eyes, took a deep breath. "Honestly, I don't know, but I'd like to think I would have. I suppose I thought it was up to you to remember. If the night had meant anything to you, you would have."

"I tried to find you," he said. "I asked about a woman named Ava in the neighborhood where we met. I tried your apartment when I came back to town. I wanted to apologize again. But mostly I wanted to see you again. I didn't deserve to, but I wanted to."

She gave him a slight smile. "I believe you."

"So that's it?" he said. "You've forgiven me for what happened that night? You've forgiven yourself?"

"Of course."

His shoulders settled into the back of the sofa, and Ava released a normal breath.

"No more secrets, Ava," he said. "We start today fresh."

She couldn't tell him that she agreed. Her precious Charlie still had to be the number one priority in her life. But she would reveal everything to Noah when the time was right, when he wasn't already doubting her sincerity. She would explain it to him and he would understand.

He moved his leg and patted the sofa next to him. She sat down beside him and he slipped his arm around her and kissed her deeply.

Yes, Ava thought. He will understand.

CHAPTER SEVENTEEN

THE LAST FEW days had been some of the best Noah could remember in a long time. Well, except for a broken leg, remnant of a concussion and broken rib, a few remaining bruises and the lectures from his daughter, which had lately softened in tone.

He'd pretty much gotten used to Sawyer not being happy about him going back to work. He just wished she'd get used to the fact that he was, indeed, going back. "Sawyer, you've got to let up. I know what happened. I know what a risk I took, but I was saving a man's life. I'm fine and so is Rick."

Sawyer had come to stay with him every evening the last three nights. Noah thought they'd talked things out. At least Sawyer had talked a lot. But she wasn't changing her mind, saying that if he really cared about the people around him he wouldn't put his life at risk every day. He certainly didn't look forward to being stuck in neutral for years to come with Sawyer, so he'd begun to think of the possibilities.

Even if he agreed to get an easier job, he hadn't any idea where to look. An office job? Not likely. Another job where he traveled? Sawyer would still have complaints. A position where his people skills were all important? He wasn't confident that he had people skills. Simply put, Noah wasn't cut out for a nine-to-five daily routine. And he'd never been comfortable in a suit and tie. So he'd thought about switching jobs but had come up with nada.

Thankfully his time with Ava more than made up for the headaches often brought on by his daughter's arguments. Ava came over in the daytime so she wouldn't interfere with his time with Sawyer. They'd had some great talks, equally great embraces and spectacular kissing sessions. There had been no more talk about deception. Noah firmly believed that he and Ava were on the same wavelength about all the things that mattered. And he was crazy about her, probably had been for years. How else could he explain the memories that were still sweet and clear in his mind? Noah couldn't wait for the cast to come off so that he could take her out and they would have a proper relationship.

One highlight of his week had been the return of his truck. His crew members had dropped off the vehicle on the weekend, and Noah had been able to keep the appointment with his orthopedic doctor on Tuesday without bumming a ride. Granted, he probably shouldn't be driving yet, but since he drove with his right leg, he headed to Boone on his own.

The doctor took X-rays and called Noah into his office afterward. Noah took the offensive in the discussion by saying almost immediately, "Doctor, I need this cast off by Christmas Eve."

The doctor gave him a puzzled look. "You mean Christmas Eve this year, the one in five days?"

"That's the one. I want to be using a walking boot by then." He'd smiled. "I have a big date."

The doctor had pointed to the X-ray lit on his wall as if the picture should be self-explanatory. "Noah," the doctor said, "you've heard the expression a 'snowball's chance in hell'?"

"Sure."

"That's about as much chance as I'd give you to have that cast off by Christmas Eve. You need at least two weeks, maybe three more in that plaster."

So Noah had returned to Holly River with a plan to find a pair of dress trousers in his closet that might cover up the cast well enough. And he'd called Jace Cahill about one more lingering problem he faced.

"I'm bored, Jace," he said. "I need something to do."

"The girls need help with the table centerpieces," he said. "I'll have Kayla pick you up."

"Thanks, but that's not what I had in mind."

Jace laughed. "I kind of thought not. So how can I help?"

"Do you need any help at the tree farm?" Noah asked.

"We're just now slowing down a bit. We've been selling trees off our lot at a rate of a hundred a day. I can barely keep track of the numbers. But sorry to say, buddy, we can't really use someone in a cast for this job."

"I can certainly plant some seedlings," he said. "Or check your books. I'm able to drive my truck now and I'm good with numbers. I work really cheap."

Jace thought a moment, and then apparently took pity on Noah. "Okay. Come on out here tomorrow and I'll put you to work in the office."

Thank goodness. Noah awoke Wednesday morning with renewed purpose and energy. He decided to drive over to the Sawtooth Home and tell Ava his good news. She'd probably warn him again about driving, but he was learning how to best trap the words in her mouth with a kiss before they all came spilling out. And he was enjoying doing it.

Noah parked and walked up to the entrance of the administration building. He opened the door and practically ran into his daughter and the little boy he'd seen Ava talk to at the hot dog luncheon.

"Hi, Dad," she said.

"Hey, what are you doing out of class?"

"Running an errand for Ava," Sawyer said. "She likes to talk to Charlie every Wednesday, and when she's done, she calls me to take him back to his kindergarten class."

"You and Charlie must be pretty tight," Noah observed, smiling at the kid. He'd already figured out that Charlie was special in Ava's eyes, and he remembered Charlie's tragic past. But Sawyer taking time with a child?

"He's a good kid," Sawyer said. "We live in the same cottage, so I sort of look out for him."

The boy stared up at Noah with incredibly wide, deep blue eyes. Strands of straight dark hair covered his forehead under his wool hat. Noah could see why Ava was taken with him. Cute kid. He raised a mitten-covered hand to his nose and sniffed.

"How's everything going?" Noah said to the boy.

"Okay I guess."

"You know the ground's pretty hard right now, and I've got this stupid cast on my leg. But maybe when things lighten up, you and I could hang out."

"What do you mean?"

"You know, throw a ball, kick stuff."

Charlie looked surprised. "You and me?"

"Yeah. That's what I was thinking."

"Do you play soccer?"

"Not really. But I'm willing to learn. Is that your game, Charlie?"

"My favorite. Miss Ava got me a soccer ball of my own."

"She's pretty nice, Miss Ava," Noah said. Charlie nodded.

"We've got to go, Dad. I'm missing Algebra."

"Okay. I'll probably see you later, Sawyer."

"Sure thing."

They headed off across the campus while Noah watched his daughter take the kid's hand and steady him on the cold sidewalks. Then Noah hobbled his way inside. The outside office was filled with huge boxes that surrounded the huge Christmas tree probably donated by Snowy Mountain. "What's all this?" he asked SherryLynn.

"Christmas presents," she said. "Volunteers from the community donate money and toys every year. And the older kids get to make up a list since they usually want games and clothes. Some of the Holly River old-timers went to the mall in Boone to find items on the list. There won't be an unhappy child on Christmas morning at Sawtooth," she added.

Noah was reminded of his own scant Christmases as a child. Never enough money for toys and never enough time to go out and buy them anyway. The kids at Sawtooth Home were lucky in a lot of ways.

"I just came to see Ava," Noah said.

"I figured as much. But she's with Mrs. Marcos, the counselor, right now. Do you have a few minutes?"

"Only just. I'm heading out to Snowy Mountain to work with Ava's brother today. I'll just stand by the door and wait until she's done." He smiled at SherryLynn. "If I miss her, will you tell her I'm at the tree farm?"

"Of course, Noah." She pointed to a bank of office chairs under a large window at least twenty feet from where Noah currently stood. "You're welcome to have a seat here in the lobby."

He evaluated the distance to the chairs and his proximity to the door. "I'll just wait a couple of minutes here," he said. "I've learned to consider every step I take with these crutches. I won't wait long. First day on the job."

He ambled over to Ava's office door, surprised to see it opened a crack. Not wanting to eavesdrop, he started to walk away. But not before hearing enough of a conversation to guess that Ava was speaking with the counselor about Charlie.

"He's doing so well," the counselor said. "His outburst the other day was a turning point for him. He was able to release a lot of pent-up emotion that had been building inside him."

"I'm very glad to hear that," Ava said. "So are you saying we can finally tell him?"

"We can't rush this, Ava. We're close. Charlie is almost ready to accept and handle your new role in his life."

"I don't want to rush him," Ava said. "But you understand how anxious I am?"

"Of course. Let me have a couple more sessions with him."

Noah stepped away from the door. New role? What were they talking about? Ava was ready to assume a role in Charlie's life beyond her capacity as administrator at the home? What bigger role could she have? As he was contemplating answers, the counselor opened the door wide and stepped into the outer office.

"Oh!" she said to Noah. "I didn't know you were waiting."

"No problem," Noah said. "I was just leaving actually."

"Noah?" Ava called from her office. "Come on in."

He entered. She stood but didn't come around her desk.

"How long have you been out there?" she asked.

"Only a couple of minutes. I was waiting until you were free."

"I see. Obviously you're still driving your truck around."

"Yep. Not having any trouble either. I'm going out to the tree farm to lend Jace a hand."

She fidgeted with a few items on her desk, arranging them as if they needed it. "That's nice. I know Jace will appreciate it."

"I should go, then."

"Yes. You know that Jace is a stickler for rules."

They both laughed at this misconception. Noah wanted to ask Ava about the new role she was contemplating in Charlie's life. What was she thinking of doing? But he figured she would tell him when she was ready. Or maybe it wasn't such a big move after all. Maybe she was just planning to give the kid more attention.

"Will I see you later?" he asked.

"I'll stop by your place. But can't stay long. So many wedding preparations and we're coming down to the wire. Mama's getting more nervous every day about all her and Kayla's plans going off without a hitch."

Noah leaned across her desk for a quick kiss. "Weddings," he said. "They might be more trouble than a couple in love really needs. But the end result is worth it."

Ava gave him a special smile. "Tell the groom I said hi."

THE NEXT TWO days progressed at a hectic pace. Ava's phone never stopped ringing with calls from Miranda, Kayla and her mother. She suddenly regretted being the logical, organized one in the family.

"What did we decide about petit fours?" Cora asked. "How many per guest?"

"Any last-minute RSVPs?" Kayla asked.

"What should I do about...?"

Ava finally had SherryLynn hold all calls so she could take care of Sawtooth Home business. She'd spent time thinking about Charlie, too. She was anxious to make him her son in every way. This meant she had to tell Noah the truth. There was no way to skirt the fact.

To tell Noah part of the story would be to tell him the whole thing. And she wasn't ready to do that. Not yet. Once the wedding was over and the fuss calmed down... Once Noah decided what he was going to do about climbing towers, or not, then perhaps Charlie would have a father who didn't take risks.

The decision to tell him about Charlie made her evaluate all her feelings about Noah. About one thing she was certain. She'd never felt this way about any man before. She'd been dreaming of finding the man for her and knowing the happiness her brothers had found. Noah certainly checked all her boxes and more. He was funny, attentive, kind, brave and strong. And good-looking. Not that Ava cared overmuch about that quality, but heck, when looks were thrown into the mix, why not appreciate them? In truth she wished he weren't quite so brave and strong.

On Friday and Saturday she spoke to Noah several times on the phone. He told her he'd found a pair of trousers that fit over his cast, and he was ready to enjoy the wedding fully, without dancing, of course. He'd even told her he was taking Sawyer shopping to find a dress for the wedding. Ava had asked him if he wanted her to go along, and he'd said, "I can handle this. We'll be fine."

Ava had smiled. Now that's progress.

NOAH PARKED IN front of Sawyer's cottage a little after noon on Saturday. He'd told Ava he and his daughter would breeze right through this shopping trip, that everything would be fine. Now he was hoping that what he'd said would prove to be true. "Buck up, man," he said to himself as he opened the door to the cottage. "It's just a shopping trip with a fourteen-year-old girl. What could go wrong?"

Sawyer came into the living room. "Hi, Dad. I'm glad you're taking me to buy a dress. I was so stoked when Ava invited me to the wedding." She walked ahead of him out the door to his truck. "I get to pick out what I want, right?"

Oh, no, was this the first hurdle? Be careful what you say, Walsh. "Actually, Sawyer, I see this as a time for you and me to work on compromising. I'm hoping we can agree on a dress."

Noah smiled. That was good wasn't it? He would show an interest in the dress she picked. And no one could argue with compromise.

She climbed into the cab. "Sure, we'll see."

They went to a shop in Boone that Sawyer suggested. The store specialized in prom dresses and clothes suitable for young women—at least that's what Sawyer had told him. Noah walked in the door and wondered why he hadn't remembered his prom date wearing something like what he saw on the mannequins. He was sure he would have remembered.

Sawyer dashed through the store, sliding hangers at a furious pace and sometimes listening to the sales lady who was trying to help. Finally she chose three dresses to try on. The clerk suggested that Noah sit in a chair by the dressing room. He sat. So far he hadn't played a significant role in this process. But that soon changed.

Sawyer came out of the dressing room in an emerald green dress of shiny material that clung so tightly to her slender frame that undergarments would have been a no-no.

"What do you think, Dad? Isn't it gorgeous?"

He frowned. "I suppose if you're going to be on the red carpet and it's being televised."

"What does that mean?"

"It's much too..." he searched for the right word that wouldn't alienate his daughter with her first pick "...short, I think."

She opened her mouth to argue, no doubt, so he added, "The color doesn't really go with your beautiful eyes, Sawyer."

"Really?" She walked to a floor length mirror and studied the effect. "Dad, you're right. I'll try another."

The next two choices were equally as shocking to a conservative father who hadn't spent much time around teen girls. Luckily Noah covered his negative opinions with comments that the dresses didn't do much for Sawyer's naturally pretty attributes. A little sugar with a bit of spice seemed to do the trick. She listened.

Finally the sales lady, who was nearer Noah's age than Sawyer's, picked up on the trend being established by father and daughter. She took a beautiful dress from a rack, winked at Noah and went into the dressing room.

Sawyer emerged looking lovely in a gauzy off-white concoction of lace and delicate ruffles at the modest neckline. The hemline came just to her knees.

Noah had never before been speechless around his daughter, but words failed him today.

"Oh, jeez, Dad," Sawyer said. "You look sappy. I guess that means you like this one." She gave him a slight grimace. "Figures."

He nodded. "I do like it. Very much."

Sawyer twirled in front of the mirror, and eventually smiled. "It's okay," she said. "It'll do."

Noah paid the bill before Sawyer would realize how accommodating she'd been. When they got in the truck, Sawyer said, "I can't wait to tell Ava about the dress."

Noah smiled. *That makes two of us.*

ON SUNDAY, CHRISTMAS EVE, the Crestview Barn was decorated with the magic of the season. The bride had chosen a color scheme of silver and white with touches of ice blue—perfect for a cold mountain wedding. Twinkle lights adorned the rafters, and trees lined the center aisle and temporary altar. Exquisite white poinsettias decked the podium where the minister would stand to deliver the vows.

Ava accompanied Kayla and Kayla's cousin to the barn where the three women dressed for the ceremony. The bride looked beautiful in a dress with a long train adorned with rhinestones and pearls, and both attendants were pleased with their floor-length satiny blue dresses. Nathan, Carter and long-time family friend, Sam McCall, were super handsome in their black tuxes.

Ava had never seen Sam so happy, and she knew that Allie, the waitress at the Holly River Café, was the reason for his euphoria. They'd dealt with their differences over Allie's falling into trouble with the wrong crowd a few months ago and now Ava didn't doubt that there would be another wedding soon.

Noah had been disappointed that he wasn't

going to pick Ava up, but he understood the responsibilities of the bridesmaids. He and Sawyer would arrive together, and Ava would be with Noah once the vows were said and baskets of glittering fake snow were released from the barn ceiling.

Shortly before the service, Ava responded to a knock at the bride's dressing room. She opened the door to see her uncle Rudy. "You came," she said simply. "I hope this means what I think it means."

He thrust an envelope at her. "You win, Ava. I can't risk losing important clients over this little dispute."

Another bright spot in a glorious day. Ava smiled at the words *little dispute*. She took the envelope. "Thank you. I'm glad this is over."

"I wasn't about to miss my nephew's wedding," Rudy said. "But I can assure you that this is the last wedding of Raymond's children that I will attend." He scowled at her. "You could have broken this family forever, Ava. I hope you're happy."

"I'm not in the least happy, Rudy. But I am pleased that justice won out for my mother."

She started to close the door, leaving him gaping at her. "Enjoy the wedding."

Every wedding is magical. But Jace and Kayla's was especially so. The processional, classical and sparkling, accompanied Carter's daughter, the flower girl, and the bridesmaids down the aisle. Ava was halfway to the altar when she spotted Noah in a dark suit and crisp white shirt. Black tie all the way.

He looked so handsome. And then he smiled at her. She held her head high and concentrated on putting one foot in front of the other. This was Kayla and Jace's wedding, and she wouldn't spoil it by practically swooning at one of the guests.

Would there be another wedding for the last of the Cahill children? She could almost picture it. But if he asked, it should only occur after she'd told him about Charlie. Ava, always known as the "pride of the Cahill kids," could not begin a future based on a lie from the past. The beauty of the wedding, the wonder of such a romantic moment convinced her. Tonight would be the perfect time to tell him about Charlie.

CHAPTER EIGHTEEN

DINNER WAS SCRUMPTIOUS. Roast duck and all the trimmings. Noah sat with Ava at the bride's table. Sawyer joined Robert at a table for special guests, and they seemed to be talking easily. Robert looked so grown-up in his sport coat and trousers. And he looked something else, too. *Proud* was the one word Ava could think of. Jace said the boy had been making phenomenal progress at the Blackthorn School.

Sawyer, dazzling in a knee-length white dress, her hair swept up in curls, seemed to have grown leaps and bounds since coming to Sawtooth. She was learning every day that to get respect she needed to give it. The change had begun with Charlie, with whom she showed extraordinary compassion that now extended to Robert and even her father. Sawyer and Noah still disagreed on Noah's future plans, but they were talking through the issues, and much of the animosity Ava had witnessed a few weeks ago had been replaced with reasonableness. Sawtooth Home had helped many young people over the several decades of its existence, but maybe none so much as Sawyer Walsh.

Noah was attentive and sweet. So attentive that Ava wondered at times if the guests might confuse the real bride and groom with them. He whispered often in Ava's ear and ended one conversation with a soft kiss. She could get used to a life with an attentive man and the bond of a wonderful family.

About nine o'clock when some of the guests started leaving, Noah asked Ava if she would like some fresh air, a walk in the lush grounds of Crestview Barn. Assuring her that he could make the trek with no trouble, he linked his arm with hers and they stepped into the cool, clean air. The lights of Holly River twinkled in the valley and glowed from the homes of those rugged souls who had built on nearby mountains.

Ava snuggled into her warm winter coat and stopped at the edge of the property, where the town below looked like a Christmas card. "What a beautiful night," she said.

"The only thing that would make it perfect is if I could waltz you around that dance floor." He chuckled. "But I have to admit, I couldn't do that with two good legs."

"Dancing is not required," Ava said. "Although all the single women here kept looking at you as if they wanted to rip that cast right off your leg."

"Funny, I didn't notice," he said. "I've only been interested in one of the ladies attending tonight. Think her last name is Cahill."

She smiled. "My mother?"

He laughed and took her hand.

"Didn't you think it was a beautiful wedding?" Ava asked him.

"Absolutely. Your brother is one happy and lucky guy," Noah said. "He gained a wife and a son just in the last few months, and I think he believes his life is complete now."

"He does. There were obstacles in their way, his and Kayla's, and it was hard at first for him to wrap his head around being a dad and everything that comes with it. But then all the problems just seemed unimportant and he jumped into his role with love and enthusiasm. Jace told me he had a sort of epiphany on the river one day, and he hasn't looked back since. He and Nathan are as close now as any father and son who'd grown up with each other."

Noah took a deep breath. Balancing on his crutch, he slipped his arm around Ava's shoulder. "So, speaking of weddings, how do you feel about getting married someday?"

She turned and stared into his eyes. "Is this a question about my general feelings on the subject, or do you have a specific reason to ask?"

He tightened his hold on her shoulder. "I guess I just can't believe that you've never met the right man. Or that I am lucky enough to have found you in time."

"I've thought about marriage," she said. "I certainly have nothing against it. But obviously it's a big step."

"Oh, obviously," he said with a hint of humor. "I can't imagine that all sorts of men haven't fallen for you."

"They have, Noah," she responded with a coy look at him. "Dozens. But I've been very selective."

"Yeah? How do you feel about a forty-year-old tower climber with a teen daughter, and a motorcycle? His baggage is filled with past mistakes, but he's trying to do better."

She leaned her head on his shoulder. "I would be more concerned about his future than his past," she said. She held her breath for a moment. She didn't believe that he was going to ask her to marry him, but they were certainly skirting around the issue, and her heart was racing faster than her mind.

He tilted her face up and kissed her. "I'm falling for you, Ava. I hope I've expressed that in countless ways, but it seems especially important to say it tonight. In a way, it's kind of scary considering my marriage track record. In another way, it's the most exciting thing that's ever happened to me."

She didn't speak, but she kissed him again trying to answer him with passion, not words. Then she looked out over the valley. "It's peaceful, quiet here in Holly River," she said. "At least, most of the time. I wonder if this place could satisfy you."

"With the right person, any place could satisfy me. I wonder if you could be satisfied with a man who hangs from towers for a living, if he decided to cut back on the more difficult climbs."

She raised her head from his shoulder. "After what happened to you, Noah, I can't deny that thinking of you doing more climbs is a very scary thing to me. But there is something I need to tell you, and it's more important than your job." The words had come from her mouth before she'd had time to think of stopping them. It was now or never.

"Really? Am I wrong or are you hinting that there is still a secret or two between us?"

She looked into his eyes. "There is one, and it may alter this conversation we're having."

"Then don't keep me waiting."

She fisted her hands and tucked them inside the long sleeves of her coat. Suddenly, even though she was so close to Noah, she felt chilled. "Remember the other day when you were outside of my office when I was talking to one of our counselors?"

"Sure." He glanced down at his crutch. "I was conserving steps that day, not eavesdropping."

"I know that. Anyway, it figures that you must have overheard some of our discussion and I'm wondering what you thought."

"Obviously what was said was between you and the counselor. But I did hear enough to understand that you wanted a bigger role in Charlie's life. I'm not surprised. You obviously care about this kid, but..." He paused. His hand around her shoulder slipped to her elbow. "Ava, I just wonder now... I don't mean to be blunt, but are you thinking of adopting Charlie?"

"Actually..." She paused, choosing her words carefully, and Noah filled in the silence.

"I know he means a lot to you, Ava. He must be a very special kid. Even Sawyer likes him. She acts almost like a big sister with him."

Ava placed her hand over her stomach in an effort to ease an ache that burned inside her. Noah had no idea how true his words were.

"If making him your adopted son is what you want," Noah continued, "then I have no reason to doubt your sincerity or question your desire to make his life better." He took a deep breath. "But it could complicate things with us, so I don't know why you didn't tell me this before now."

"Noah. I'm not thinking of adopting Charlie."

"You're not? Then…what?"

"I don't have to adopt him." Ava stepped out of Noah's embrace, faced him squarely and held both of his hands. "Charlie is already my son."

Noah's brow furrowed. "What? But he had parents. They were killed in a plane crash you told me."

"Yes, that's true. He was adopted by the Marshalls when he was born. They are the only parents he has ever known."

"And you're telling me that you are his biological mother? You gave birth to him?"

"That's right. I wasn't married, and I was scared. Getting pregnant wasn't what I'd planned at all. I'd set my goals, there was a lot I wanted to achieve, and I wasn't in the right place to be a mother. A good mother. And I knew my baby deserved much better than me. I chose the Marshalls from among many candidates and only agreed to an open adoption."

Noah's face reflected his disbelieve and even his disappointment. "So you gave him away?"

"I thought it was the best thing I could do for him."

He swallowed, croaked out his next question. "What's an open adoption?"

"It means I have had access to news of the child his whole life. I can request pictures, reports. I can't see him, of course, and I certainly can't identify myself to him, but I can know that he is okay and happy and being well cared for. That's how I knew that his parents had been killed."

"And his parents agreed to that?"

"They did, and they kept me aware of the major achievements in his life. They were excellent parents, and as much as I came to regret my decision, I would never have tried to take Charlie away from them."

"You regretted the decision?"

"I did. Almost from the moment he was taken from my arms. I have agonized over Charlie for so long."

Noah slowly shook his head. "I have to tell you, Ava, this is a tough one for me to get my head around. You had money. You came from a supportive family. You could have raised the child. But you gave him up."

"I could have provided for him, but not

in a way that was best for him. I loved him, Noah, from the moment I knew he existed. But I also knew I would not be a one hundred percent mother to him. I would always be lacking. And no child deserves a parent who cannot commit one hundred percent."

He closed his eyes and took a deep breath. Perhaps he was wondering if he had committed one hundred percent to Sawyer for fourteen years.

"And then..." She paused, breathed deeply. "There is the fact that I wasn't in a relationship at the time."

Noah's eyes reflected his confusion and his pain. "Ava, knowing you as I do, I can't imagine you becoming involved with someone you didn't care deeply for." He looked up, his eyes appearing dark and guarded in the evening lights. "Ava, did a man force himself on you?"

"No, no. Nothing like that." She smiled and realized that probably only confused him more. "Charlie's father is a good man. I know that now. In fact, I wouldn't be telling you this if I didn't totally believe that."

"Okay. It was six years ago, right? One indiscretion. I have no right to judge you.

I've never been one to uphold double standards of any kind. After all, you and I, that one night…"

She struggled to keep her expression neutral, to wait until she was certain he was ready to hear. But she knew the truth had a way of breaking through the most determined calm.

He stopped talking, his gaze never leaving her eyes. His face paled. He looked as if someone had sucker punched him. "Ava… the timing. Charlie is five. Are you trying to tell me…" He bit his bottom lip. "Ava, is Charlie my son?"

Ava's eyes stung. One tear rolled freely down her cheek. She didn't know if she was crying from relief that it was out in the open or if a fear of the future now that Noah knew made her regret the confession. But it was done. She had expected that he would figure out his connection to her—and perhaps ultimately to Charlie. But now that it had happened, her blood felt as cold as the wintry breeze rustling through the trees.

CHAPTER NINETEEN

NOAH JERKED HIS hands from Ava's grasp. He looked around for a place to sit. He needed a seat before his one good leg collapsed under him. But there was no place to rest. He and Ava were on the edge of a mountain. And he felt like he was going over.

"Are you all right?" she asked him.

"All right? Are you kidding? How do you think anyone would feel having learned that they're suddenly a parent...again?"

"I've told you before... Jace went through the same thing."

"Well, I'm not Jace, am I?"

"No, you are not." The chill in her voice only made her colder.

He turned away from her, struggled to maintain his balance on the cumbersome crutches. "I've only just started to get through to Sawyer, and I find out I have a five-year-old son! I can't have this now. Not now."

Ava rested her hand on his arm. "Maybe we should go inside, find a warm, quiet place to talk."

"Right. Let's go inside where everyone is celebrating. Let's find a place to hash out the biggest betrayal that's ever happened in my life."

"Noah, this isn't a betrayal. No one is asking you to be a parent to Charlie. I haven't said a word about that, have I?"

"Then why tell me at all?"

"You have a right to know. And because you and I are getting close. I have every intention of making Charlie part of my family. And if you…"

"What? You think I want to be part of the Cahills? No, thank you. I can't imagine I'd ever measure up."

Her mouth opened but no words came out. For a moment Noah wondered if she were even breathing. And then he realized it was the shock. She let out a long, trembling breath, her expression turning cold and hard.

"Get one thing clear, Noah. I don't need you to help raise this child. I don't need your money, or your false compassion for a boy you obviously don't even want to get to know. And most of all, I don't need your questionable parenting skills. Charlie and I will be much better off if you don't become involved at all." Her voice quavered. Her bottom lip trembled. But she wasn't done. "I can see I've made a terrible mistake in telling you about Charlie. But at least—" she gulped back a sob "—I know without question how you feel."

She whirled away from him and hurried back toward the barn.

He kicked a clod of snow with his good foot and almost lost his balance. Not surprising. And he was nearly freezing to death. He wasn't a mountain man, never wanted to be. And the woman he'd thought he loved had just delivered about as shocking a piece of information as anyone could ever get.

So why was he feeling like the heel? He didn't even know Charlie. Had only seen him a couple of times. One of those times he'd offered to play soccer with the kid. That was the kind of thing a dad did, but Noah had just volunteered his time to be nice. Well, at least now he wouldn't have to bone up on his soccer skills.

AVA RUSHED INTO the ladies' room as soon as she reentered the barn. Thankfully no one was in there. And thankfully no one had spoken to her when she beelined for the safety of a bathroom stall. Or maybe someone had spoken to her but she hadn't heard. And she didn't care.

Regret felt like sandpaper on her tongue and tasted as bitter as vinegar. At one time she'd believed the worst regret she'd ever feel was when she realized the consequences of that one night with Noah. But this was worse. She'd told him about Charlie and he'd reacted with confusion and fear and cold-hearted shock. There was no other way to put it.

Well, fine, she'd told him she'd raise Charlie on her own, and she meant it. She would have the support of her family, and that's all she would need. She and her son would be safe and happy, and all the family she'd ever desire.

Ava slammed the toilet seat down and sat. Her eyes burned. She grabbed a piece of toilet paper in case they started leaking, but she sure as heck hoped they didn't. Noah wasn't worth the first tear. True, she'd allowed herself to imagine a future with him, the kind of future that her brothers had. And she knew if that were to happen she'd have to tell Noah about Charlie.

It's not like she could have told him before, at least not before he'd come for Sawyer at Thanksgiving. Thanksgiving? Just a few weeks ago, and so much had happened. She'd helped a troubled fourteen-year-old find a place of comfort. She'd advanced her ties to Charlie. She'd tried to understand Noah. She'd fallen in love…

No! Stop it. You're not in love, she told herself. *In fact, you're lucky you've seen the true side of Noah Walsh.* Sawyer had been right all along. He was selfish, self-serving. He'd spent years not considering his daughter above all else. What parent did that? Even if he was doing better now, that didn't make up for years of neglect. Charlie was better off without him. She was better off…

Ava wiped her eyes.

A terrifying thought suddenly occurred to her. What if Noah told Sawyer about Charlie? Would Sawyer tell everyone about her connection to the boy? Would she feel even more animosity toward her father? Would she think Ava was too judgmental against her father? Or would she feel like Charlie had dodged a bullet by not having Noah Walsh for a father?

Surely Noah wouldn't do that. Surely he understood how this knowledge could affect all of them. Surely he would jump in his truck and head back to Chapel Hill, cast or no cast and return to the life that stroked his ego and made him a hero in the eyes of every one of his crew members.

Noah had to go. Ava couldn't risk running into him if he stayed in the little cottage next to the school. It would hurt too badly. She would be reminded of his rejection of the beautiful boy they'd conceived together. If only she hadn't begun to care so deeply for him.

"Where's Ava?" She heard Jace's booming voice through the bathroom door and the haze of her anguish. "I want to dance with my sister," he bellowed.

She had to leave the bathroom. This was Jace's wedding after all. She was a bridesmaid. She was beyond happy for Jace and Kayla. She was beyond miserable for herself... She dried her eyes, blew her nose, plastered a smile on her face and went into the decorated barn. Greenery, blue and silver lights, candles on every table. A slow waltz coming from the four-piece band.

"There you are." Jace grabbed her arm. "This song is just about your pace, *big* sister," he joked. "I wouldn't want you to sprain an ankle with a rock number."

She practically fell into his arms and let him awkwardly dance her around the barn floor. For a guy who played guitar and once claimed music was his life, he was unbelievably clumsy. The only man who would dance worse tonight was Noah, with his cast. She stared over Jace's shoulder looking for Noah, for Sawyer.

"I don't see the Walshes," she said into her brother's ear.

"They left. I heard Noah go up to his daughter and say, 'We're leaving.' Kinda strange, don't you think?"

Not strange at all, she thought.

"Don't worry, sis. If your escort turned out to be a jerk, we'll get you home safe and sound."

The song ended and Jace actually dipped her in a flourish of gallantry. "How about that move?" he teased when she was upright. "It's been a great night."

"WHAT'S WRONG WITH YOU, Dad? I was having fun."

Other than a few unintelligible grumblings, Noah and Sawyer hadn't spoken for several miles. Now that they were approaching the school, Sawyer apparently decided to open up.

She tried again. "Is your leg hurting?"

"No."

"Then why did we leave?"

He breathed deeply, calmed his escalating emotions. "Look, I'm sorry, okay? Something happened, that's all."

"What? You were having fun with Ava, weren't you? And then you two just disappeared…" She halted. "Ohhh, so that's it. You had a fight with Ava."

Deciding it might be better to admit some of the truth to his ultraclever daughter, he gave her a slight nod. "A little disagreement, that's what it was."

"*A little disagreement*, and I would still be there waiting for cake. Now I'm hauling my butt back to Sawtooth with only memories of that three tiers of sugary perfection to lull me to sleep. Geez, Dad, it's Christmas Eve!"

"I'm aware of the date," he said.

"What's going on with you and Ava anyway? I thought something might be happening between the two of you when you wanted to see her after dinner the other night and made me go in my cottage. And she always goes to see you at the house when I'm not there."

Sawyer took a great gulp of air. "Oh no! You've been hooking up with her and she dumped you!"

She dumped on me, is more like it. "She didn't dump me, and not that it's any of your business, but we haven't been hooking up, so get that notion out of your head."

"But you do like her?"

I did. Very much. I do. I don't know. "Of course I like her. She's accomplished and caring and organized and…"

"So what did she do tonight?" Sawyer interrupted. "Failed to care enough for you? Or did she—" Sawyer pretended to be aghast "—act a bit disorganized?"

He pulled in front of his daughter's cottage. "Will I see you tomorrow?" he asked as a way to steer the conversation away from his shock and confusion. Knowing Sawyer, she'd probably blurt out the truth. *I know what happened. You and Ava met before and had a thing one night. And Charlie is your son.*

Good grief, Walsh, what's happening to you? Even Sawyer couldn't guess the details of this turn of events.

"I have some Christmas gifts for you," he said. "Ordered them all online since I wasn't in any shape to go shopping. But I think you'll like them. Some of them, anyway."

"That's all you're going to tell me?" she said in her most challenging voice.

"That's it. So I'll see you tomorrow?"

She got out of the truck. "Tell you what, Dad. You keep the gifts. I'll bet you can return every one of them. I'll just take a few from the mountain of donated stuff in Ava's office. Even a stupid stuffed animal would be better than putting up with your mood tomorrow." She slammed the truck door.

After she was inside, he backed the truck out of the parking lot and headed to his rented house with its lonely little tree. He'd have a big glass of whatever he had in that top cupboard over the refrigerator and drink until he fell asleep on the couch. One thing was for sure. He wasn't about to hear any tidings of comfort and joy tonight.

CHAPTER TWENTY

CHRISTMAS DAY STRUGGLED to dawn through a layer of gray clouds and misty rain. Ava rose early, put on her red dress and made the rounds to all the cottages visiting with the few residents who hadn't gone home for the holiday. Try as she might, she couldn't find the energy or attitude to feel merry on this bleak wintry morning.

Her mood improved the instant she saw Charlie though, still in his pj's sitting in a mound of torn wrapping paper near the tree Snowy Mountain had donated to each cottage. He looked like any other five-year-old on the happiest day of the year, showing off his gifts. He seemed especially excited about the extra-large interconnecting blocks Ava had bought for him and put under the tree.

"I'm going to make the biggest thing ever," he told her.

She ruffled his hair. "I don't doubt that for

a minute. Merry Christmas, sweetie." She wrapped him in a hug and almost cried when his little arms came around her and squeezed love right into her heart.

This is why I woke up feeling so miserable, she told herself. How could anyone not see the goodness in this boy's heart? *This is why I have to forget Noah. No sacrifice is too great to make a life with this precious boy.* Soon. Today would be a giant step forward in making her dream a reality. She was going to tell her mother everything.

Now she had a second chance and life didn't offer too many of those. She truly was lucky this Christmas morning. Before leaving Charlie's side, she had an idea, which suddenly seemed so right. She told Mrs. Carmichael that she was taking the boy with her to her family Christmas at the Cahill farm. A second giant step.

"That's wonderful," the cottage mother said. "He'll have a great time visiting with the animals."

And he'll meet his grandmother, his two uncles, perhaps his stepuncle, Robert, and two adorable cousins. When she told Charlie about their special adventure, he popped up from playing with his toys.

"I have to get dressed. Today will be the best day ever!"

And Ava made a silent wish that it would be for all of them.

Noah awoke with a pounding headache and the deepest regret that he'd taken that bottle down from the cupboard. He got out of bed and made it to the kitchen where he spied the empty bottle, uttered a mild curse and tossed it in the trash. Then he found his container of aspirin, swallowed three tablets and made coffee.

"Pull yourself together, Walsh," he said after the first sip of really strong brew. "You've got some serious thinking to do. And some situations to make right." Truly he didn't have a clue how he would make amends with the people he'd angered last night. But he would start with his daughter.

"What do you want, Dad?" she said when she answered her cell phone.

"I'm not giving up, Sawyer. I'm coming to get you and you're coming over here to open presents."

She sighed, remained silent for way too long. "You can't do that," she said. "Mrs. Carmichael won't let me leave with you unless Ava approves it."

"What? That stupid rule is still in effect?"

"Yep, 'fraid so."

"That's hogwash…"

"Hold on. I'll sneak out and walk over to your place."

Good for Sawyer. She hadn't lost all her spunk. "Great idea. Don't get caught."

She snickered. "Dad, come on. It's me."

She showed up an hour later. Noah's heart swelled when he spied her coming through the trees, her hoodie pulled tight against the mist.

"I made cocoa," he said. "When you were a kid…"

"Coffee, please," she said. She had a few sips, and then switched to hot chocolate. "Your coffee is terrible."

They opened presents. She even had stuck a couple for him under the tree, hiding them beneath a throw rug. His sneaky, clever daughter. He complimented the sunglasses she bought him and claimed he really needed a new wallet.

Either she liked the things he bought her or she pretended to. Either way, Noah couldn't help letting a bit of Christmas spirit into his damaged soul. Maybe like Ebenezer Scrooge, he actually had a chance of having a few good holidays in the future. If he only knew what it would take to guarantee that.

When they were finished, Noah asked his daughter to stay awhile. "Sit down, Sawyer. There is something I have to tell you."

His heart hammered. His palms sweated. He was more frightened than he'd ever been on an Air Force jet or a five-hundred-foot tower.

"What is it?" she asked.

"It's about Ava and that little kid, Charlie," he began. "You deserve to know the truth."

If Sawyer had been another type of kid, maybe he wouldn't have been able to tell her about his past. But she was smart and worldly for a fourteen-year-old so he just had to trust his instincts on this one. He started with six years before and continued to when he'd faced Ava on the threshold of her apartment several weeks ago.

Sawyer didn't interrupt, a rarity from her. She listened intently, without judgment, so he concluded with an admission that he was developing long-lasting feelings for Ava.

Sawyer snorted. "Is that what you said to her? 'Ava, I think I have long-lasting feelings for you.'?"

"Good grief no," he said. "I can be more romantic than that."

"I hope so." She tucked one leg under her and leaned back on the sofa. She looked as casual as if she didn't have a care in the world. Noah, on the other hand, was a trembling, aching mass of nerves.

"So what now?" Sawyer asked. "You've made Ava mad. She thinks you don't want to have anything to do with her son, *your son,* my brother—who, by the way, is a really cool kid. What are you going to do?"

"Honestly? I don't know. You are aware, more than anyone, that I'm not exactly a prizewinner in the parenting department. Taking on another kid, maybe raising another runaway, another offspring who hates me…"

"Now who's a drama queen?" she said.

"I'm just stating the facts, Sawyer. Maybe my job isn't conducive to raising a kid."

"Ya' think?"

"But it's what I do, and I'm good at it."

"I'm not used to complimenting you," she said. "But here goes. Dad, you'd be good at anything you did." She smiled. "Except maybe parenting. But it's not in you to be anything less than the best at what you do."

He stared at her a moment before saying, "Thank you, Sawyer."

"Don't thank me. What I'm saying is that I'm not going to buy that 'can't get another job' line anymore."

He sighed. "Okay, I guess I could get another job. I'm not really over the hill. I do have a few skills."

"So what's your plan from this point on?"

"I don't know but I can't leave things this way. I've got to see Ava, try again to explain my shock at what she told me, my fear about what it means. I didn't use the right words yesterday. Maybe they will come to me today."

"I don't think that's all you need to do," Sawyer said.

"What do you mean?"

"I think you ought to get to know one

pretty cute little boy. He just might make up your mind for you."

He didn't say anything for a long minute. Just sat there considering what Sawyer said. "I suppose Ava is out at her family's place," he said. "It is Christmas, and I'm sure those people make a big thing of it."

"I imagine."

"I figure I'll go out there."

"Seems like a good plan to me," Sawyer said.

"Can you get back to the cottage without getting caught?"

She shook her head. "Dad, seriously?"

He stood. "Give me your hand." She did and he gently pulled her up from the sofa. "I feel this incredible urge to give you a hug."

"Go for it."

He brought his daughter to his chest and held her close and long. The gesture reminded him of when Sawyer was a little girl, before the hugs had stopped, before the feelings between them had been severed beyond repair—or so he'd thought. If he could get this feeling back, maybe there was hope for all of them.

THE SUN HAD finally decided to break through the gray cover of clouds when Ava drove up to her mother's house at noon.

"Wow, this place is really neat," Charlie said. "Is that a real barn?"

She smiled at him. "It certainly is. And inside we have a cow and a horse and a goat or two. Would you like to see them?"

He nodded with enthusiasm.

"And inside the house we have Buster. He's a big dog, but he's got a soft spot in his heart for little boys."

"So I can meet him, too?"

"It's more likely that he'll be running around like crazy trying to meet you. I just want to make sure you understand that you don't have to be afraid of Buster."

"Okay. I like dogs."

Ava noticed that hers was the last car to park in front of the house. The car with out-of-state plates obviously belonged to Kayla's parents. Her brothers and their families had already arrived. Even Jace, who'd put off his honeymoon so Kayla and Nathan could experience a true country Christmas.

"I want you to meet some people," Ava said. "My two brothers, my mother, and my niece and nephew. Maybe you and Emily and Nathan can play a game together."

They went into the house and Emily and Nathan ran from the kitchen. "Who's this?" Emily asked.

"This is Charlie," Ava said. "He's going to have Christmas dinner with us."

Emily reacted just as Ava knew she would. "That's cool. But we're gonna play first." She gave him a secretive look. "Grandma calls playing 'staying out of her hair,' whatever that means."

"I like to play," Charlie said.

Jace came into the living room next, completely at ease with seeing a stranger with his sister. Since she'd been a little girl, Ava had been bringing uninvited guests to the house, both two-legged and four-legged, so the appearance of another wasn't a big deal. "Hi, kid," Jace said, shaking his hand.

Soon everyone in the house except Cora had met Charlie. The boy seemed to beam under all the attention.

"Where's Mama?" Ava asked her brother.

"Kitchen. She's setting out snacks sent over in a huge gift basket from Uncle Rudy."

Jace grinned. "Looks like you taught the old bird a lesson."

"Great. Then we should all start the New Year with forgiveness in our hearts."

Jace chuckled. "Sure. Until the next time Rudy screws up. Then Carter and I are going to send you back to deal with him."

Ava took her brother aside. "Jace, would you watch Charlie for me for a few minutes? Maybe set out a game all the kids can play together? I need a few minutes alone with Mama."

"No problem. Maybe I'll even play, if the game is easy enough."

Before Ava could get to the kitchen, Cora came out with a tray of crackers, cheese and Christmas cookies. She set it down on the coffee table and looked at Charlie. "Who is this little angel?" she asked.

"He's one of the residents at Sawtooth," Ava explained.

"Welcome, darling'," Cora said. "I hope you're hungry."

"Can I have a cookie?" he asked.

"You may have one, maybe two. But no more or you will spoil your dinner." Charlie responded with a nod and a longing look at the tray of goodies.

"Mama, I need to talk to you…alone," Ava said. "Can we go in the kitchen?"

"Sure, Ava. Kayla and Miranda are upstairs doing some last-minute wrapping, and Carter and Kayla's dad are taking turns riding the horse. We won't be bothered."

Cora sat at the kitchen table after bringing a cup of coffee to Ava. "Is something wrong, sweetheart?" her mother asked. "You look like you're carrying the weight of the world on your shoulders."

"I'm fine," Ava lied. "And I hope that what I'm about to tell you is good news. It is for me. It concerns Charlie and Noah and me. And a history that seems pretty bizarre to me, and I lived through it."

"Start at the beginning," Cora said.

Ava told her about the night in the cocktail lounge. Cora's brow furrowed and she frowned. "Oh my, Ava, that doesn't sound like you."

"I know. And the man I…*was with* that night is Noah. We parted company, and I never thought I'd see him again."

"Okay. I understand so far," Cora said.

"Good." Ava took a deep breath and admitted the details about Noah's marriage and her own regret when he left her that night. "But the thing is—" she swallowed "—I was pregnant."

"What?" Cora leaned across the table and covered Ava's hand. "Oh, sweetheart, why didn't you tell someone? Why didn't you tell me?"

"I was ashamed, unsure of what to do, unable to get in touch with Noah, and truly I didn't want to tell you. I was torn between feeling sorry for myself and a determination to take care of everything without help. In the end I decided to have the baby and give it up for adoption."

Cora sniffed loudly. "That must have been a heartbreaking decision."

"It was. But at the time it was also the right decision. The baby went to a wonderful home. I followed his progress through letters and pictures. And then the unthinkable happened. His parents were killed in a freak plane crash. I heard about it and arranged for the child to be brought to Saw..."

Ava stopped when she realized her mother was openly weeping. "Oh, Mama, I didn't mean to make you cry." She got up, took the chair next to her mother and put her arms around Cora.

"I just feel so bad for you, Ava. You went through this alone. I would have helped."

"I know, Mama, but I couldn't ask. Don't cry for me, please. I'm okay. In fact…"

"I'm not just crying for you, Ava," Cora said. "Some of these tears are happy ones."

Ava waited until her mother had wiped her eyes and regained some control. "I'm crying because it's come full circle, sweetheart. You have your son with you now, and Charlie is that boy."

Ava couldn't speak, so she just held on more tightly to her mother.

Cora blinked several times and blew her nose, and then asked Ava for a glass of water.

"Mama, you never disappoint me," Ava said, bringing the glass to the table. "I didn't know for sure if you would understand why I did what I did, but I felt sure you would try to."

"I love you, Ava. I will always try to understand." She stared into her daughter's eyes with the comforting love Ava had always relied on. "What are you going to do now, sweetheart? I sensed that you had feelings for Noah. Will you two get married?"

Ava shook her head. "No, Mama. That's not going to happen."

"He doesn't know? You don't love him?"

Ava felt her eyes begin to well up. She steeled herself with several deep breaths. "I told him last night. Maybe I should just say that he didn't react as I'd hoped he would. He didn't even say he wanted to get to know Charlie."

Cora's spine straightened like a stick. "What's the matter with that man?" she asked. "Doesn't he realize how amazing you are and how terrific that boy must be...?"

"Mama, we have to understand how this news affected Noah. Remember he had no idea..."

She was interrupted by Jace who just then came in the kitchen. "I hope you ladies aren't talking about Noah. He's standing out on the front porch."

Cora stood, started toward the kitchen door. "I'll take care of this, Ava. You stay here."

Ava gave Jace a pleading look. He intercepted his mother's determined path. "Oh no, Mama. He wants to see Ava."

"I'll go," Ava said.

Cora looked disappointed. She was definitely ready to do battle for her oldest child. And Ava had never loved her more.

"All right, Ava," she eventually said. "But if you need any help, you have a small army behind you in this house, and every soldier is on your side."

CHAPTER TWENTY-ONE

AVA WALKED ONTO the porch, mindful of the gray clouds gathering again over the mountains. Because of the Christmas lights hanging from the eaves, the porch was bathed in a soft white glow. She spotted Noah looking out at the yard, his back to her.

"What are you doing here, Noah?"

He turned toward her. "Is there a place we can talk? It's cold out here. Maybe the barn…?"

She remembered what happened the last time they were in the barn, the smiles, the kisses. "This is fine," she said. "Have a seat on one of the chairs." She picked up a throw from her mother's swing. "You can use this if you're cold."

He waved off her suggestion. "Never mind. I can stand. Please, you use the blanket. I'll be fine."

"Suit yourself." Ava wrapped the blanket

around her shoulders and stood beside Noah at the porch railing. "You want to talk?" she said. "I have about five minutes before Mama serves Christmas dinner."

He rested his crutch on a post and leaned against the railing. "Five minutes is very generous of you, Ava."

She searched his words for sarcasm, but he seemed to be serious.

"I might not need all that time," he continued. He stared at her for a few moments and began. "I'm looking at you now, the set of your lips, the spark in your eyes. You're obviously angry, hurt, determined to make a family without me in it. Maybe you even hate me."

"I don't hate you," she said. "The rest? Okay, there is an element of truth in what you say."

"I have a few points to make about all that," he said. "And it's not easy for me to get the words out."

"It wasn't hard for you to express your opinion last night, Noah. When it came to Charlie, you were perfectly clear."

"I was shocked, rattled. At first I didn't know whether to believe you. But I do now.

I did then after the news sank in." He looked like he might take her hands but she kept them folded under the blanket. "I'm sorry for the way I reacted, Ava. Truly. Since then I've thought of several things I might have said that would have been kinder."

She didn't argue. She wished he had said those kinder words also.

"Ava, I love you. I have since I walked into the café that day and confronted you about our past. Heck, maybe I have loved you since that special night we first met."

He paused. Ava sensed him looking at her deeply, and it was all she could do to keep staring out over the ice-crusted lawn. Maybe it was the cold that was getting to her, but her breaths were becoming more difficult to take.

Could she finally trust him?

"I told you I tried to find you," he said. "I didn't deserve to see you, but I wanted to. I needed to." His gaze stayed locked on hers. "And now I want to shout my feelings from the rooftops. Since that isn't logical, I decided to tell the other incredible lady in my life."

Ava turned to him. "You told Sawyer about us? About Charlie?"

"I did. You're part of my life, Ava. And because of a quirk of fate, Charlie is part of my life. It's only fair to Sawyer to let her know what's going on. She won't talk about this at Sawtooth. You may not believe this, but that kid has her own sense of family loyalty, which is pretty amazing since I'm her only family."

"I believe it," Ava said.

"And, for what it's worth, she's nuts about Charlie."

"You're wrong about one thing, Noah. I am not part of your life. You have no obligation to me, nor do I have an obligation to you beyond telling you the truth."

His eyes narrowed. "Is that what you truly believe?"

"It is now. I had thought that perhaps… Well, it doesn't matter now. My life has to be about Charlie. I owe him a home, a family, a chance for happiness among people who love him."

He looked sad. But he needed to know that he'd hurt her last night. And he had to understand her priorities.

"And so," he said, "because of our conversation, which I admit was awful, you're assuming that I can't contribute anything to Charlie's happiness, his well-being?"

Ava drew the blanket more closely around her. She was shivering, but not from the cold. "You are the kind of man you are, Noah—a risk taker, a man who sees challenges as a way of life. And Charlie is the kind of boy he is—wounded, alone, confused." She laughed bitterly. "I had thought that once you knew about Charlie, once you'd accepted that you have two children who need you, you would give up your job, your reckless hobbies. I was a fool for thinking that. I had assumed something that I know now is never going to happen."

"It all comes back to that one little accident…"

"The one that could have killed you?" she said. "The one that left you unconscious while your daughter and the woman that was falling in love with you sat by your bedside and begged you to wake up—that accident, Noah?"

He shrugged and tried for a smile. "Can I have part of that blanket now?"

She opened her arms and let him wrap

himself in the comfort of her mama's old quilt. "Why are you smiling?" she asked.

"Because you were falling in love with me even then and I didn't realize it. Sure would have saved me a lot of frustration if I'd known, but better late than never."

"This situation was never about loving you," she said.

He put his arm around her shoulders. "Funny. For me it's always been about loving you. Of course, until last night I figured I only had to share that love with an obstinate fourteen-year-old. Now I realize I'm supposed to split it three ways."

"But you don't have to do that," Ava said. "I'm letting you out of your parenting responsibilities. I'm letting you go, Noah, back to Chapel Hill, back to tall metal towers that seem to draw you in like a magnet, back to motorcycles, speedboats, even mountain climbing if that suits you. You can pretend you never heard of Charlie or of me. And it will be much easier for you to forget us than it would be for a five-year-old insecure little boy to lose another father."

"So now you're making decisions for me, Ava?"

"What? No. I'm freeing you..."

"On one hand I have Sawyer telling me to quit my job. On the other hand, I have you telling me to go back to it." He smiled, looked up at the sky. "What's a guy supposed to do? You both make a convincing argument."

"You can't make light of this, Noah."

"Oh, I'm not making light of it. I'm trying to make sense of it. And I'm beginning to. I just learned of my new role last night, and I don't want to screw it up for any of us."

"Miss Ava?"

They both spun around to the front door where Charlie stood bathed in the light from the fireplace. Ava's heart was filled with love for both of the males who stood near her. If only she didn't have to let one of them go.

"Yes, sweetie?"

"Miss Cora says it's time to eat." He stopped, stared at Noah. "Hey, you're that man, the one who's going to play soccer with me when his cast is off."

Ava snapped her head back and stared into Noah's eyes.

He chuckled. "You don't know everything that goes on at that home, Miss Ava. Some things are just between us guys." Then he bent slightly at the waist. "As soon as my leg is all better, buddy."

Charlie stared at the cast. "How'd you hurt yourself?"

"Doing something I should have let someone else do. Someone younger, someone who'd been specially trained," he answered.

He took the blanket from Ava's shoulders and laid it on the chair. "Go on in, Miss Ava. Have a good time with your family. I'll see you tomorrow."

He grabbed the crutch and hobbled down the steps to his truck. Before getting in, he looked back at the two of them and said, "Tomorrow, Ava."

Ava THOUGHT TOMORROW would never come. All through Christmas dinner she laughed with her family, saw to Charlie's needs, aware that her mother had taken each one of the adults into the kitchen and explained about Ava. What she had done and what she planned to do now. The family reacted as Ava knew they would—accepting, loving, making room for Charlie at the dinner table and in their hearts.

She was just waiting for word from Marjorie Marcos that Charlie was ready to hear the news that he would be part of a family again.

All through the opening of packages Ava thought about the day she could be Charlie's mother. She would make the necessary changes in her life to accommodate him. Maybe she would even rent the house next door to Sawtooth where Charlie would have his own room. She'd loved the house from the first time Noah took her to see it. Once Noah was gone…

Yes, her heart ached for a lost love that had begun to grow into its potential. But she would fill the hole in her heart with Charlie. And what about Noah? She kept wondering. Could a man change overnight? She'd never known it to be true, but according to Cora, miracles happen every day.

Just before dusk, Ava and Charlie left the farm and drove back to Sawtooth Home. Charlie was sleepy, his head nodding to his chest several times on the way. Ava took the quiet time in the car to study the beauty that was her son—the dark, straight strands of his hair that were so like his father's, the strong jawline so like his uncle Jace's, the eyes that were unmistakably her own.

She couldn't wait to start this chapter of her life. She would get over Noah if only because of her determination to make a home for Charlie. Still, as darkness fell over the mountains, she wished things could be different. She wished for a full, complete family of love and comfort and security. A girl could wish, couldn't she?

TUESDAY THE TWENTY-SIXTH of December dawned with a sparkling clarity that made the world seem new and bright and hopeful. Classes had been canceled for the week at the school, and activities were planned for the children who had remained at Sawtooth over the holidays.

Ava watched the kids from her office window. She was always quick to pick Charlie out of the crowd. She'd grown so accustomed to his movements, the way his legs churned in the snow, the colorful rainbow of his hat. She supposed all parents instinctively knew their children and could pick them out from among many. Recognition was just a part of bonding.

At ten o'clock Noah came to her office. He said a quick hello, but seemed taken with something outside. "Look at that guy, will you?" Noah said from the window. "He's not about to let a little snow slow him down."

So, Noah knew, too. He'd picked his son out of the crowd. She couldn't help but smile.

"I've come to a decision," Noah said after a few minutes.

"I thought you might." Her words were calm. Her heart was hammering.

He pulled a chair close to hers, sat down and took her hands in his. "Probably this should be more romantic, but if that counselor is right about our son, we don't have all the time in the world."

"What are you trying to say, Noah?"

"I want you to marry me, Ava. I love you. We've already established that fact and it's something I'm certain will never change, along with the additional fact that we will raise two great kids." He shook his head. "Yeah, definitely this should be more romantic. Sawyer would be kicking my butt about now."

"You want to marry me?" The question held a world of disbelief.

"Yes. Today, tomorrow, whenever you decide. Just please marry me. I'll propose again and do it better if it will make you trust and believe me. I'll have a ring. I'll get down on my knee. I'll hire a skywriter."

She managed a small chuckle. "Those things might help."

"Just say yes, Ava. Say that what started in a bar in Charlotte led us to this day, this moment. I'll never let you down again."

Suddenly Ava was seeing Noah and everything through a lens of watery brilliance. She blinked hard. She wanted—she *needed* to see his face as if she would be looking at it for years to come.

"I guess I've surprised you," Noah said. "You probably need some time to think it over. I understand that…"

She almost shook her head, denying that she needed time at all.

"We can wait awhile, a week or two if you want to.

She sputtered a most unladylike laugh, and reached up to touch his face. He kissed her palm and she suddenly thought he was the most romantic man in the world. At least, he was perfect for her. But there were issues they hadn't settled.

"Noah…"

"You admitted you were falling in love with me last night," he said.

"I know, but our problems still exist."

"Maybe not," he said. "I spoke to the owner of Maxicom this morning. He and I have gotten close over the years. I think he respects me."

"I'm sure he does."

"Anyway, I told him I was through climbing towers. I still want to be a crew chief. I can send crews out from my desk. And I can check on them. Still have to travel some, but that's doable, right?"

She didn't trust her voice but managed to get the words out. "Oh, Noah, are you sure?"

"Ava, I'm sure." He grinned at her. "The two women in my life have finally knocked some sense into my head. Daredevil stuff is for younger men, men that don't have a bunch of kids to raise."

"A bunch of kids?"

"You never know. If I am suddenly sure of myself in the parenting department, I just might want to try it again. Who knows?"

"Have you told Sawyer?"

"Oh heck no. If I'd told her, she would have given me a mile-long list of instructions of what to say so I wouldn't blow it."

Ava swiped at the tears going down her cheeks. "Noah, sweetheart, you haven't blown it. Your words were from your heart. Your proposal was perfect. *You* are perfect."

"Not perfect, Ava. I'm never selling my bike. You can live with that, can't you?"

"I can...happily. Can you reach the tissues on my desk?"

He handed her one.

She blew her nose. "I love you so much, Noah. I love you as a friend, a husband, and I'm ready to love you as the father of our son."

"It will happen, Ava. Before we get married, I will prove myself to that kid and then to you. You won't have any doubts."

She stared into his eyes, memorizing everything about this moment, this utterly dream-fulfilling moment.

"So, I've left a proposal on the table," he said. "What's your answer?"

"It's a yes."

He smiled. "That's good, because I don't

think I can breathe right now. I know you're working, but can I pick you up later? If it's okay with you, I'm going to talk to my landlord about buying that little house next door. I'll tell you his decision as we drive out to your mom's place. There are a lot of Cahills that need to know what we've decided."

She laughed. "And Sawyer?"

"Definitely Sawyer. She'll be over the moon. You are about as far from a wicked stepmother as anyone could be."

"I love her, Noah. I really do."

"I know. You saved her, Ava. I know that, too."

"Maybe I helped, but you would never have stopped trying."

He raised her to her feet and kissed her deeply. "We'll make this work, Ava. There's enough determination in this room to make failure an impossibility."

Ava kissed him back. "*Failure?* The word never entered my mind."

EPILOGUE

SPRINGTIME ALWAYS PROMISED BIRTH, regrowth, possibilities and love. And this March was no different in the mountains. The trees hadn't started to bud yet, but they soon would, and the cycle would begin again. And on the highest peaks, snow still dusted the slopes and brought the last of the skiers.

Miranda's baby was due any day. She was happy for two reasons. She would give Emily a sister and Carter a daughter. And she would be able to fit into her bridesmaid dress for Ava's wedding.

The wedding was set for the end of April and today, March 30, was the day Ava had waited for, thought about, for many months. She and Noah sat in Marjorie Marcos's office. When a knock sounded on the door, Marjorie got up from her desk and walked to let in her visitor, one bright-eyed, smiling little boy who'd just turned six years old.

"I'll leave you three alone," she said, and followed her words with a nod of encouragement at Ava and Noah.

Charlie brightened instantly when he saw who was waiting in the office. "Hi. Are we going somewhere today?"

Their custom had been to take Charlie somewhere for an adventure in the mountains each Sunday. Now he looked forward to the outings and to the times he and Noah would kick the ball around after school. They had become special moments for father and son.

"No, sweetie," Ava said. "Today we just want to talk to you."

"That's right, buddy," Noah said. "Come sit down, okay?"

Ava and Noah had talked endlessly about the way they would approach this important announcement to Charlie with Marjorie's advice. They would save the biological details for later. For now it was enough for Charlie to know he was wanted and loved.

Ava took his hand. "Sweetie, you know how sometimes children from this school go home to be with their parents? And sometimes children are picked by new parents to go home with them?" She smiled. "You know all this, right?"

He nodded.

"Well, I'm so happy to tell you that brand-new parents have picked you."

His eyes rounded. "No. I don't want to go. I want to stay here with you and Noah."

Noah lifted him up and settled him on his knee. "That's the best news, Charlie." He grinned with all the happiness in his heart. "For better or worse, kid, we're the new parents, and we want you to live with us."

"We want to be your mom and dad," Ava said. "We love you, sweetheart, just like we love Sawyer. We'll be a family, the four of us."

Charlie blinked several times. His bottom lip trembled.

"Aren't you happy about this?" Noah said. "Because I gotta tell you, kiddo, that I've pretty much set my mind on this whole thing."

Charlie reached his little arms up and wrapped them around Noah's neck. "I get to live with you and Miss Ava?" he said, his words muffled by Noah's throat.

Ava put her hand on Charlie's back and patted gently. "Forever and ever, sweetie.

Noah and I are getting married soon. You'll come to the wedding and then we're all moving next door to Noah's house—you, Sawyer, Noah and me."

"And I get to be your little boy for real?" Charlie said.

Tears gathered in Noah's eyes. With Charlie's head tucked against his collarbone, Noah ran his hand down the boy's silky hair and smiled at Ava. "I feel like you already are, sport."

* * * * *

For more stories about the Cahills of the High Country, check out these fabulous titles from author Cynthia Thomason:

High Country Cop
Dad in Training

Available at www.Harlequin.com.

Get 4 FREE REWARDS!

We'll send you 2 FREE Books plus 2 FREE Mystery Gifts.

Love Inspired® books feature contemporary inspirational romances with Christian characters facing the challenges of life and love.

Their Family Legacy
Lorraine Beatty

The Rancher's Answered Prayer
Arlene James

FREE
Value Over
$20

Get 4 FREE REWARDS!

We'll send you 2 FREE Books plus 2 FREE Mystery Gifts.

Love Inspired® Suspense books feature Christian characters facing challenges to their faith... and lives.

FREE Value Over $20

Get 4 FREE REWARDS!

We'll send you 2 FREE Books plus 2 FREE Mystery Gifts.

Both the **Romance** and **Suspense** collections feature compelling novels
written by many of today's best-selling authors.

YES! Please send me 2 FREE novels from the Essential Romance or
Essential Suspense Collection and my 2 FREE gifts (gifts are worth about
$10 retail). After receiving them, if I don't wish to receive any more books,
I can return the shipping statement marked "cancel." If I don't cancel, I will
receive 4 brand-new novels every month and be billed just $6.74 each in the
U.S. or $7.24 each in Canada. That's a savings of at least 16% off the cover
price. It's quite a bargain! Shipping and handling is just 50¢ per book in the
U.S. and 75¢ per book in Canada.* I understand that accepting the 2 free
books and gifts places me under no obligation to buy anything. I can always
return a shipment and cancel at any time. The free books and gifts are mine
to keep no matter what I decide.

Choose one: ☐ **Essential Romance** ☐ **Essential Suspense**
                  (194/394 MDN GMY7)   (191/391 MDN GMY7)

Name (please print)

Address   Apt. #

City   State/Province   Zip/Postal Code

Mail to the **Reader Service:**
IN U.S.A.: P.O. Box 1341, Buffalo, NY 14240-8531
IN CANADA: P.O. Box 603, Fort Erie, Ontario L2A 5X3

Want to try 2 free books from another series? Call 1-800-873-8635 or visit www.ReaderService.com.

STRS19R